A MATTER OF LOVE AND DEATH

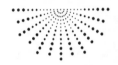

CARMEN RADTKE

ISBN : 978-1-9162410-0-8

Cover design: Fiona Leitch, Cover Image: Annalise Batista

For Kathrin Bartelt, who brightens up the dullest day

CHAPTER ONE

*F*rances stepped out of the house a good quarter of an hour early. After an interminable week when heat held Adelaide in a relentless grip, the temperatures had tumbled, making walking to work tolerable.

She strolled along at a pace that made sure she arrived at the telephone exchange unflustered and, for once, cool. Only this shift and then she'd be off duty for two whole days. Tomorrow unfolded in front of her in all its unhurried glory. She'd help her mum with the laundry – it took two people to feed sheets into the mangle – but they should be done by afternoon tea time. She'd reward herself with a long soak in the roll-top bath, before putting on her print dress with the low waist and the quarter sleeve and meet Pauline to go to the talkies.

Frances wondered what the Empire Theatre would show. She rather hoped for something lighthearted, with one of her favourite stars, like William Powell or Jeanette

MacDonald. But it didn't really matter. As soon as the room fell dark and the velvet curtain opened, she was sure to escape the dreariness that was 1931.

'Another stick-up,' yelled a newspaper boy at the top of his lungs. 'Another stick-up. Read all about it.' He held out a paper to her, hope in his too thin face. Frances shook her head. Her pennies were too few to be spent without necessity, and besides, she'd hear all about the latest crime soon enough, if there really was one. One good thing about scraping by, she thought. No robber would mistake the Palmers for anything but poor.

On impulse, Frances decided to walk around the post office building where she worked. That way, she passed the small shop where Tilda and Martha O'Leary sold barely-worn clothes. For valued clients, they looked out for desired items. That's how Frances got the smart, lime green cotton dress she wore today. Two bob, and there'd been nothing wrong with it apart from a tiny tear at the hem that anyone could mend in a blink.

An elderly lady, with grey wisps of hair escaping from a bun, bent down to put a pair of leather driving gloves in the window display. Frances knocked on the window to get her attention. The lady looked up and shook her head.

Frances shrugged as she gave Tilda a smile. After all, they were just coming up to Easter. There was plenty of time for someone to bring in the nice woollen winter coat that she hoped to purchase for her mother, and the sisters knew what to look out for.

Still smiling, she unlocked the back door of the post office and headed towards the narrow staff room. She put down her brown paper bag with her two lunch sandwiches. How lucky they were to have an ice-box.

One last glance in the mirror, to make sure her light-brown hair, worn in a tight bun at the nape of her neck, was tidy, and she was ready to take over at the switchboard.

Loud sobs brought her up short before she could enter the room.

'You can't do that. I've done nothing wrong.' The voice on the other side of the door belonged to Gussie, the part-time girl who'd started a fortnight ago. Frances' hand rested on the door handle, but she couldn't bring herself to waltz into the room. Being forced to listen in was bad enough, but intruding would be worse by miles.

'I'm sorry,' Mr Gibbons said from behind the closed door. 'But you've left me no choice but to dismiss you.'

'I only told my friend, and she wouldn't breathe a word to anyone.'

Mr Gibbons' tone grew grave. 'It doesn't matter if it's the Prime Minister you've been talking to. This is a government agency, and we maintain strict confidentiality in every respect. Good Lord, babbling about something you've overheard on the telephone switchboard ...'

'But I need this job. Please!'

'You should have thought about that earlier. I'll write you a cheque for your wages, and nobody needs to know about your indiscretion when you apply for a job somewhere else, unless they ask me for a reference.' Mr Gibbons paused. 'That is the best I can do for you.'

The door swung open. Frances had barely enough time to move out of the way as Gussie thundered past. Her eyes were swollen, but her jaw was set in a mulish line.

'Come in, my dear,' Mr Gibbons said. His face looked drained. 'I'm afraid you've overheard a few things that should have been best kept quiet, but I trust I can rely on your discretion.'

He sank on to one of the three straight-backed chairs that stood in a line. 'Not that Gussie is much of a loss, but I did hope it would work out, for her family's sake. And how I'll fill her chair at such short notice is beyond me.' He sounded almost as if he was talking to himself, having forgotten all about her own presence, Frances thought, or he wouldn't have been so embarrassingly frank.

She took pity on her superior. Mr Gibbons always treated her fairly, and she'd never seen him this downcast before. 'I've got two days off coming up,' she said, watching the silent switchboard. 'If it's any help, I could come in and do some extra hours.'

'Are you sure, my dear? You'd get paid extra. And it'd only be from twelve until five.'

'I'll be here.' Frances gave him a reassuring smile as she pressed the headset down on to her hair, switched it on, and answered the first signal.

By lunchtime, her ears buzzed from all the noise and her eyes smarted from the flashing lights. She lifted her headset off and got up, moving her neck from side to side to prevent any stiffening. Lately, she'd taken to eating her sandwiches at the small table in the exchange, allowing her to keep an eye on the switchboard. She worked alone on her shifts these days. They'd become pretty quiet anyway, except for Fridays and Mondays, the days when tradespeople and business managers made phone calls. Not that long ago, there used to be three girls on busy days and two girls on slow shifts, but the depression had gotten too bad to allow for that. Calls during her lunch break were rare, the girls at the main exchange knew how short-staffed Mr Gibbons was and told callers to try again later, unless it was urgent.

With the unemployed roaming the country in ever growing numbers, it was beyond Frances how anyone could be stupid enough to jeopardise a steady job. A shudder ran through her. She called herself to order. The Palmers were fine, as long as she earned enough to meet the mortgage and the regular bills. Not to worry.

She bit into her ham and pickle sandwich. The bread tasted soft and fresh. She savoured the quiet around her as much as her meal. Mr Herbert, who worked behind the post office counter, preferred lunch in one of the small tea shops that somehow managed to survive on customers like him, but Frances hated the idea of spending two whole pennies on a simple sandwich and have even more talk wash over her.

Another light flashed on the switchboard. She took her headset and went to answer the call, fingers dancing as she worked the plugs.

The air felt crisp as she left. It cooled her cheeks as she rushed home. She'd promised her mother to try and pick up a leftover loaf or two at half price from the German bakery, halfway between the telephone exchange and Grenfell Street.

'Whoa, steady there.' A tanned hand grabbed Frances' arm as she slipped off the kerb to avoid colliding with a ragamuffin boy chasing after a ball.

'Thank you,' she said, catching her breath. 'You can let go now. I'm fine.'

The man relaxed his grip. 'At least let me see you safely across the street. What's with the big rush?'

'I want to get to Kessler's bakery before closing time.'

'What a coincidence,' the man said. 'I could do with a loaf myself. Just show me the way to this bakery of yours.'

Frances glanced up at him. He seemed respectable enough, with good clothes and a broad jaw that reminded her of her brother, Rob.

'Sorry, I forgot my manners,' he said, taking off his grey fedora to her. 'Jack Sullivan at your service. It'd be my pleasure to accompany you, but if you prefer to be rid of me, I understand perfectly well.'

There was a hint of amusement in his cool voice. Frances raised her head, openly scrutinising him. She shaded her eyes against the fast-setting sun. A dark-haired man in his thirties, pretty much the gentleman, as her mother would say, with sleepy blue eyes and a nose that had obviously been broken at one stage. The dark blue suit and buffed leather shoes were neat, but not flashy.

'Well,' he said, 'will I do? I promise you I don't bite.'

She felt the corner of her mouth curl up against her will.

He offered her his arm. 'And your name is?'

'Frances Palmer,' she said, relaxing a bit more.

They entered the bakery in silent harmony. Mrs Kessler stood behind the counter, piling up the remaining half dozen loaves and a few pies and bread rolls in front of her. Her hair was pulled back into a bun, fiercely enough to raise her eyebrows. She looked like she herself was made of dough, thought Frances, with her round dumpy body and that shiny face with eyes like currants.

She said, 'One crusty loaf, please, Mrs Kessler, and one sourdough.' She turned to Jack Sullivan. 'Mr Kessler makes the best bread for miles.'

A pleased flush crept into Mrs Kessler's plump cheeks. 'You're a good girl, Frances,' she said. 'You found yourself a very good girl, sir.'

'But Mr Sullivan is not ...'

Mrs Kessler ignored her. They both did. Frances snapped her mouth shut. Setting the record straight with Mrs Kessler would have to wait until the next time they were alone. But she would mention it. She didn't want people to talk about her, simply because she turned up with a personable man in her wake.

She gave Mr Sullivan a sideward glance. He seemed unruffled as he asked Mrs Kessler to fill a bag with the remaining rolls.

'What do you usually do with the leftover bread?' he asked

'We give it to soup kitchen,' Mrs Kessler said in the heavy accent she hadn't lost in twenty-five years, rubbing her ample stomach. 'It is good bread, made for filling hungry mouths.'

'That's very kind of you.'

'Kind, I do not know. We do not like waste.'

7

~

'Is there anything else you need to buy?' Mr Sullivan asked after they'd left the bakery.

'The greengrocers over there,' Frances said, after a moment's hesitation. 'But I wouldn't want them to get the wrong impression as well. You know how people talk.'

'I see.' The corners of his eyes crinkled. 'In that case, I'd better say goodbye before I harm your reputation.'

She felt her cheeks grow warm. 'Well – yes. Goodbye.' She gave him an apologetic look and walked away from him, to the shop.

'Nice-looking fellow I saw you coming out of the bakery with,' Mrs Jacobs said, as she splashed water on the cabbages to keep them fresh.

Frances ignored the remark. 'Do you have some old potatoes or carrots for half-price, Mrs Jacobs? Anything that'd do in a stew?'

'I've got some turnips and onions that need eating. And I could let you have a bag of potatoes if your mum doesn't mind sorting out the odd one that's already sprouting. Mind you, that's a lot to carry, even if your young man gives you a hand.'

'Mr Sullivan is not my young man.' Honestly, these people. 'He asked for directions to the bakery, that's all.'

'It's always good to have someone lending a hand, that's all I'm saying, seeing as he's still waiting around. I can see him through the window.' Mrs Jacobs wiped her hands on her apron. 'That'll be sixpence, love.'

Mr Sullivan strolled towards Frances as she struggled to

carry the heavy bag with her arm outstretched to protect her dress from getting dirty.

She didn't even bother to protest as he took it off her, or ask why he'd hung around. It was kind, after all. 'Where do we go now, young lady?' he asked.

'Home. Off Grenfell Street, if you're sure you want to carry my bag. But then I really have to say goodbye to you.'

'Fair enough,' he said. 'But I promise you, I'm perfectly house-broken and harmless.'

She felt herself smile as they fell into a perfectly matched step. 'We're here,' she said finally, stopping in front of the sagging wrought-iron gate that her godfather, Uncle Sal, cared for with black-lead and twisted wire.

He put down the bags.

'Again, goodbye, Mr Sullivan,' Frances said, with something close to reluctance to see him go. 'And thank you for your help.'

'Any time.' He tipped the brim of his hat with two fingers. 'I'll see you around.'

The front door creaked open while she still fumbled with the gate-latch. Uncle Sal must have kept a look-out for her, she thought, as he rushed to help her with the bags.

'You've got no call to lug all that heavy stuff,' he said, his mouth set in an obstinate line. 'You tell 'em folks I'll be along to pick up those things.'

'You know as well as I do that I had help, you sly fox.'

'I might.' Uncle Sal pushed the door wide open with his shoulder.

Frances followed him into the big kitchen and sat down at the table. She propped her chin up with her hands, watching the dapper little man busy himself with storing the food in the wire baskets that hung from a beam. She knew better than to offend his sense of Italian manhood by helping. For a man who was two years shy of his old age pension, his movements were graceful, despite the gammy right leg.

Uncle Sal always said the steel in his ankle was better than any weather vane when it came to predicting rain. Hard to believe he'd barely been able to hobble along on crutches three years ago, courtesy of a drunken driver who ended the stage career of Salvatore the Magnificent. That's when he moved in for good, and she couldn't imagine life without him. They were a team.

Uncle Sal paused to sniff at the potatoes. 'Some start to smell a bit. Only good for pig-swill.'

'That's why they were cheap. Where's Mum?'

'Run over to give Bertha a hand with old Henry. It takes two these days to lift him out of his chair, and he won't let anybody but the girls do it.'

Uncle Sal dropped the offending potatoes back into the bag, took three of the onions out of their basket and began to juggle them, catching them on the way down. 'So,' he said, keeping a steady rhythm with his hands, 'who was that young man and why didn't you ask him in? It's not because of me, is it? I may not be much to look at, but I wouldn't embarrass you in front of a friend.'

'You wouldn't, and he's not a friend,' Frances said once more. 'Mr Sullivan was being polite, carrying my bags for me, that's all there is to it. I wouldn't dream of inviting a stranger in, as you well know. You helped Mum set out those rules, remember? If you could stop being silly now we might get supper on the table as soon as Mum's back.'

Her right arm shot up as Uncle Sal flung an onion her way.

'Good catch,' Uncle Sal said. 'We'd have made a nice double-act, you and me, if we'd ever put our show on the road. Salvatore and Francesca, the billboards would have read in bright lights.' He sighed. 'We came so close to the big time, my love.'

She planted a kiss on his thin cheek.

Maggie rushed into the kitchen as Uncle Sal lifted the stew-pot off the burner.

'Sorry it took me so long,' she said, grabbing her apron from the hook on the wall. 'You sit down, love, and I'll do the rest.'

Frances propelled her mother onto a chair. 'Uncle Sal and I can manage perfectly well.'

'That was wonderful.' Maggie put fork and knife on to the empty plate. 'You spoil me.'

Uncle Sal said, 'Easy enough to cook for the three of us, with no one getting under your feet and talking me silly.'

'Then we'll do our best to keep our new lodger out of the kitchen.'

Uncle Sal groaned. 'Oh, Maggie, not another Mr blimmin' Hoskins? You'll end up running a nursing home soon.'

'Oh, no!' Frances stared at her mother, open-mouthed. Mr Hoskins had stayed with them for five months, making nights miserable for everyone with his pneumatic snores, and days as bad with his stories about all the misadventures that seemed to have befallen anyone who came into close contact with himself. Despite the undeniable help that his twelve bob a week for board and lodging had constituted, she did somersaults when he left.

How she wished they could afford to have the house to themselves. A deep crease developed between her brows. She did what she could to take care of her mum and all the bills, but sometimes that wasn't enough. They didn't run a proper boarding house, of course, although it had been no trouble at all for them to get the required references and pass all the regulations when they first were introduced to get rid of rat-infested dumps where men slept four or more to a room. But the Palmers had one spare bedroom that they let out if the opportunity arose.

Maggie said, 'This time it's a much younger man, I suppose. Your Uncle Fred sent a letter from Melbourne, saying that he'd recommended me to Mr Anderson, who's moving to Adelaide. Fred says we won't regret it, and if there's one thing you learn in the police, it's how to judge people.'

'When's he coming?' Frances asked.

'Tomorrow afternoon, I'm afraid. It is short notice, but we'll manage, won't we?'

'Sure.' Frances forced herself to sound chipper. 'It's – Gussie got herself the boot and I've promised to work her shifts. That means I'll have to be in the exchange at noon.' And if they didn't get the housework finished in the morning, they'd have to do it later, meaning giving up her night at the pictures. It wasn't fair. Now that her best friend worked at the Top Note, she hardly saw Pauline at all.

She needn't have worried. When she got up at dawn to tackle the spare bedroom on the other side of the landing, her mother had already aired the bedding and was pulling the linen bed sheet taut. It was the only sheet in the house that was as good as new, she realised as she helped her mother, folding in the corners under the mattress. The fabric felt as smooth and cool as mornings on the Adelaide Hills where they once spent a blissful week's holiday.

Frances took the pillow and buried her face in its snowy softness, breathing in the sweet smell of sun-dried laundry. If she ever came into money, she'd take Mum and Uncle Sal and head straight to the hills with them. And she'd buy enough sheets and eiderdown and pillowcases to dazzle them with white sumptuousness. As things were though, she'd have to put up with a stranger enjoying the linen that, by right, ought to belong to her mother, while she herself made do with a sheet that had been turned and washed so often, you could read a newspaper through the fabric.

Maggie snatched the pillow from her, plumping it down on the bed. Next came the eiderdown – no scratchy woollen blanket for lodgers in Mrs Palmer's house – and then her mother stepped back to cast a critical glance over her handiwork.

'It looks fine, Mum,' said Frances, who knew her mother's fastidiousness. True, the striped cream-coloured wallpaper had faded in the fierce Adelaide sun and the chest of drawers had a chipped leg, but the ash floorboards were sanded down and polished, the brass bedstead gleamed, and freshly cut dahlias, in a gold-rimmed vase, lent the wash-stand, with its daisy-patterned ewer, a cheerful air.

'That should do it,' Frances said. 'Why don't we have breakfast now, and then I'll sweep the rugs and mop the floors while you and Uncle Sal take care of the laundry? I don't want you trying to work that mangle on your own.'

CHAPTER TWO

'Honestly,' Pauline said, rolling her eyes, when Frances explained her belated arrival at the Empire, 'your mother's house would be fit for the governor himself.'

Poor Pauline, Frances thought. She, her mother, and her granny had been forced to leave their comfortable rented house two streets from Frances just before New Year's Eve, moving to an ice-box of a two-up, two-down house. It was squeezed into a long row of small, depressing buildings that hardly saw any sun in winter, with yards barely big enough for a chicken to scratch in. Not that any chicken would survive for long in that neighbourhood. It'd soon find its way into a pot, no questions asked.

In comparison, the Palmers' spacious four-bedroom brick house with its two storeys and an indoor bathroom, as well as the outdoor dunny, felt like a palace. Frances hoped that Pauline's new job at the night club worked out and that no one bothered her.

Frances had never been to a smart place like the Top

Note, apart from one time at the no longer existing Floating Palais, but she'd heard stories about lecherous customers from Uncle Sal.

Pauline seemed happy enough. Maybe she'd get a pay rise soon. She might be able to leave the horrible house and rent a nicer one.

Frances frowned. The next time she grumbled because it was so hard to meet the mortgage payments, she'd better remind herself how lucky she was.

On a whim, she turned to her friend. 'Shall we go for an ice cream after the pictures? My shout.'

They settled with their bowls at a window table. 'That was so romantic, when the brother fell in love with the chorus girl,' Pauline said, starry-eyed. 'I'm glad you chose *Fast and Loose*. Do you think I should change my hair colour? Not that I'd ever look like Carole Lombard.' She dipped a spoon into her chocolate ice cream.

'Bleaching your hair platinum blonde would be expensive,' Frances said, pondering her friend's smart, dark bob. 'You told me yourself, when Miss Arnold did it? She had to go to the beauty parlour every four weeks, because the roots showed up, and that on a teaching assistant's salary.' She let a spoonful of ice cream melt on her tongue. Funny how something this cold could warm your heart.

Pauline sighed. 'I know.' She'd worked as a shampoo girl for almost two years, picking up a lot of skills when it came to doing hair, before the salon closed. 'But, Frances, remember what happened when that waitress from the Floating Palais got her hair done just like Greta Garbo, only much lighter.'

'I don't know what you're talking about.'

'She's married now, with a house in Glenelg and her own maid, and she's got a chauffeur who drives her around in a tan-coloured Packard. She had the car especially painted to match her brown mink coat.'

Frances suppressed a giggle. 'What a good thing she doesn't wear black and white rabbit. Imagine how ridiculous a matching car would look then.'

'It does look ridiculous all right, when she waves like this at people.' Pauline gave a languid wave with her hand. 'But like I said, she caught the eye of a rich man as soon as she swanned around like a movie star.'

Frances felt a stab of alarm. Surely Pauline wouldn't be stupid enough to spend a fortune on her hair in the hope of finding a wealthy husband at the Top Note? And what about her boyfriend Tony? He was still travelling, searching for work, but they'd been as good as engaged when he left.

She scraped the last bits of ice cream out of the bowl before she pushed back her chair. 'I think we'd better get going,' she said. 'They'll be worrying at home if I stay out too late.'

Pauline peered at the wall clock. 'Quarter past ten. Shall we walk or take the tram?'

'The tram.' Frances pulled a face. She'd promised her mum that she'd never walk home in the dark. That was tempting fate for a pretty girl, her mother said, with so many vagrants passing through who might get ideas. Safety was more important than saving a few pennies, she said. Frances gave in, to keep her mum happy, although she'd never felt anything but safe on the streets.

Pauline linked her arm with Frances'. 'So,' she said, 'what's your new lodger like?'

'I haven't seen him yet. I went to meet you straight after work.'

'Don't tell me it's another old codger?'

'He's supposed to be young, but why don't you come and see for yourself? He might still be awake. If not, you can interrogate Mum about him.'

'Frances Palmer!' Two pink spots appeared on Pauline's cheeks. 'I only asked to see if you'd care to try my new powder, to look nice for him. It's scented.'

The tram was already waiting as they reached the stop. The girls boarded the brightly-lit wagon and took a seat as far removed as possible from the two other passengers.

Pauline pulled an enamelled box out of her handbag and flicked it open with an experienced hand. 'Can you smell violets?'

Frances took the small box, admiring its smooth feel in her hand and the satiny powder inside, which had nothing in common with the lumpy talc they sold at the chemist's in her neighbourhood. 'It's wonderful. How did you get it?'

'All the girls at the Top Note get one. The boss says it's to make sure we all smell nice and we all smell the same.' She took the puff and dabbed a few grains of powder on Frances' nose. 'There's nothing cheap and tawdry about our club, believe you me.' She perched her head to the left. 'Why don't you come along one night, and bring your lodger with you? If he's handsome, of course.' She fluttered her lashes seductively.

The house lay almost completely in darkness. A single light

shone in the hallway, casting a feeble glow through the stained-glass panel in the top of the front door.

Frances stood still for a moment, hesitating whether to invite Pauline in and risk waking the others.

'Don't mind me,' Pauline said. 'I'll come another day to meet your mysterious stranger.'

'Wait. You'll take the tram again, won't you? Do you have tuppence?'

When she came down in the morning, she found her mother alone in the kitchen. The table was already set for four people and the kettle steamed.

'Where is everyone?' Frances pushed her loose hair behind her ears. She'd slept longer than planned, which meant that grooming would have to wait until she'd helped Maggie. As a result, she already felt annoyed with Mr Anderson who, when she steeled herself to make an unflattering first impression, simply wasn't there.

'Haven't you told our lodger that we've got set meal times?' she asked. 'He hasn't cried off, has he?' She hoped not, because although lodgers were a nuisance, they could do with the money.

Maggie patted Frances' hand. 'Don't fret, love. Uncle Sal's showing Phil around. It shouldn't be too long until they're back. How is Pauline? Did you girls enjoy yourself?'

'Oh, yes. I'll tell you later after I've made myself presentable.' Frances dashed upstairs to brush her hair and dab on a pinch of her own powder. Cheap and unscented as it was, it did cover the bothersome freckles on her nose.

19

~

'We're back,' Uncle Sal announced, flinging the door wide open. 'Our gracious hostess you've already met, my boy, but let me introduce you to our little Frances, one of the fairest flowers in our fair city.' Uncle Sal winked at her while making an exuberant bow.

She laughed. 'You'll need to ignore Uncle Sal when he's in one of his theatrical moods.' She held her hand out to the dazed looking man who entered in the old artiste's wake. 'Welcome, Mr Anderson. I hope you found everything to your liking.'

'Better than I'd dared hope for,' he said. 'And please, call me Phil.' He had a nice voice, rich, without being loud. Add to that broad shoulders, open, regular features, slicked-back hair, and an air of solidity. Yes, Pauline would approve of him. She'd make sure to introduce them, but only if Tony was yesterday's news, which she fervently hoped he wasn't.

She stole a glance at Phil's left hand. No wedding band.

'Frances?' Maggie said.

She sat down with a thump.

Maggie busied herself pouring tea.

'What brings you to Adelaide, Phil?' Uncle Sal planted his elbows on the table, butter knife upright in his right hand.

'A new job. I'll start after Easter.'

'Doing what?' Uncle Sal asked.

Phil took a second slice of toast. Maggie offered him the jam jar, giving Uncle Sal a reproachful glance for interrogating their new lodger. 'Strawberry,' she said. 'It's home-made.'

He spread the jam thin enough for the bread to shine through and took a bite before he turned to Uncle Sal. Frances reached for the honey pot, listening with unashamed curiosity. After all, they'd have to live with this man, so it was only fair that they should know something about him.

'Sanitation,' Phil said, with an air of finality, after he'd finished his toast. 'I'm helping keep Adelaide clean.' He turned towards his hostess. 'Is it all right if I'm not back for dinner? I'd like to use my week of freedom to get acquainted with my new surroundings.'

Maggie smiled. 'I'll leave the light in the hallway burning for you. The front door will be unlocked.'

'But you shouldn't do that.'

Her eyes widened in surprise. 'Why ever not? We're all decent folks around here, not as in some parts of town I'm sure, and how else are you going to drop off something for your neighbours if they're out? Like this jam, that Edna Brown left for me on the kitchen table last week?'

She gave him a pitying look. 'This isn't Melbourne or Sydney, where, I dare say, the most horrible things happen. You can still feel safe in this part of town. It's not like Hindley Street, or parts of Sturt Street, where I wouldn't go on my own.' She hesitated for a moment. 'Although, to tell you the truth, even we did have a few thefts in the last months. Bicycles, mostly, and a few odd pieces of clothing from the laundry line, but surely that happens everywhere.'

'And the stick-ups?' Frances heard herself say.

'But that was jewellers' shops, and on the other side of the river,' Uncle Sal said, giving Frances a warning look. 'As long as you girls don't flout your tiara you'll be safe.'

21

'Still,' Phil said. 'Lock the door, please. To humour me.'

'Sal?'

The old man wagged his head as if to weigh the options. 'He's right, Maggie. You can't be too careful these days, not with so many desperados out there. You don't just have to worry about being out and about.' He furrowed his brows. 'How about I make a little hidey-hole for the key under the roof overhang of the dunny? That's set back where no one can watch you put it there. Suits you, my boy?'

'Good-oh.'

'Give me the key,' Frances said, 'and I'll get a couple of spares cut on my way to work.' Thank goodness, she'd offered to do the extra ten hours, with all these unforeseen expenses.

She perked up. She could even go and tell Tilda and Martha that she'd be willing to go to a whole pound for a winter coat for her mother, if the coat had a fur collar. But first she needed to get the cleaning out of the way before she set off to work.

She attacked the banister and ceilings with vigour. There was something soothing about clean, cobweb-free walls and ceilings that made this one of the few chores she enjoyed. The long broom she used made quick work of the few half-hearted attempts any spider had made since last week.

Frances put the broom down, resting her hands on the handle. The sun's rays painted golden swirls and stripes on the floorboards. Singing under her breath, she ran up to her room and changed into a clean skirt and jumper.

She gave herself an approving look in the mirror as she adjusted the butter-coloured felt cloche that her mum and

Uncle Sal had given her two Christmases ago. One slick of pale pink lip-paint – maybe not as fancy as Pauline's bright red lipstick, but good enough for a girl from Grenfell Street.

Phil waited for her in the hallway. 'Do you mind if I join you?'

'Are you sure? I've got to warn you I've got a bit of a walk ahead of me. You'd be more comfortable taking the tram if you want to go into town.'

He gave her an ingratiating smile. 'But it's so much nicer to walk, especially in the sunshine, with a pretty girl as my guide.'

She raised her eyebrows, hoping he didn't mean to flirt with her. He seemed spiffy enough, but it would upset her mother, and Uncle Sal had quite a temper when it came to protecting their honour.

Phil held the door open for her. 'Shall we go?'

Frances knew she was being watched, as good as if she saw the glances that followed her from behind flimsy curtains. She resigned herself to her fate. Being seen with two different men in the span of a few days was bound to set a few tongues in motion.

Phil interrupted her thoughts. 'Are there any public phone boxes nearby?'

'There is one on the upper part of King William Street, if that's convenient, Mr Anderson.'

'I told you to call me Phil, or else I'll feel as old as your Uncle Sal.'

'Don't let him hear you call him old. There's no

knowing what he'll do to prove you wrong. He has his pride, you know.'

'I got the impression. He doesn't resemble any of you, does he?'

'Oh, no, he's my godfather, not my real uncle, if that's what you mean. But he's as good as one or even better. Uncle Sal is brilliant.' She pointed towards a metal box next to a street lamp. 'Here's your phone box, and now I'll better rush, or I'll be unable to get things done before I go on duty.' She jingled the two keys on their wire ring. 'Front and back door. Will two sets do?'

Phil held out his hand. 'Three would be better. I'll take care of it.'

That would save her the hassle of finding a locksmith. Maybe having a lodger around had its good points after all. She gave him a grateful smile. 'Thanks, if you're sure it's no bother. I'll pay you back tonight. I'll be home as quick as I can.'

~

Ten minutes early. She took off her cloche and put it over a hook on the coat stand.

She entered the telephone exchange room as noiselessly as possible, signalling Clara that she was ready to take over. Clara raised one finger, pulled out a plug and jerked the headphone off her frizzy hair.

'You're a life saver.' Her shoulders heaved in a sigh. 'I was afraid I'd have to pull a double shift when Mr Gibbons said Gussie no longer worked here, and Mum needs me.'

Frances arranged her own headphone. 'Can you believe anyone'd be so daft?'

Clara leaned back in her chair, obviously ready for a bit of gossip while there was a lull. 'She did it on purpose, if you ask me.'

'Never!'

Clara lowered her voice. 'From what I've heard, she thinks she can make more money somewhere else.' Her sallow face blushed with excitement. 'In a hotel on Hindley Street, that's where you'll find her in the evening, behind the bar.'

'But that work's illegal for a girl.'

'Oh Fran, you're such an innocent. As if anybody cares about laws like no drinking after six o'clock or no girls serving in hotels.' Clara pushed herself off her chair. 'I'll better run and look after the baby while Mum goes on her cleaning tour. She's got a new lady and she's that hard to please, Mum says.'

'Right-oh.'

'Oh, and Fran, you make sure you stay on the line a bit longer, to make sure the connection works all right. I had one call cut off twice, and they were livid when they got through again.' The first light began to flash.

'Thanks, Clara,' Frances mouthed as she listened to the operator at the other end who gave her a number.

With the thoughtless skill born out of practice, she plugged the jacks in, sent the ringing signal and waited for the other party to pick up. Usually she flipped the switch to cut off her headset straight away, but after Clara's warning she'd decided to listen in for a few moments before she let people talk in privacy. It didn't matter anyway, because all she did was let the words wash over her.

That's why she'd already flipped the switch before the meaning of the words sank in. She sat there, heart racing. Her hands trembled hard enough to make it difficult to operate the switch again.

Crackling noises, and then again, the voice that had given her such a fright. 'Next ... after Easter,' a man said. 'When she's with friends in the valley. Make it look like another stick-up.'

The line crackled louder. 'Could be easier to take our cove lakeside,' another man said, in a croaked, nasal voice. 'Make him go for a swim.'

Frances clapped a hand to her mouth, setting Clara's tin mug flying with her elbow. It hit the floor with a thud.

'Hey,' the nasal voice said, 'did you hear that, boss? Think somebody's listening?'

She held her breath.

'No,' the first man said, just as she was starting to see spots dancing in front of her eyes. 'Don't be a fool. And don't forget, you get paid to do your job. Leave the thinking to others.'

'Good-oh. Sure, you didn't hear anything?' A slight pause. 'All right, boss. Where do you want me to do the job? The jeweller's shop or home?'

'Suit yourself.' The man hung up.

CHAPTER THREE

A stick-up? She bit her knuckles. There could be little doubt about what was going on. If only she could remember the number she'd been given by the other operator, and where that call had come from. She needed that information for the police.

Another thought pierced through the fog that filled her head. It hit her for six. She couldn't tell anyone – she'd get sacked, like Gussie. They'd lose the house. Mum, Uncle Sal, they'd all be out on the street and it would be her fault.

Her hands still trembled as she locked the door of the telephone exchange at five o'clock. Only the switchboard at the big General Post Office stayed in service at night. She walked home in a daze, hardly paying any attention to the Sunday afternoon bustle around her.

Usually she enjoyed afternoons like this, with the sun giving a warm glow to the Victorian brick and limestone buildings and enough of a breeze to move the clouds along at a pace that kept the heat at bay. Today it was all she could manage not to bump into people and to stay clear of cars when she crossed the streets.

She dug her nails into her sweaty palms. She must have misunderstood. No one in their right mind would plan a crime in such a casual way. There'd been a lot of crackling noises on the line, so the words had been slightly mangled. A misunderstanding, that's all it was. Like a game of Chinese whispers, where you could rely on the meaning being distorted.

Her pace quickened. She'd read too many sensational stories. The books had given her ideas. And the newspapers. *The Advertiser* was full of articles about shoot-outs and underworld figures with nicknames straight from the silver screen. But that was in Sydney, or Melbourne at a stretch.

Frances stopped in her tracks, nearly causing a young man to collide with a tree as he swerved on his bicycle to avoid hitting her.

'Watch out what you're doing, lady,' he yelled.

Frances gasped. 'I'm dreadfully sorry!' She had to pull herself together. She wouldn't think about that phone call any more before tonight, in the privacy of her own room.

By the time she opened the front door, she had calmed down. Sunday evening was the best time in the week, when they all sat down together in the parlour after dinner, listening to the radio programme. Frances and Maggie would share the deep settee, with its comfortable upholstery and the warm plaid rug that covered the worn blue fabric. They'd sew or knit, while Uncle Sal, settled in one of the two oak-framed armchairs that Grandpa had brought with him from Scotland, would sit and look at his old scrapbooks, dreaming of past glory. There'd be tea and biscuits or fruit, and contentment.

She took off her cloche, patting her hair back into place.

'Mum?' She went into the kitchen where her mother attacked a lump of dough with her rolling pin. A floury streak ran down her left cheek.

'What are we having?'

'Apple pie. Edna had some windfall fruit to spare,' her mother said. 'And Yorkshire pudding, with lots of pudding and gravy and a wee bit of braised beef.' She pushed her hair back from her forehead, leaving another trail of flour. 'Tell Sal and Phil we'll eat in half an hour. And take the pipe-cleaners with you, please. Sal left his new packet in the cupboard.' She prodded her pastry and nodded satisfied. 'Oh, and there's a letter for you under the bread bin. I forgot to tell you yesterday.'

Frances picked up pipe-cleaners and letter and shoved both without a glance in her shirt pocket.

She found the men sitting on the back porch, smoking their pipes and chatting. She flung the packet with the pipe-cleaners without a word of warning.

Uncle Sal snatched them in the air. 'That's my girl,' he said. 'You've got the eye, and you're quick. We'd have gone far together, love.'

She felt the heat rising in her cheeks. Why did Uncle Sal have to be so talkative? Nobody knew about the vaudeville act they'd worked on in secrecy, until the Post Office took up most of her time. Even Maggie was blissfully unaware of Signorina Francesca's blonde wig and the sequined costume that were stowed away in Uncle Sal's stage trunk. Nobody but Uncle Sal knew how much Frances longed to travel and see new, exciting places, a world removed from her real life.

She kept her voice lighthearted. 'Don't pay him any heed, Phil. It's one thing to juggle a few balls or fling a knife or two, another to have someone fling them at you.' She gave Uncle Sal a warning glance. He winked at her, raising both thumbs in the air.

Phil grinned. 'Thanks for the warning. I'd better mind my manners around the house, before I set myself up as an unwitting target.'

'Rest easy,' Uncle Sal said. 'We never perform our tricks without a paying audience.' He put the parcel down, dug deep in the pocket of his shapeless brown cardigan, and flung Frances a set of keys. She caught them in mid-flight. Uncle Sal motioned her to follow him as he got up and went down the porch steps to the retired dunny. Well-tended flower beds flanked it. They'd tried growing vegetables there, but the soil wasn't right.

'Look here, Frances.' He tapped a fingernail on a piece of pipe he'd nailed directly underneath the roof overhang. 'I plugged her up good and proper, so she'll stay dry inside, and that's where we'll keep the spare keys. Mind you, plug her up again when you've put the keys back in. You too, young man.'

'I promise,' Frances said. 'You'd better tell Mum as well, after we've had our dinner.'

Frances peered under her lashes at Phil while her knitting needles clicked away. She couldn't imagine going to stay with strangers. He must feel lonely.

If he did, though, he hid it well. He'd changed into slippers and looked, for all the world, as if he'd spent many an evening spread out in the armchair, absorbed in reading the paper. The pages rustled as he turned them.

'Not much worthwhile in there, except for the sports pages,' Uncle Sal said.

Phil folded *The Advertiser* and laid it down on his lap. 'It's still the best way to learn about a place.' He flicked his fingers on the paper. 'Less than half an hour, and you know where to buy your shaving cream or your socks, which pictures are shown and where to go for an outing. Anything one needs to know about a city, confined to a few pages.'

'You could ask us,' Uncle Sal said. 'There's not much we don't know between us three, eh, Maggie?'

Maggie cut off the thread she used to sew new buttons on an old white blouse, to freshen it up, and nodded while rethreading the needle.

'If there's anything you'd like us to tell you, you're more than welcome to ask.' She squinted at her handiwork. 'Are the buttons in a straight line, Frances?'

'Hold the blouse up.' She ran her finger down the seam. 'It's fine,' she said. 'You'll be the best-dressed lady in church for Easter.'

She turned to face Phil. 'Mum's one of the ladies in charge of the flowers, so she has to leave earlier than we do most Sundays, to make sure everything is as it should be, lest a flower might have wilted overnight.'

Her mother cut off the last thread and put the scissors into her sewing basket. 'If you and Sal aren't busy otherwise, having to miss the service again, you mean. Are you a regular churchgoer, Phil?' She folded the finished blouse. 'There's no need to pretend if you aren't. But if you are, you're welcome to join me.'

Frances tried to concentrate on her work. Sometimes she wondered why she bothered with knitting. Her efforts were slipshod at best, with practice not making a whit of difference. But it made her mum happy, to see her perform homely tasks like that. It helped reconcile her with the fact that it was Frances who paid the mortgage and bought their bread.

What her mother, and many of her generation, couldn't understand was that Frances, along with most of her unmarried friends, enjoyed earning money. Any job was better than running yourself ragged with keeping the home nice and clean, looking after husband and little ones, without getting recognition or independence in return. Even Pauline, with her romantic notions, half-agreed with her.

Frances stifled a yawn. She cast a critical glance over the scarf she was knitting. She'd made good progress tonight. A couple more nights should see it finished, and Uncle Sal could be presented with the result. Those few uneven rows would be invisible once he tucked the scarf under the collar of his jacket.

Her eyelids began to droop. 'Good-night, everyone. I'm sorry I haven't been better company tonight.'

'Nonsense, dear.' Maggie rose to switch off the radio. 'It's almost ten, time we all turned in. Do you have tomorrow off instead, to make up for the days you gave up?'

'No, those were extra hours I did. I'm on the early shift this week, but I'll try and sneak down without disturbing you.'

At a quarter to six, she stepped out on to the quiet street. She loved these mornings, when a sparkle seemed to be cast over the city, as yet undisturbed by the stench of coal fires and car exhausts, and the noise of the human race.

She drew in a deep breath. Nothing could spoil this. True, most houses could have done with some paint or new pointing, but the trees hadn't lost their splendour, the cockatoos greeted each new day with glee, and the people kept their heads high because they'd get through this together. That's what she hoped her mother had told Phil. That it was the schools and the churches and the neighbours that bound Adelaide together. You stayed true to your community, and the community stayed true to you.

Two shadows moved in an alleyway. 'Morning, miss,' one man said, touching his worn cloth cap with a trembling hand. His mate gave her a toothless grin. A bowl sat at their feet, with a halfpenny inside.

They looked older than the hills, with their dull eyes and careworn faces. Frances dug in her coat pocket. She kept a few pennies loose in there for just such a case. She dropped a penny into the bowl. 'Good luck,' she said.

'Thanks, miss,' the first man said. 'Bless you.'

Up close, the men seemed shrunken, as if their clothes had grown without them. Frances bit her upper lip. She'd have loved to give more money, but there was the winter coat to think of, and roof tiles to be replaced.

She opened her lunch bag. Two sandwiches and two apples; more than sufficient to keep her going until supper. She took a sandwich and an apple and handed them to the man with the cloth cap. 'It's not much,' she said, feeling apologetic, 'but I thought you might be hungry.'

'Thanks again, Miss.' He tore the sandwich in two, handing the other half to his mate.

Frances reached the telephone exchange without further delays. During the whole shift, the lights kept flashing, making her wonder how people had dealt without a phone.

The Palmers still hadn't got one in their home though, and they coped fine. With neighbours and friends you visited at home, or chatted at the market or in the shops, wherever you ran into them, and you had to be destitute to be unable to afford the stamp for a letter.

The letter! She still hadn't read it. Well, whatever it was would keep until she was home.

She rolled her shoulders to loosen them up, accepting yet another request from an operator up north. The voice could have come from next door, the connection was so clear. She flicked the off switch once the other party had answered. She had no reason to stay on the line as a silent third any longer than necessary. If only she'd done that the day before. Try as she might, Frances couldn't shake off the sickening feeling that washed over her whenever she thought of that phone conversation. Last night she'd been tired enough to nod off straight away, but her dreams had been filled with faceless men chasing her, with phone cords dangling from their hands. It had been a relief to wake up.

After Easter, the man had said. Four more days to go until Good Friday. A chill crept over her. She glanced at the clock; another hour until she could escape into the sunshine.

CHAPTER FOUR

*H*er shift over, Frances resolutely pushed every thought about the phone call aside, as she made her way to the O'Leary's shop. A browse through the racks full of frocks and skirts might chase away the lingering fear, and Martha and Tilda always made her feel better. The sisters loved a good chin-wag, and because she'd known them all her life, there was no awkwardness involved if she left without spending anything.

A bell above the door tinkled as she entered the shop. It smelt of the incense the sisters burned to cover the cloying odour of moth powder some of the clothes were sprinkled with.

Martha hurried towards the counter, spectacles askew on her thin nose. Sticking plaster held the frame together, at the expense of the correct shape.

'I'm so glad you came in today.' She beamed at Frances, pushing the spectacles further up the bridge of her nose. 'We need to go through to the back. Tilda, love! You'll have to mind the shop.'

Her sister appeared from behind a crowded rack.

'This way,' Martha said, almost touching Frances' head with hers as she led her through a maze of shelves and boxes, into a makeshift changing room. 'You won't believe your eyes, my dear. I won't be a tick.'

Frances sat down on the straight-backed chair, handbag on her lap. Her curiosity increased. The last time the old dear acted this mysteriously, before Christmas, she offered her a padded bed jacket in a crimson that flattered Maggie's olive skin and brown hair shot with grey. At tenpence, she'd snatched it up.

Martha drew the curtain of the changing room. Her whole face glowed with happiness as she presented the coat hanging over her arm.

Frances stretched out her hand before she could stop herself.

'We got it in this morning,' Martha said, 'and I said to Tilda, why, this was made for darling Maggie.' She rubbed a sleeve between two fingers. 'Real wool. Feel the quality. And the collar's real fur, and the right size too, if I remember correctly. Do tell your mother she must come in and see us one day. It's been too long.'

'She'd love that.' Frances stroked the soft butter-coloured material. 'And she'll adore this coat.' She hesitated. 'That is, if I can afford it. New, it must have cost a mint.'

'That's true,' Martha said, nodding so eagerly her spectacles slipped again, 'but quality pays for itself, I always say. This coat should give your mother good service for years and years, and she'll look a treat in it. Oh, before I forget, there's something else I want to show you.'

She bustled away, giving Frances no chance to protest.

The coat was lovely. She imagined her mother in it. Her mum deserved nice things, and a warm coat was a necessity for winter in Adelaide, when temperatures could dip below freezing.

'Tadaaa!' Martha pulled back the curtain.

Frances held her breath. In front of her dangled the most elegant frock she'd ever seen. Rippling and shimmering like the ocean, azure satin flowed down from the padded hanger Martha held as high as she could. The only ornaments were thin golden threads woven into the narrow shoulder straps.

'I haven't shown it to anyone else,' her old friend said. 'You simply must try it on.'

She opened her mouth, but no sound came out. She wouldn't buy it, because even if she had money to burn, where would she wear a frock like that? But somehow it seemed wrong to disappoint Martha, who'd already slipped out again, closing the curtain behind her.

The satin slid over her body like a caress. Frances turned towards the mirror, waltzing a few steps. The frock moved with her, the material molding itself around her without clinging to her shape. The back was deeper cut out than the front, but it, too, barely hinted at exposed skin.

She put her hands on her hips and twirled around once more.

'May I have a peep?'

Frances drew the curtain aside.

Martha clapped her hands in excitement. 'I knew it. I knew this frock was made for you the moment I saw it.' She sighed. 'It almost makes me wish I was young again.'

Frances left the shop ten shillings poorer, with the promise to bring another ten bob the next day.

Her conscience kept remarkably quiet over this extravagance, but it might kick in later, she thought. Especially since this frock was made for sipping champagne and dancing the night away, both events that didn't occur in her life.

Still, she told herself, she didn't have to wear that dress to enjoy it. She could put it on in the privacy of her room and let it work its magic in secrecy. Because for the few moments that she'd stood there, in front of the mirror, Frances had felt glamorous, the way she used to in her secret role as Signorina Francesca, future world-travelling stage assistant to Salvatore the Magnificent. This dress rekindled her dreams. She hugged the wrapped frock as close to her chest as she could, suddenly unwilling to go home to the predictability of her everyday life. She turned around and changed direction.

'Hello?' Frances lifted the brass knocker and let it fall against the door.

A middle-aged woman inched the door open, with a resigned look on her pretty, skillfully made-up face. Pauline's mother would rather go hungry than let herself go, she always said, and she was true to her word.

Ruth Meara brightened when she recognised Frances.

39

CARMEN RADTKE

'Why, what a nice surprise, and in time for a cuppa, too. The brew's just ready. Pauline! We've got a visitor.'

The house was as shabby as Frances had expected, but every inch was scrubbed with a vengeance.

She followed Ruth into the parlour, which would have been cramped had the Meara's possessed more to fill it with than a battered oak sideboard and three mismatched cane chairs, one for each of them.

The chipped brown paint on the walls didn't help, but Ruth had done her best by putting up a few colourful prints she'd cut out from old magazines.

She met Frances' discreet look with a twinkle in her wide-set eyes. 'Pretty awful, isn't it? But believe you me, love, it could be much worse, and, say what you will, it'll make our next place feel like paradise.' She patted a chair, shrugging off the squalor with unquenchable good humour. 'You sit down, and I'll fetch the tea tray. I won't be a twinkle.'

Pauline rushed into the room, squealing with delight. 'I didn't expect to see you this week, Fran. What a shame I've got a measly twenty minutes before I must run to work.' She plopped down on a chair. 'Do tell me everything. How is your new lodger? Young and handsome?'

'Yes,' Ruth chimed in, carrying a laden tea tray. 'Do tell us all about him.'

Frances put sugar in her tea and stirred it. 'Well, he is tall, broad shouldered, and tanned. He's a bit older than I thought at first, in his early thirties I'd reckon, but you'd like him, Pauline. He's got a moustache and dark hair, and he wears it slicked back like Ramon Navarro. He's got nice

40

manners as well, and before you ask, he's not tried to flirt with me.'

'Pah,' Pauline said. 'Early days. Maybe he's still gathering his courage to ask you out.'

'Pauline!'

Ruth sipped her tea. 'What does Uncle Sal say to the lad? He's so used to being the man around the house, poor pet.'

'Oh, he seems to enjoy having another fellow to talk to, whatever it is that men do talk about when they're on their own.' Frances set her cup aside. 'But Phil's been with us such a short time I can't really say much. To be honest, I've popped in because I want to show you something.'

She unwrapped the unwieldy parcel with as much care as possible. A jingle of excitement shot through her whole body as her fingers touched the satin.

'Oh my gosh, it's marvellous.' Pauline drew in her breath. 'You'll look like a movie star. When are you going to wear it?'

'That's the snag. I won't, because it's not something I can wear to work or to the pictures with you, can I?' She pulled a face. 'I shouldn't have bought it, but I couldn't resist.'

'Of course you had to buy it. Otherwise you'd spend nights agonising over that evening dress.' Pauline stroked the fabric. 'Have you ever seen anything like it, Mum?'

'I'll ask Martha and Tilda to look out for an evening dress for you, if you want to,' Frances said, seeing the longing in her friend's dark eyes. 'You'd look dashing in lime green or lemon.'

'Never mind me. I know exactly the right occasion for

your new dress,' Pauline said. 'There's a new swing band playing at the Top Note, this Thursday night. They've played all over Europe and in Sydney and Melbourne and it'll be a really flash affair.'

She gave Frances a cheeky grin. 'Get that Phil to take you there and you can dazzle him. Come early and make sure he wears an overcoat so he can hand it to me, because I'll be attending to the cloakroom for a bit.'

She checked the wall clock and jumped up. 'Look at the time. I've got to dash. Bye, Mum, bye, Frances, and do come on Thursday.' Off she went, letting the door slam behind her.

Ruth shook her head. 'Always in a hurry, and on those heels, too. If I had a penny for every time I told her to wear solid shoes and keep those flimsy things at work where they belong, we'd be in clover.'

She chuckled as she noticed Frances' furtive glances at the shabby room. 'Never mind that, love. This,' she made a sweeping gesture with both arms, 'is temporary. A soon as I can take some sewing and washing in again, we'll move up to a decent place. I can almost bend my wrist like I used to.'

Frances smiled at her. She'd yet to see Ruth admit defeat. 'Rain today means a good crop tomorrow,' she always said, like the farmer's daughter that she was. Pauline took after her, living on hope and the unshakeable confidence that good things were waiting around the corner.

'I'm sure you'll be fine. But I'd better go now,' Frances said, sliding the dress back in its tissue paper.

'Can't wait to show your new finery to your mum, can

you? You'll be the belle of the ball at the Top Note, that much I can tell you.'

'I can't go to a night club. At least not on my own, Mum wouldn't like it, even if I could afford to waste money, which I can't, and it wouldn't feel right to ask Phil. I mean, he's a paying lodger, that's all.'

Ruth gave her a sympathetic look. 'Margaret needs to relax a bit more. You all deserve a bit of fun.'

Frances pulled a face. 'There'll be other opportunities.'

'Pity. The Top Note is the most marvellous place. Ask your Uncle Sal. There's not much he doesn't know about what's what, the old rascal. There's no flies on him.'

Ruth rose. 'Say hello to him and your mum, and tell her I'm on the mend.' She wrinkled her nose at the smell of frying onions coming from next door. 'I'd better get going myself. There's a new revue on at the Empire, and a friend of mine has a spare ticket.' Her brown eyes sparkled.

Bubbles rose in the big stew pot as Frances came home. Maggie gave it a quick stir. 'I was beginning to wonder what kept you so long,' she said. 'I didn't want to put the potatoes on before you got back, or they'd have turned to mush by now.' She wiped her hands on her apron.

'Sorry I'm late,' Frances said, 'but there were a few things I had to do on the way home.' A big grin stretched across her face. 'You wait and see.'

Frances kept her air of mystery until they'd finished their meal. For once, the women had nothing left to do. Phil had banned them from the kitchen, cheerfully announcing that he and Uncle Sal would clear away and do the dishes.

She grabbed her mum's hand before she found other things to keep busy and propelled her towards the staircase.

'Close your eyes,' she said as soon as they entered Frances' bedroom. Maggie obeyed, stretching an arm out against the wall for support.

'Now you can open them.' The coat hung from her wardrobe.

Her mother's eyes widened with delight. 'What a wonderful coat. Mind you take good care of it, and don't put it too close to the heater in the telephone exchange.'

'It's for you, Mum. My coat is good for another dozen winters, but your old one is past anything. I've seen warmer handkerchiefs. And before you say a word, I've got a confession to make. I lost my head over a frock.' She picked up her parcel and undid the tissue paper.

'Oh, Frances! Put it on, quick.'

'I will if you show me how you look in your new coat.'

Maggie chuckled and put on the new coat, while Frances changed into the frock.

They entered the parlour together. Frances felt slightly self-conscious as she swanned into the room in her new finery, but it did her good to see the look in Phil's eyes as he saw her in all her elegance.

Uncle Sal poked his head around the corner. 'Nearly there, and the kettle's on already,' he said, before he took in their changed appearance. He whistled through his teeth. 'Holy cow! Now look at you girls. You're a sight for sore eyes, you are.'

Frances took her time taking off the evening frock. She put it on a hanger, smoothing the folds with loving strokes before she could bring herself to close the wardrobe doors. Her brown skirt and yellow jumper that used to feel so comfortable and pretty, now seemed as dull as dishwater. That was the trouble with spoiling yourself. Once you got a taste for it, the cravings started.

She wondered how wealthy women coped. Not that she was likely ever to find out, she told herself, firmly relegating the dress and its implications to the back of her mind. She was gaining a lot of experience shutting out unwanted thoughts lately. She pushed the wardrobe shut and went downstairs to join the others.

'That's settled,' Uncle Sal said to Phil as Frances walked in. 'I'll see to it that we're getting a good table.'

She sat down in her usual place and took up her knitting. She had just found her rhythm, needles clicking away, when her mum said to her, 'Don't forget to get a darker lipstick, love. Not too dark, you don't want to look fast, maybe a deep rose.'

Frances stared at her, confused.

'Well, you want to look your best, don't you, when we're going out?'

'What are you talking about, Mum?'

'Phil has invited us and Sal to go out with him, dear. It seems there's a special band playing on Thursday, at the Top Note.' Maggie beamed. 'It's been ages since I was last out dancing. Aren't we lucky?'

45

~

Frances sank into her bed with a wide grin on her face. How surprised Pauline would be when Frances turned up on Phil's arm. It would be nice if Maggie had a beau, but the only unmarried men the right age were the milkman, who flirted with every woman he met, and the postie, who saw sin and depravation everywhere, especially when it came to Uncle Sal.

The postie. Frances jumped out of bed. She'd forgotten the letter again.

She switched on the light, slit the envelope open with a nail file and took out a typewritten sheet.

Two minutes later she let the letter drop. She put her head between her knees and took a deep breath before she picked the letter up again.

'Dear Miss Palmer,'
'A recent inspection of our books has shown that as to date you are behind with your mortgage payments to a total of seven £ and six d.
Please contact us at the earliest possible time to discuss the repayment. Otherwise we would regrettably have to consider other measures.
Kind regards,
M. Smith
Bank manager'

A faint taste of bile crept into Frances' mouth. This must be a mistake. She always made sure that she handed her mum enough money to settle mortgage and utilities bills. She'd seen enough people turned out off their homes for missing payments, or having to fend without electricity for months.

She switched off the light and went back to bed, like an automaton. An error, a horrible error, that's all, she told herself over and over again. She'd visit the bank in her lunch break and then – what then? *Seven pounds and six shillings. Where could she find that much money? Even if she returned coat and dress and got a refund, it wouldn't be enough – and Mum needed that coat.* She pulled the duvet over her head, the way she used to as a child when something frightened her.

CHAPTER FIVE

*A*fter a night of recurring dreams, where Maggie and Uncle Sal lay half-starved under a bridge, pointing with skeletal fingers at Frances, waking up brought no relief.

She barely brought herself to face them both at breakfast. The one relief was that Phil was still asleep.

She toyed with her toast. Every crumb swelled up in her mouth, making it awkward to swallow.

'Are you unwell?' Maggie asked. 'You look peaky. Maybe you should stay—'

Frances shook her head. She took a deep breath and shoved the letter over to Maggie. Maggie scanned the contents. The colour drained from her face. 'But that is – oh, no.'

Uncle Sal took the letter.

'Mum?'

'It's all my fault,' Maggie whispered. 'How could I?'

'How could you what? Please, tell me what's going on. I

haven't got much time left before I need to go, and if I don't sort this today ...'

Maggie trembled slightly. Frances got up and sat down on the armrest of Maggie's chair.

'You remember when I was ill a few months ago.'

Frances nodded. As if she could forget the worry that her mother's cough might turn into pneumonia. Or the doctor's bills that swallowed up most of her meagre savings.

'You see, Bertha was at the doctor's too. With her grandchild. She couldn't afford to pay for the treatment, or the medication. I was heading for the bank straight after my appointment, so I had money in my bag.'

'You gave it to her? And you didn't tell me?' The anger in her voice surprised Frances herself.

Maggie stifled a sob. 'I didn't know how to tell you, and Bertha was going to pay me back as soon as she could.'

'What's done is done,' Uncle Sal said. 'What matters is that we pay the money now.'

Maggie blinked away tears and fished in her bag for money. She brought up two ten-shilling notes.

Frances took the money. She had a hard time calming down.

Uncle Sal limped to the dresser and took out a battered tobacco tin. He tipped the contents on to the table. 'Three pounds and seven, no eight shillings. I'll make sure you get the rest by lunch-time.' He gave her a reassuring wink and patted Maggie on the head. She managed to smile at him.

'Thanks,' Frances said. 'We'll talk about everything tonight.'

∾

True to his word, Uncle Sal waited outside the post office at lunch-time. He offered Frances his arm, which she took gratefully. She knew she should feel guilty about being less than understanding to her mum, but she couldn't.

The bank was a five minute walk away, but every step took ages.

'Do you want me to come in with you?' Uncle Sal asked as they reached the stucco building. 'Or I can wait in the foyer.' He slipped an envelope with money into her hand.

She squeezed his hand. 'Thank you. I shouldn't be long.'

Uncle Sal settled in a patched arm-chair, apparently at peace with himself and his world. Frances marveled at his acting skills. She knew that deep-down he'd fretted all morning about her.

'Miss Palmer? In here please.'

The bank manager smiled at her in a paternal fashion that partially relieved the worry lines in his face.

'I've come to apologise,' she said, putting letter and money on his desk. 'and to settle the outstanding debt.'

'Thank you, that was very prompt.'

'I'm much obliged to you, for your patience.' She swallowed. 'I'll make sure something like this won't happen again.'

'I trust it won't,' he said. 'We try to be lenient, but headquarters ...' His sentence trailed off. 'Anyway, there's no harm done. Of course, we prefer if our clients let us know in advance if they will fall short on a payment.'

'I understand.'

'I wish you a pleasant afternoon, Miss Palmer.'

'Thank you, Mr Smith. And good-bye.'

∽

She almost dragged Uncle Sal out of the bank. 'Phew!'

'All sorted?'

'Yes! That poor man – I think he was at least as relieved as me.'

Uncle Sal juggled imaginary balls in the air. 'See, nothing to worry about.'

'Thanks to you coming to my rescue.'

'We're a team, eh. Salvatore and Francesca.' A bank note appeared in his hand. 'And now you'll go and buy that lipstick your mum was talking about.'

Frances stared at the ten-shilling note. 'But where did you get that money?'

'I'm not a pauper. And,' he put a finger over her lips, 'I had a chin-wag with Bertha. Three quid's worth of chin-wag, and she's very grateful to Maggie for her patience.'

'You didn't tell her about our trouble?' Tongues wagged freely around Grenfell Street, and if people thought the Palmers couldn't pay the mortgage, and then Frances suddenly waltzed around with strange, prosperous-looking men, they'd put two and two together and come up with a baker's dozen.

'We talked about my ankle, and if I should go and see the doctor again.' His eyes twinkled as he led her towards Rundle Street, right up to John Martin's Big Store. 'In you

51

go, Signorina Francesca, and promise me to stop worrying about anything. You'll be the belle of the ball.'

He smiled to himself as he watched her lift her head up high and glide through the revolving door. She needed to be allowed to be a carefree girl of twenty-two sometimes.

Maggie, he crossed himself hastily, possessed a kind heart and a generous spirit, but she expected the girl to be a child at home and a grown-up outside the house. It wasn't fair how she allowed Frances to carry all the burden of caring for them. Including himself. If only he were less of a burden, although he did his best to make himself useful around the house.

Maybe he should push on, he thought. But where to? Frances and Maggie were all he had. He pushed his hat further up his forehead. He'd think about his future another time, once he'd fixed the gutter. And the shed. The veggie patch in the garden also cried out for attention. A lot of work. But first, a night on the town.

For a moment, the bright lights in the Big Store shone directly into Frances' eyes as she stared at the high ceiling. She lowered her head and caught her breath as she inhaled the perfumed air. Nothing she'd ever experienced could rival this. Even the shop girls were special. They could have stepped right out of a fashion magazine, with their bobbed, glossy locks, perfect arcs of pencil-line eyebrows emphasising lightly shadowed eyes. Their dresses fit like a second skin and were the latest chic, with floppy bows and dainty piqué collars.

Frances' spirits surged as she fought the urge to take the lift to the top floor and work her way aimlessly down, as if she had a pocket full of cash. Reason won, although she stole a few glances at the fetching mid-calf skirts that came in all colours of the rainbow.

Clutching her purse, she made her way towards the beauty counter when a pair of silk stockings caught her eye.

The bleached blonde shop girl behind the stocking counter smiled at her invitingly. 'Come and have a look at these, miss.' The girl held a gauzy stocking closer to a lamp. The light caught in the fine thread and bounced back. 'Aren't they lovely? We got a new consignment two days ago, and they fly off the shelves.'

Frances gazed at the stockings with unexpected longing. The sight of the price tag stopped her reverie. More than two bob a pair, for stockings as fragile as spun sugar. 'Artificial silk for me, please. Two pairs, one in size eight and one in a ten, please.'

The sales assistant opened a drawer and took out two cardboard boxes. 'There you are, love. Can I help you with anything else today?'

'No, thank you.' Frances put a shilling on the table and headed straight to the beauty counter. This was the right thing to do, she thought, keep busy and concentrate on the positive things instead of fretting about things she couldn't change. She'd make her mum promise to talk to her before she gave away any money, and she really would stop being influenced by mystery dramas on radio, or sensational newspaper headlines, like the ones she'd read lately in *The Advertiser* about stick-ups. They gave her silly ideas.

～

Her calm mind-set lasted until Wednesday night when Frances came home to find her mother gone.

'A boy came to fetch Maggie,' Phil said. 'She left me in charge of tea and told me we shouldn't wait for her.'

'Is it about old Henry again? Mr Cooke?' She took an apron off the wall hook and tied it around her waist. 'Let me peel the vegetables. You can slice the onions if you don't mind your eyes watering. Where's Uncle Sal?'

'Outside, inspecting the broken tiles on the roof.'

'He's doing what?' She nearly dropped the pie dish she'd taken off a shelf. She put it down and ran outside.

Phil followed her, frowning. 'Is there something wrong with that?'

'Apart from the fact that he's old and lame and might fall off the ladder, breaking every bone in his body?' Frances tried to stay calm. 'Why didn't you stop him?'

'He looks fine to me. Besides, what right do I have to order your Uncle Sal around?'

'None whatsoever, mate, so you calm yourself down.' Uncle Sal climbed down the ladder and planted his feet wide to support himself. 'As for you, love, you'd better have some faith in me. I may not be as spry as I used to be, but I'm not drawing my pension yet.'

Frances put her hands on her hips, exasperated. 'You promised you wouldn't try to tackle the roof.'

Uncle Sal gave her a hurt look. 'When have I ever broken a promise? I simply took a geek at the damage, that's all. And the sooner you stop treating me like a cripple and get our supper on the table, the better it'll be for all of us.' He limped off.

She bit her lip. Now she'd hurt his feelings. What was the matter with her? No, to be honest, she knew what bothered her. It was that stupid talk she'd overheard. She'd tried so hard to put it out of her mind but it was still there, lurking in a recess, ready to pounce.

She needed to talk to someone she could trust with anything, someone who'd laugh at her and tell her she was seeing ghosts, all because of a few words on the phone line. Only one person fit that bill.

She knocked on Uncle Sal's door.

'Yes?' He still sounded tetchy.

'May I come in? Please?'

He opened the door with less than his usual exuberance. He looked smaller, as if the harsh words between them had deflated him, but his gaze held hers without flinching.

'I'm sorry,' she said, stepping into the room. 'I didn't mean to belittle you. It's ... It's hard to explain, really, Uncle Sal, but something's happened that makes me feel, well, silly and anxious at the same time.'

'I knew something was eating at you.' He shut the door behind her. 'Let's sit down and have a talk.'

Frances sat down on the sea chest that doubled as a window seat and hugged her knees. Uncle Sal pulled up the chair in front of his battered dressing table and turned it so he faced her.

'Spit it out, love,' he said. 'What's wrong? Something at the phone exchange?'

Her bottom lip began to tremble. She nodded. 'It's all because of Gussie,' she said. 'If only she hadn't gotten herself the boot. You see, Uncle Sal ...' Something caught in her throat.

'Hush, love,' he said, as he got up to sit down next to her. He hugged her, cradling her like a child. She closed her eyes.

'You don't have to say anything,' Uncle Sal said, with the special tender note in his voice he had for her. 'You worry too much, love. You'd never do anything stupid and lose your job. I know it's not easy to have us all relying on you. But things will get better and then we'll go travelling the world, just you and me, the way we always planned.' He planted a kiss on her forehead. 'I count my blessings every day, that I have you and Maggie in my life. I don't know what I'd do without you.'

She hugged him back with all her power as the knot in her chest tightened.

'Are you feeling better now?' he asked. 'Or is there anything else you wanted to tell me?'

She stretched her lips apart, trying hard to sound cheerful. She couldn't tell him. He'd only get nightmares too. So, instead, she said, 'Just that I'm happy I've got you, Uncle Sal.'

Mum must have been up with the Cookes all night, Frances thought, as she put on the kettle for breakfast. If her mother hadn't been fit to drop she'd never have tolerated her dirty plate, cup, and cutlery to sit in the sink come dawn, next to the soaking pie-dish.

Ten past five. She wondered if she had enough time to spare to wash up the few things, but then she might be cutting it a bit too fine. At least Maggie was asleep now, and tonight they'd go out together for the first time in almost two years.

Her mood brightened, and she was determined to keep it that way. She'd spent enough time tossing around in her bed, repeating in her mind what she'd heard. Long past midnight it had come to her in a flash, the one explanation that made sense. The man had said pick up, not stick-up, and obviously they wanted to meet a friend and take him for an outing, lakeside or somewhere else. Imagine if she'd gone to the police with that! They'd have laughed at her all the way to Timbuctoo.

What a fool she'd been to lose sleep over that. It didn't bear thinking about that she'd nearly confided in Uncle Sal, burdening the poor darling with her crazy ideas. Well, she wouldn't go down that path again. Instead, she'd be back to her normal sensible self.

'You're sounding pretty chipper today,' said the operator of the telephone exchange in Port Adelaide, while Frances tried to get through to the China Gift Store for her.

'I'm going out dancing tonight.' Her grin widened. 'And then I've got all of Good Friday off, and Saturday and Easter Sunday as well.'

'Gosh, you're lucky,' the other operator said. 'I wish I had someone to take me out, but my boyfriend says as we'll have to make do with a picnic this Easter.'

'I'm not going with a boyfriend, just Mum, Uncle Sal, and our lodger.' She listened for the ringing tone. 'China Gift Store? You've got a phone call from Port Adelaide.' She flipped the switch on her headset, still smiling.

~

Mr Gibbons handed her a brown envelope when her shift was over. Because of Easter they got paid a day early.

'Happy holiday, my dear,' he said. 'Enjoy yourself and thanks again for helping me out last weekend.'

'Have you found a replacement for Gussie yet?' she asked.

He shook his head. 'The head office hasn't yet decided what to do. We aren't as busy as we used to be, and if the revenue doesn't add up ...'

Fear shot through her as his words sank in. 'They're not going to close us down, are they?'

Mr Gibbons took a quick step forward. 'You needn't worry, Frances. Your job is safe, and even if this exchange gets closed, I'd see to it that you'd be put on another switchboard.' He patted her shoulder. 'Your father was with the Royal Post until the day he died, and you're the best, most reliable operator I have. It's simply that there might be no new girls joining us.'

'But what about Gussie's shift?'

Mr Gibbons took off his spectacles to give them a polish with his handkerchief. 'Either the main exchange will take over or I'll ask around who can help fill in, until it has been decided if she'll be replaced. Gussie was only doing twelve hours a week.'

58

'I could help out,' Frances said, eager to show her gratitude, and earn some extra money. 'You'll let me know if I'm needed, will you?'

'Thanks, Frances, I might have to take you up on that. But I won't keep you any longer. The sky doesn't look too promising, and we don't want you to get drenched on my account.'

A brief glance out of the window told her that Mr Gibbons was right. The clouds that were clearly defined, snowy-white and briskly moving when she arrived, now loomed grey and bloated. She took the umbrella she kept in a stand for such cases and gritted her teeth. After almost a month of rainless days and nights, the weather had to turn sour on the one day when she needed it to be fine.

Frances wondered how far it would be from the tram stop to the Top Note. She could carry her ankle-strap satin shoes in a bag and wear her wellies on the way, but what about her frock? She'd rather stay at home than risk spoiling it with water stains, and her raincoat fell a good ten inches short off her hem.

She looked up at the sky with a sinking heart.

The grey clouds expanded, until there was barely a patch of blue left, but the rain held off.

She ran up the stairs. 'Mum, you need to get your rain gear out,' she said. 'I'm going to have a bath now, and then I'll help you dress your hair.'

She didn't wait for a reply. Instead she locked the bathroom door, plugged the enamel roll-top bath and opened the chrome taps as wide as possible. From a stoppered glass-bottle she poured a handful of rose scented bath salts that her mother had given her for Christmas into the bathwater.

She sank into the foaming water. She stretched luxuriously. The bathroom was less than ten years old, and had been ingeniously converted from part of the landing and a broom cupboard. Until then, they'd used a zinc bath tub in the kitchen, filled with hot water from the copper and topped up with cold rain water from the butt in the garden.

She sank deeper until her chin touched sudsy bubbles. Heavenly to stretch out like this, she thought. She rarely allowed herself to fill the tub more than ankle-deep, with the hot water boiler using so much electricity.

The water had cooled to lukewarm when she roused herself and grasped a striped cotton bath sheet to towel herself off. She wrapped in her green flannel dressing gown and wound a towel around her wet hair.

Back in her room, she opened the drawer and took out the new stockings. 'Mum?' She knocked on her mother's bedroom door before she went inside.

'I'm downstairs,' Maggie sang out. 'I'll be with you in a minute.'

Frances sat down on the edge of the bed. Her mother's dress, a low-waisted affair in a golden brown that had been fashionable in 1925, hung ready on the wardrobe. She wished her mother had a new frock as well, but at least the colour suited her, and she always looked distinguished. A rush of pride swept over her, as Maggie joined her.

She patted the spot beside her. 'You sit down and I'll

bring brush and hairpins,' she said, giddy with anticipation. 'I thought we'd do your hair up with the diamante combs I got at the jumble sale.'

Her mother gave her a weak smile. 'We'd better get you ready first. Is your hair dry?'

She unwound the towel. 'Almost,' she said, touching her hair. 'If we do it in rollers while I get dressed, it'll just need ten minutes in front of the fire.' She peered at Maggie's anxious face. 'We are going, aren't we? Don't say something has happened.'

Maggie sank down next to her. 'It has, but that won't spoil your fun. I can't wait to hear every little bit tomorrow morning.'

Frances opened her mouth.

Maggie fingered the quilted bedspread. 'Henry Cooke passed away this morning at a quarter past three, while I was sitting with him. Bertha is beside herself. I promised I'd come and stay with her until she can cope. She needs help with the arrangements.' She took Frances' face into her hands. 'You understand, love, that I can't go out with you tonight. They'd been married for fifty-three years, poor soul.'

Frances felt tears well up in her eyes. 'Oh no. Poor Bertha, and poor you, watching him die. I'll come with you. There must be something I can do to help. I'd feel like a beast enjoying myself at a time like this.'

'There's no need,' Maggie said. 'Stop acting all tragic and silly, my darling. You'll go out and have a great time with Uncle Sal and Phil, and maybe we'll all go out together another day.'

She rose, pulling Frances along. 'You put your frock on, and then I'll do your hair and make-up.'

'Are you sure?' A tiny part of Frances felt bad about enjoying herself when someone she'd known all her life must be devastated, but she had looked forward to this treat so much that giving it up would have been a hardship, especially after her own turmoil these last days.

'Very sure,' Maggie said. 'Now hold still while I do your hair.'

Frances felt self-conscious as she glided down the stairs. It was the dress, she decided. It made her feel almost like a butterfly that had emerged from its chrysalis.

Uncle Sal made a formal bow, while Phil's lips formed themselves into a whistle.

'You look beautiful,' Uncle Sal said. 'I wish your father could see you.'

Frances felt a quick stab of pain. She'd loved her dad, but somehow, she was so busy taking care of things, that whole weeks passed without her thinking about him. It must be different for Uncle Sal. He had too much time on his hands, and he and her dad had always been close, right up to his death in 1928, even if they didn't meet up for months because Uncle Sal was on tour.

She took Uncle Sal's arm and gave it a light squeeze. 'You don't look too shabby yourself.' She gave him the once-over, admiring the white silk scarf and old-fashioned black dinner jacket with the wide velvet collar. It was hard to believe that these garments used to be part of Uncle Sal's vaudeville costume. She had to look very hard to spot the faint stains left by sweat and stage grease.

'I'm beginning to feel a bit like a swagman,' Phil said,

adjusting the bow-tie that sat uncomfortably tight on the unstarched collar of his dress shirt. His brown suit had seen better days, but it was well-cut and of good quality, as were the brown leather shoes.

Frances gave him a dazzling smile, basking in his obvious admiration. 'Shall we go now? I'll just fetch my rain coat.'

'You won't need that,' Uncle Sal said. 'Didn't you hear the wind puffing like a steam engine? It's blown the rain clouds right up against Mount Lofte. Don't wait up for us, Maggie.' He made a few uneven dance steps. 'I can feel the old soft shoe routine coming up through my soles.'

CHAPTER SIX

The Top Note was a brisk five-minute walk from the tram stop. Frances and Uncle Sal emerged in high spirits. They left Phil to follow them, carrying, on his insistence, the bag with Frances' satin dance shoes. She'd decided against wearing them on the way, for fear they might get dirty. The low-heeled brogues she wore everyday were at odds with her dress, but Frances didn't care. She bubbled over with happiness.

The club occupied the first two floors of a three-storey, sandstone building erected in the eve of the war in classical style, with brick detailing and strapped gables. In less than two decades, its fortunes had changed from a private gentleman's residence to vaudeville theatre and, since the end of 1928, to the Top Note, a popular night club. It held a place of its own, ranking between a frightfully exclusive club, notorious for its excesses, and the establishments that catered to the seedier elements.

An impassive giant in a black suit guarded the glossy, black-painted door. Frances' eyes widened as Uncle Sal ushered her inside the building. Two discreetly signed doors to the left and right made her turn towards Phil and ask him for her bag.

'I'll be right back,' she whispered to Uncle Sal.

He gave her a wink. 'We'll wait for you at the door, love.'

The powder room drew a gasp from Frances. One whole wall was covered from halfway up until a couple of inches under the ceiling with a gilt-framed mirror. Two shell-shaped marble basins stood on top of a marble shelf that was placed directly underneath. Plush chrome-legged stools sat at regular intervals.

A girl about her own age sat on a stool. She had one eye closed, reapplying a thick coat of turquoise eye shadow. Her open evening bag on the counter revealed a golden powder compact, a bejewelled lipstick case, and a purse made of a golden metal.

Frances sat on a stool and took her satin shoes out of the bag. She still needed to put on her new stockings. She gave the other girl a quick sideward glance. The girl raised her eyebrows. 'Don't mind me,' she said, painting the other eyelid. 'I'm almost done anyway.'

Frances slipped into a cubicle and opened the cardboard box. She took off her socks and slid on the stockings, fastening them on to her garter belt, before she put on her dance shoes. She stepped out of the cubicle as the other girl glided out of the room.

Frances smoothed her frock and took a comb out of her evening bag. In this artificial light, her hair looked more bronze than light brown. Its soft waves touched her shoulders, curling inwards.

She examined her face. The powder hid the dusting of

freckles on her nose, but with her glowing skin she'd never achieve that pale, mysterious look other girls sported. She'd tried to suck in her gently rounded cheeks, for that hollow effect, but it only made her look and feel foolish.

She took out her compact and snapped it open. A quick dab of powder on nose and chin, another coat of lipstick, and she was done. She gave herself one last satisfied glance in the mirror.

'That was quick,' Phil said as she joined them. He leant over the wooden counter that separated the cloakroom from the corridor. 'Uncle Sal has gone to secure us a table, after he introduced me to your charming friend.'

Pauline, who stood on the other side of the counter, gave Phil a wink and a smile. Frances suppressed a grin. Trust Pauline to flirt mildly with any personable man.

Pauline turned to Frances. 'I'm sooooo glad you came.'

She handed Phil a metal plate with an engraved number, fluttering her lashes at him, before she addressed Frances again. 'You know, I might be able to join you later for a bit. I'll ask after I've done my spell here and helped Miss Bardon backstage.' She lowered her voice. 'I'm sure she'll let me go once I've helped her dress, when I tell her I've got friends here. She's so nice, and she sings like an angel. You've never heard her, have you?'

Frances shook her head. Miss Bardon's name was well-known to her, it was through her that Pauline got this job, but she'd never seen her in person. The singer used to be a regular at the beauty salon where Pauline was employed as a shampoo girl and general dogsbody, until the business folded.

Pauline leant over to Phil. 'She's the best night club

singer in Adelaide, if not the whole of Australia, and everyone is crazy about her, in a nice way, I mean. Otherwise Mr Jack would be sure to teach them what's what. He's the boss.' Footsteps interrupted her. 'New customers,' she said. 'See you later.' She put on a professional smile as she turned to a slick man with a pencil moustache and two-tone shoes.

They found Uncle Sal waiting for them at a small table close to the dance floor. Phil said, 'Your friend's a nice girl. Very chatty, and very pretty.'

'Pauline's been my best friend since we started school,' Frances said. 'I'm glad you like her.' She looked around her with delight. A dozen tables were scattered along the white-washed walls. Sconces fitted with electric candles and chandeliers spread enough light to chat and dance, without casting anyone into sharp and unflattering relief. The hardwood floor was partly covered with crimson rugs, making it easy to roll them up to enlarge the dance floor.

The place filled up rapidly, Frances noticed. People were in a high old mood, the men meeting and greeting each other, the women embracing while appraising the other's fur stoles and jewels. Hardly anyone gave Frances a glance. She didn't mind. It offered her the opportunity to soak up every detail without being scrutinised herself.

Uncle Sal gave her hand a little squeeze. 'Happy?'

'Very.' She blew him a kiss.

Phil said, 'We'll wait to order our drinks until the hubbub dies down a bit.' He relaxed into his chair.

The five-man band moved on to the small stage while people were still milling around.

To Frances, it seemed rude to chat without giving the musicians a single glance. She frowned, but Uncle Sal shook his head a fraction of an inch. 'It's not like a theatre,' he said, 'where you get a bell ringing and the curtain comes up.' He pulled a wry face. 'Glory days, love.'

She smiled at him, her gaze directed towards the dapper looking band who seemed so cool despite the heat of the limelight. She'd try and memorise as much as she could, to share with her mum.

A slight young man with slicked back hair and a tuxedo stepped in front of the band, raised his baton, and the concert was in full swing.

She tapped her feet under the table. Her fingers drummed on the tablecloth. The first couples took to the dance floor. Her gaze followed them.

Phil held out his hand. 'Shall we dance?'

Uncle Sal nodded. 'Off you go, child, but mind to save the first foxtrot for me.'

Phil was a fabulous dancer, matching his step to hers. It was heaven to glide across the room without having to worry if she'd step on his toes. She hadn't been to a dance in ages, and her knowledge of the one-step, two-step, and Lindy Hop was limited to what she and Pauline had seen at the pictures and practiced in Frances' parlour, to the sounds of the radio.

The band was bonzer, too, playing all of her favourite tunes, like 'Three Little Words' and 'Ten Cents a Dance'. Phil's hand grasped her waist tighter. Her cheek came up to his shoulder, and for a second he pulled her close enough for the top of her head to rest against his chin.

Her pulse quickened. She made a wrong step.

'Would you like a break?' he asked.

Frances nodded as he led her off the dance floor, confused about her own reaction. For an instant, the image of another man had flashed inside her mind, a tanned man with dark hair and a nose that had once been broken. Silly.

She sank down onto her chair.

'Thirsty?' Uncle Sal asked.

'Very. It's hot with all those chandeliers above the dance floor.'

'I'll get us something to drink from the bar,' Phil said and got up.

Uncle Sal held him back. 'No need. I've already seen to that.'

Frances still felt flustered. 'I'll be back in a jiffy,' she said, picking up her bag. On her way to the powder room, she looked for Pauline, but she'd been replaced by a stout man.

Two women stood in front of the mirror. Their conversation stopped as they saw Frances. Cold eyes took in every inch of her appearance, before they dismissed her with a shrug and a yawn.

'And then,' a brunette, with jutting hips in a cut-out, pink, silk dress that revealed every bone in her back, said, 'I told her to take her hands off my man. As if he'd look twice at a scrawny bit of used goods like her. I bet you she's been around the block more often than a bobby on the beat.'

Her heavily peroxided friend dabbed perfume behind her ears. She ran her fingers through a frizzy halo of bleached hair. 'You should have slapped the little hussy once and for all. She's been after your Harold for ages, and Will said she's been trying her luck with him as well, as soon as Nancy's back was turned.'

The brunette said, 'Who cares about trash like that anyway?' She touched a sparkling choker around her thin neck. 'What do you think of this? Harold's little surprise to make up for finding him with that vulture almost on his lap.'

The blonde's eyes were hungry. 'Where did he get it from?'

'Who cares? He didn't stick anyone up to get his hands on it, that's all I need to know. I'd hate to have the force sniffing all over me.' The brunette smoothed her dress over her hips and grabbed her bag. 'Let's go before the boys start to get naughty ideas.' Their heels beat an aggressive staccato as they sashayed off.

Frances' mouth gaped open. Those words again. Her mind must be starting to play tricks on her, or maybe that kind of talk was fashionable among the fast crowd those women obviously belonged too. It had nothing to do with her, anyway. She swiped her lipstick over her mouth.

A silver bucket and four glasses stood in front of Uncle Sal.

He winked at her. 'I thought you might be a while,' he said, filling a glass with a pale-yellow liquid.

She picked it up and held it under her nose. A fruity scent tickled her nostrils.

Uncle Sal and Phil raised their glasses. 'Cheers, love,' Uncle Sal said. 'And go easy on it.'

Frances took a sip. She wrinkled her nose. 'It's sourer than I thought,' she said. 'What is it? Champagne?'

'I couldn't order a schooner of beer for you, love, now could I?'

'But isn't that terribly expensive? And what if the police turn up and arrest us for illegal drinking?'

Uncle Sal gave her a chuck under the chin. 'The police have got better things to do. And I'm not skint yet, Frances. There's a few quid left from the money that grogged up toff paid for mowing me down.'

'Yes, but ...'

'Wipe that frown off your pretty forehead. Do you think your mother would let you come along if she didn't trust us?' Uncle Sal drained his glass with a few sips. 'Mind the table, Phil. The next dance is mine.'

Feet aching, Frances made her way back to their table only when the band announced the last dance before their break. They'd played for over two hours.

She felt giddy, even though she had forbidden Uncle Sal to order another bottle of champagne and stuck to iced water after her second glass.

'There you are.' Pauline's dimples deepened as she pulled Frances down on the chair next to hers. 'Isn't this bonzer? I told you you'd love it.'

'How long have you been sitting here?' Frances dabbed her hot forehead with a lace handkerchief.

'Only long enough to have had one drink. Iced water! Frances, honestly, how can you?'

'Why not? Don't tell me you have champagne all the time when you're working.'

'As if!' Pauline stuck out her lower lip. 'I've had a sip once, that's all. We're not allowed to drink with the customers, not even if they invite us.'

'I'm glad to hear that,' Uncle Sal said. 'Your mum would not be happy if you start picking up bad habits.'

'I can look after myself, thank you very much.' Pauline pouted. She swivelled around to face Phil. 'Don't you think he treats us like children?' She fluttered her eyelashes at him, the way they did in the pictures.

Phil gave her an amused smile.

'Anyway,' Pauline went on, 'Miss Bardon said it doesn't do to mix business and pleasure, and she's always right.' A drum beat interrupted her. She cocked her head to the left. 'Quiet, now,' she said, in a hushed voice. 'It's her turn.'

Loud applause greeted the singer, interspersed with whistles. Dolores Bardon stood motionless in the centre of the small stage, until the noise calmed down.

She was older than Frances had thought she would be from Pauline's stories, probably in her early thirties, and of a luminous beauty. A black dress hugged her curves which defied the current fashion for boyish slimness. Eyes like molten chocolate scanned the crowd. Dark curls pinned up in a careless fashion brushed prominent cheekbones. The brows were arched but not plucked, and the deep red mouth was as unfashionably generous as Frances' own.

Peardrop-shaped diamond earrings and a matching pendant sparked off tiny rainbows whenever the light fell on to them. Frances stared, spellbound.

She clasped her left hand to her heart as Dolores Bardon began to sing. There was a haunting quality to that rich, velvety voice. A warm sensation rose in Frances' stomach, as she listened to the 'St Louis Blues' and then to 'Stardust'. With all her experience of vaudeville shows, Frances had never seen or heard anything like it. She held her breath as long as possible, anxious to break the magic.

'Care to dance?' Phil asked.

She shook her head, her gaze fixed on the singer.

She heard him ask Pauline, and then Pauline's skirt rustled, but it was all in the background. People milled around, hogging the dance floor. The smoke of cigarettes drifted by, twisted columns in the air that burnt in Frances' throat. It didn't matter. Nothing did, but the music.

When Dolores Bardon took her final bow, Frances felt drained of all emotion.

Uncle Sal blinked back tears. 'What an artist,' he said. 'What a beaut.' There was longing in his voice, as if he ached for those days when he'd shone on the stage. He got up and bowed, his hand almost sweeping the floor, before he sat down again.

She felt for his hand and pressed it. Together they watched Miss Bardon receive a bouquet she had to hold in both hands, made up completely of white flowers.

Frances gave Uncle Sal's hand another squeeze, wondering if he remembered the first time she'd given him flowers on stage, when she was eight years old and he performed for two weeks at the Empire Theatre. Uncle Sal had forever been part of her family, because his father had worked as a waiter in London and he and his folks had come over from England on the same boat as her grandparents and her dad. Whenever he performed in Adelaide, he'd drop by, but that was the first time she'd been allowed to come along to a matinee.

He'd looked like a matinee idol then, with his black and silver hair setting off the deep tan of his skin, the thin black moustache curled up at the ends. The dinner jacket could have been the same he wore today. She looked at him with pride. He still was Salvatore the Magnificent, where she was concerned. Maybe she'd tell him so, but without an audience.

Pauline and Phil returned. He appeared unruffled and cool, but Pauline was flushed. 'I'm off to the powder room,' she said. 'My nose must be all shiny. I'll be back in a twinkle.'

She glided off, weaving her way expertly through the crowd.

CHAPTER SEVEN

'Phil? Is that really you?' A male voice, relaxed but with a hint of doubt. Frances' heart beat faster. She'd recognise that voice anywhere.

'Yes?' Phil said. 'Do I – but of course, we've met before. Sorry, I forgot the name.'

'No wonder, after all these years. It's Sullivan,' the man said. 'Jack Sullivan.' The men engaged in a firm handshake. Frances' head swivelled towards the man as Phil whistled in amazement. 'Jack Sullivan! Last time I saw you was on a ship. Fancy meeting you here.'

Mr Sullivan sounded amused. 'I'm always here. This is my joint.'

'Lucky you,' Phil said. His eyebrows shot up. He looked around as if he saw the room for the first time.

'Lucky me. But I don't want to keep you from your company.'

'Don't go,' Phil said. 'Unless you must, of course. Jack, let me introduce you to Sal Bernardo and Miss Palmer. Jack and I came back home together after we'd been demobbed.'

Mr Sullivan stretched out his hand. His sleepy eyes opened a fraction wider as he saw Frances. 'My pleasure, Mr Bernardo. Well, Miss Palmer, it's nice to meet you again.'

Frances took his hand, not sure what to say. A half smile spread over Jack's face. A few crinkles fanned out in white lines around his eyes. He slid his left hand into the pocket of his perfectly fitting white evening jacket. Despite the warmth of the room he appeared cool and in control.

Uncle Sal gave him a critical glance. 'So, you're White Jack. Fancy you knowing my Frances.'

'We've met, briefly.'

'Mr Sullivan is the man who helped me with the shopping last week,' she said, hoping her colour hadn't changed.

She needn't have worried about that; Jack had already switched his attention to Phil. 'I can't tell you how glad I am to bump into you, of all people,' he said, 'but we can't talk here.' He scanned the crowd. 'Why don't we all go upstairs and have a bite. There's someone you might want to meet, Phil.'

Frances followed in Phil and Jack's wake, with Uncle Sal at her side. She heard his laboured breathing as they climbed the broad staircase to an upper balcony. She shouldn't have kept him dancing for that long, she admonished herself. He'd wake up in pain.

~

Jack Sullivan ushered them into a niche. A velvet curtain could be drawn across to hide them from prying eyes. Another five niches and a small bandstand, placed right in the middle, took up the rest of the balcony. Only two niches were occupied, but all the tables shone with gleaming silver cutlery and crystal glassware.

He pulled out a chair for her, amused by her open astonishment. 'We do a bit of dining here as well, Miss Palmer. Downstairs you can get light snacks to go with the drinks, but it'd be hell for a waiter to press through that crowd with a fancy meal.'

She sat down, careful to smooth the frock over her legs, the way they did in the talkies. 'You don't seem to be doing too much business here tonight.'

'It's a bit early for the night revellers, and downstairs everybody's having too much fun to come up to dine. Now, what would you like? Steak? Ham and veal pie? Lobster? Or something fancier?'

She waited for the men to reply, but obviously they wanted to leave the decision to her. She wished she could see a menu. This evening would be expensive enough for Phil, without her going overboard with dinner because she had no idea what to order.

Mr Sullivan watched her with an encouraging twinkle in his eyes.

She took the plunge. 'Could we have a cold pie, or a sandwich or two?'

'Sure,' he said. 'Nothing easier. Drinks?'

'Beer'll do me,' Phil said. Uncle Sal nodded.

'And for you, Miss Palmer?'

She hesitated, embarrassed.

'Well?' Mr Sullivan asked.

She fixed her gaze at a point over his left shoulder, careful not to look away, but also not to meet his eye. 'Could I have lemonade?'

Phil opened and closed his mouth with a loud snap.

Frances stuck her chin out. 'You did ask,' she said to Mr Sullivan, turning her head just enough to make eye contact.

'And you shall have your lemonade,' he said, regarding her with something like a new-found interest. 'What's more, I'll join you.'

Phil guffawed. 'Don't tell me, Jack, you of all people are a wowser.'

'I'm not. You might even call me a sly-grogger, but as a custom, I don't drink booze when I'm working. I've seen too many men in my business become their own best customers.'

'But what about the police?' Frances glanced around nervously, half expecting to see a posse of burly men in uniforms bearing down on them.

'They're already here, Miss Palmer.' He nodded downstairs, where the crowd seemed to be swelling by the minute. 'I could point out at least three high-ranking officers and a couple of members of the council swilling champagne cocktails right now. Does it bother you very much to be in the company of a hardened sinner? Even if I'm one of a million law-breakers, and only after six o'clock, because of the way our prohibition works?'

'No.' She shook her head. 'I've had some champagne, so that makes me a law-breaker as well, doesn't it? And I think it's stupid to believe someone who likes his beer would stop being thirsty because the clock says so. But I wish you'd call me Frances.'

He touched her shoulder for a heartbeat. 'I will, if you'll call me Jack.'

'Here you are. I've been looking everywhere. You should have told me you're going upstairs.' Pauline pressed her lips together the way Clara Bow did in the pictures.

'We didn't know it then,' Phil said.

'Well, it doesn't matter,' Pauline said, mollified. 'This is nice. At least one can have a real chin-wag here, without having to yell. I swear, sometimes I think I'll go deaf in this place.'

'Sorry to hear that,' Jack said as he returned with a laden tray.

'Mr Jack!' Pauline had the grace to blush. 'I didn't mean to be rude.'

Frances giggled in a most undignified manner. Blasted champagne, she thought.

'That's not funny, Frances Palmer.' Pauline glared at her. 'This is my boss, Mr Sullivan, and I don't want him to get the wrong impression.'

A hint of surprise crept into her tone of voice. 'What are you doing here, Mr Sullivan, now I think of it, doing Danny's job? Is something wrong with him?'

He sat the tray down on the table. 'Danny is fine, but I'm sure he'll appreciate your concern, and these people are my guests.' He pulled out another chair. 'As it seems you're a part of the company, you'll be my guest as well. But just this once, don't forget that, young lady.'

Pauline gazed at him with wide-eyed gratitude. She sat

down on the edge of a chair, inching as close to Frances as possible.

Downstairs, the band struck up another tune. Pauline jumped up. 'I'll go and see if Miss Bardon needs help.'

'Do that, and please ask her if she'll join us, Pauline.' Jack dismissed her with a nod and leant against the waist-high railing, hands in his pockets. 'So, what brings you to Adelaide, Phil? I seem to recall you being a big town boy.'

'There's a lot to be said for places like this, and these days you got to go where you can earn your living.' Phil replied.

'Got the spear in your old place? It's no shame in these hard times.'

Phil hesitated. His neck muscles tightened. 'No. I left for health reasons.'

Frances began to feel light-headed with the heat, and she wished everybody would sit down. Her mouth watered looking at the spread. Bundles of grapes, apple slices, and pears garnished the three-tiered stand bulging with crust-less bread triangles.

Uncle Sal had less scruples. He reached for the beer pitcher and filled his glass.

'Sorry,' Jack said. 'Here I stand, yacking away, instead of being a good host. We'll soon fix that.'

He poured lemonade for himself and Frances. 'I'd bring out a toast, but seeing as Miss Bardon and Pauline aren't here yet, I'd better wait for them.' He raised the glass to his lips and took a big gulp.

She sipped her lemonade. It had exactly the right amount of tartness, coupled with a generous dose of sugar.

Jack smiled at her. He had a comfortable face, she

decided. Not movie-star handsome with brooding eyes, and a pencil-thin moustache like Phil, but his features, under the thick, wavy dark hair were regular, and his mouth spoke of a ready sense of humour. He seemed completely at ease with himself, but at the same time in control. More and more did he remind her of her big brother, Rob. It was more to do with his air instead of his looks, but he inspired trust.

'Darling!' The velvety voice tingled with laughter. Dolores Bardon stretched out both her hands for Jack to kiss, before she bestowed a dazzling smile on the rest of the company.

She was even more beautiful up close, Frances decided. The singer had changed into a black and white dress, with a cinched waist and a matching jacket. The ruby-red paint on her fingernails matched her lips.

Phil's and Uncle Sal's eyes widened in open admiration, both emulating Jack and kissing Miss Bardon's hands as they were introduced.

Frances got up from her seat, curtsying as she touched Miss Bardon's outstretched hand. 'I'm honoured to meet you, Miss Bardon.'

The singer laughed again. 'There's no need to treat me like royalty, darling. If Jack says we're among friends, then that's what we are.' She sat down, smoothing her frock over her crossed legs. 'Besides, Pauline has told me all about you.' She reached for Jack's cigarette case.

'Allow me,' Phil said, snapping open his own case.

She took a cigarette and put it between her lips. Phil flicked a silver-plated lighter.

'Thank you,' she said, blowing perfect circles. The

crinkles at the corners of her eyes deepened. Miss Bardon hadn't even tried to mask the first lines with make-up, Frances noticed. She didn't have to. She'd always be lovely. And she was nice as well, Frances thought, as Miss Bardon offered to squeeze a little closer to Uncle Sal, so Pauline could fit in more comfortably. No wonder the men were smitten with her. One only had to watch Phil's face. Tony used to look at Pauline with that same expression on his face. She felt a pinprick of envy.

'Well, Jack?' Miss Bardon rested her cigarette in an ashtray. She spun the revolving sandwich stand around with her fingertips and selected a couple of roast beef sandwiches and a bunch of grapes. 'Where is my surprise, darling?'

'He's sitting right across you.' Jack jerked his head towards Phil. 'The fellow here served with Simon.'

Miss Bardon's hand hung suspended in the air. 'So that's how you met Jack. The Big Stoush.' Her voice sounded choked. She put grapes on to her plate without looking.

Phil's eyes filled with understanding. 'What do you want to know?'

'Everything.' Miss Bardon picked up her cigarette again with a trembling hand. She inhaled deeply. 'Everything you can tell me about Simon Grant.'

No one else said a word. It was as if they were all bit-players, placed there to support the actors in a drama that was played out right here. Frances tensed, feeling very much in the way. She gave Uncle Sal a questioning glance. He shook his head.

Phil lit a cigarette for himself. 'Simon Grant. I met him

first in the training camp and later, in the trenches. Early 1918,' he said. 'Good man. Everybody liked him. He'd share his last shirt if you asked him. Or his socks. One day he got a parcel, with a tin of tobacco and two pairs of hand-knit socks. A few days later there was this New Zealander, a kid who'd lied about his age to enlist, rubbing his feet raw in his boots, because he'd wagered his socks in a craps game, the silly mug. Simon handed him a pair, just like that. Didn't want to hear a word of thanks in return.'

He drew on his cigarette, staring straight ahead. 'Hell of a man, Simon Grant. Boss cocky, and he didn't need the stripes, that's for sure.' Frances reached for Uncle Sal's hand. He gripped hers tight.

Dolores Bardon leant over the table, her lips parted. She blinked back tears. 'He always was like that, he and Jack both.' She pressed the knuckles of her left hand into her mouth. 'How did he – how did he die?'

A nerve on Phil's temple twitched. 'Quick,' he said. 'He wouldn't have felt anything.' He clasped Miss Bardon's hand with both of his hands. 'Everybody loved Simon.'

'Yes.' Tears began to trickle down Miss Bardon's cheek. 'Yes. Thank you.'

She blindly wiped the tears away with the back of her hand before she turned around to face Jack.

He put his hands on her shoulders. 'It's all right, love, it's all right,' he said as she buried her face against his chest.

The scent of Miss Bardon's perfume wafted towards Frances, almost overpowering her. She felt like the worst form of intruder, watching someone's private grief. 'Shouldn't we better leave?' she whispered in Uncle Sal's ear.

Jack must have heard, because he shook his head, holding up his hand as if to stop them.

'I'm sorry.' Miss Bardon took the proffered handkerchief from Jack. 'It's just – I always wondered, you know. About Simon. If he suffered.' She dabbed her wet eyes with angry movements. 'All the telegram said was that he'd been killed.'

She got up to walk around the table. 'Thank you,' she said, brushing Phil's cheek with her lips. 'You don't know what this means to me. Maybe we can talk again, another day?' She bestowed a trembling smile on Frances, Pauline, and Uncle Sal. 'And now we shall eat and drink and be merry.' Her smile became steady. 'After I've done some repairs. I must look a fright.'

'You could never do that,' Frances said, feeling the colour creep up from her neck. 'You look like a star in the pictures, Miss Bardon.'

'It's Dolores for you, darling. No, I don't need any help, from anyone. You enjoy yourselves, and I'll be with you before you'll miss me.' She blew them a kiss and swept off.

'Thanks, mate.' Jack seemed unfazed by all the emotion swirling around them as he took a sandwich. He bit into the bread. 'Call me unfeeling, but I'm starting to feel a bit hollow.'

CHAPTER EIGHT

*T*he other niches had filled by the time Dolores came sweeping back up the stairs. 'Have I been this long?' she said, with a strained smile. 'I ran into some people, and you know how hard it is to extract oneself.'

Jack arched an eyebrow. 'Anyone I'd care to hear about?'

Her hand fluttered to her throat. 'These were new ones, Jack, darling, otherwise Bluey would have stopped them.'

A muscle on Jack's jaw twitched. Frances began to feel puzzled. Something obviously was wrong. She wasn't the only one to pick up on the change in atmosphere, because Phil moved closer. 'Trouble?' he asked.

Jack said. 'Nothing we can't handle. Lots of people out there would love to lure Dolores away from the Top Note, and not all of them are welcome news.' He pushed back his sleeve to look at his watch. 'Long past midnight. It's time we see the ladies safely home. Bluey'll take you along, Pauline.'

'He doesn't have to,' Pauline said with the half smile, half pout she'd copied from Clara Bow. 'I'm fine on my own.'

Most men would have smiled back at that pretty face, Frances thought. Not Jack, though. He said, 'Not if you value your spot here. As long as you work for me, you play by the rules. Not every man's a nice bloke out there.'

Pauline lowered her gaze. 'Yes, Mr Jack.'

'That's better. Run and join Bluey.' He dismissed Pauline with a wave of his hand. She ran off, fluttering her fingers at Frances.

Phil rubbed the bridge of his nose. 'I thought this is a pretty clean area. Do you think the girl'd run into trouble?'

'We don't want to find out. The rules are, no girl working for me walks home alone at night, and anyone getting ideas about them answers to me. I don't tolerate any funny business.'

Frances stifled a yawn. Jack patted her shoulder. 'Car'll be there in ten minutes.'

'Already?' Dolores raised huge, pleading eyes towards Phil.

'We can talk tomorrow,' he said. 'Jack suggested to meet in the park, if Frances' mother doesn't object to a picnic on Good Friday?'

'She won't,' Frances said, confused. 'Mum never says no if she can help it. But you don't have to ask her for permission. Just because you're lodging with us doesn't mean we hold you accountable.'

Jack smiled at her. 'That's good to hear, but I'd rather have your mother agree to your coming along, too. You'd be in safe hands, with Dolores and your Uncle Sal to look after you.'

He took her hand, put it in the crook of his arm and led her towards the stairs. 'Do me a favour and say yes,' he said as they went down. 'Please. Dolores and I would both appreciate it. She doesn't get the chance to see many people outside the business, and she likes you.'

'She does?' Frances said, feeling a light flutter in her stomach. 'I like her, too. I'll come if I can.'

He walked her to the cloakroom. 'Uncle Sal and Phil will be with you in a minute. I'll wait outside in the car as soon as I've made sure that Dolores won't be bothered again.'

Frances watched his retreat. Uncle Sal instead of Mr Bernardo? The old man must have taken to Jack Sullivan in a flash. Maybe he'd also felt the resemblance to Rob. They both exuded the same sense of comfort. Jack hadn't even laughed when she'd asked for lemonade.

After the hot perfumed air of the Top Note, the air outside felt fresh and crisp. Jack bundled Frances in the passenger seat of the Ford saloon, while Phil and Uncle Sal shared the back. The streets were almost devoid of life. Occasionally was there some movement in the darkness, when the headlight of a car hit upon a shadowy figure who'd sidle away. Jack's jaw clenched in these situations, she noticed out of the corner of her eye before her lids shut of their own accord.

The Ford came to a halt. Before Frances could rouse herself, Jack had opened the door, half pulling her out. She stumbled into his arms.

'Steady there,' he said.

'Thanks for everything,' she said, with her eyes still half-closed.

'My pleasure, kiddo. Phil? Careful how you go. The poor girl is half-dead on her feet.'

She felt herself propelled up the stairs. It was all she could do to take off her dress and her new stockings, change into her nightgown and have a quick wash before she tumbled into bed.

'I'm glad you enjoyed yourself.' Maggie spooned scrambled egg on to four plates. She'd stretched them as far as she could, using plenty of milk.

Frances gave her a swift hug, careful not to dislodge the plates. 'It was splendid, but I still wish you could have come. Poor Bertha! I hope she's feeling a bit better.' She put the plates on a tray. 'I'll take these. Do we need anything else for breakfast?'

'The hot cross buns.' Maggie lifted a metal sheet out of the oven and slid the steaming buns on to the blue and white serving plate they kept for Easter and Christmas. 'They need to cool off a bit.'

Frances carried the tray into the south-facing dining room. They rarely used it these days, because it needed too much heating, and the kitchen was much cosier, but the holidays needed to be celebrated properly.

Maggie had spread the best table cloth on the rosewood table. Frances set the cutlery in even distances next to the plates. Tea and coffee stood ready on an electric hot plate, and a vase full of flowers on top of the piano added a festive touch.

She went along the wall, adjusting the framed music hall pictures celebrating Uncle Sal's days of glory so they hung straight. She loved these pictures, with their gaudy colours and promises of giddy pleasure. They shone brightly on the faded duck egg blue wall. Most of them featured exotic dancers or comedy acts, but two had a small portrait of Uncle Sal a few inches under the top billings. She traced the outlines of his portrait with a finger when the door opened.

'Good morning, love,' Uncle Sal said. 'None the worse for wear, I hope.'

She kissed him on the cheek. 'It was bonzer, wasn't it? I hope the dancing didn't hurt you.'

'No worries, my darling. I told you I'm still pretty nifty on my feet.'

Phil sprung the invitation on Maggie as soon as they'd started breakfast.

'I don't know,' she said, putting down the half eaten hot cross bun. 'Going out with people you just met?' She turned to Uncle Sal, a deep crease between her brows. 'I'm not saying they're not perfectly nice and decent, but mixing with a nightclub crowd, why, that's courting trouble.'

'She'll be fine, Maggie.' Uncle Sal chased his bun down with a mouthful of almost black tea. 'White Jack's no more a crook than you and me, and if the law's stupid enough to make honest coves turn crims with its half-baked prohibition, I say bugger to the law. To be honest, you probably met worse sorts backstage in my heyday, and you never minded them, rum lot that they were.'

'Yes, but ...'

'Why don't you come along and have a geek for yourself? After all, what can happen on an afternoon in Elder Park?' Uncle Sal reached for the teapot. 'It'll perk you up to get away for a bit, and you said yourself that Bertha's got other company today.'

Maggie and Frances tidied the bedrooms. Good Friday or not, the mattresses needed turning and that was easier to do as a team. Uncle Sal turned his hand to whatever needed doing around the house, and he gladly donned an apron in the kitchen, but he'd never entered their bedrooms. People might start to get the wrong idea, he said.

'Mum?' Frances pushed a lock of hair behind her ear. 'Are you all right? You look all in.'

'I'm a bit tired, that's all.' Her mother flipped the mattress over and pummelled it into place.

'You spend too much time cooped up in this house or taking care of the whole street.' Frances shook out the fresh sheet, handing her mother the other end. 'Uncle Sal's right. You should come with us to the picnic.'

Maggie wavered.

'Please? You already missed last night's fun.'

Her mother gave in, as Frances had known she would. 'If you think it won't be a bit embarrassing, having us old folks around, when you go out with a young man.'

'You're not old, Mum, and whatever gave you the idea that I'm going out with anyone but Uncle Sal?' She pulled the sheet taut with force. 'You don't think that anyone will get the wrong idea?'

'Of course not,' Maggie said after a moment's pause. 'And anyway, you'll have Uncle Sal and me to chaperone you. Nobody would dream of talking about you.'

She blew her a kiss. 'You'll see, Mum, it'll be a bosker day. The best we've had forever.'

Maggie insisted on packing a picnic hamper, despite Phil's pleas not to.

'One doesn't turn up empty handed,' she said, pushing him gently but determinedly aside. 'We've never bludged anything, and we're not going to start now.' She took four leftover hot cross buns and put them next to a bottle of home-made lemonade. Frances rummaged in a drawer for the cut-up handkerchiefs Maggie had bought as napkins from one of the endless stream of hawkers.

Maggie lifted the lid off a ceramic jar and peered inside. 'I should have enough sugar left to make an apple and rhubarb crumble, if you can face sugarless tea tomorrow morning.' She pulled a mixing bowl out of the kitchen cabinet.

Phil gave Frances a helpless look. She shrugged, mouthing, 'Don't worry, it's fine.' He winked at her, before he turned his attention to Maggie. 'I'll peel the apples for you,' he said. 'Unless you've got another chore for me.'

The door-bell rang as Maggie put the cake tin into the oven. 'Can you answer it, Frances?' she said, taking off the headscarf she wore for housework. A big-boned, elderly woman stood on the doorstep. Her callused hands clutched a black-rimmed handkerchief.

'Edna?' Maggie brushed past. 'Do come in. Is anything wrong?'

Edna swallowed, her baggy cheeks working. She gave Phil and Frances a quick glance. 'If I could have a quick word? Between you and me and the lamp-post?'

Frances said, 'Phil and I'll see how Uncle Sal's getting on in the back yard. If you'll excuse us, Miss Edna.'

They found Uncle Sal sitting on the veranda, eyes closed against the sun.

'Have you come to pretty yourself up, my lad? I'll have first dibs at the bath just so you know it,' he said, without moving.

Uncle Sal and Phil had their own bathroom, a small affair built as an annex to the main house, making the old dunny obsolete, unless the electricity was out. Cold water was laid on to the bathroom, which offered enough space for a tub, a sink, and a toilet. Bathwater needed to be topped up with hot water from the kitchen, but at least it gave the women free rein of the indoor bathroom and prevented trouble with any lodger over long, expensive baths.

Frances decided to leave the men alone. 'If Mum's asking, I'm upstairs,' she said.

Uncle Sal stretched. He peered at the sky. 'Past noon,' he said. 'I reckon there won't be any lunch today unless we make it ourselves.' He shook his head. 'Don't forget, love, we won't be leaving for another couple of hours. And remind Maggie. If she puts on her finery now she'll get all fidgety, not knowing what to do with herself until we leave.'

'Mum's got a visitor. Edna's with her.' She turned around to go inside.

Uncle Sal said, 'On Good Friday? Well, well.'

Once inside the house, Frances lingered. She sat on the top of the stairs, sunlight streaming in from the window behind her, while she waited for Edna to leave. She didn't want to ear-wig on Maggie and her visitor, and Phil and Uncle Sal were cosy enough, which left her alone with her thoughts. She usually didn't mind letting her hands and her brain idle for a bit, but today felt different. Unwanted thoughts kept pushing their way into her head. And she'd done so well since she'd come up with an innocent explanation for the words that still replayed in her head, like a stuck gramophone record. But in her mind the words were clear. They said, stick-up, stick-up, stick-up.

Goosebumps dotted her arms, despite the warmth of the sun on her exposed skin. She clamped her hands down on her ears, to shut out the unwanted voice. She'd think of something else instead, like the picnic. What should she wear, so she wouldn't look too dowdy compared with Dolores?

The front door banged shut. She brushed off her skirt and went downstairs.

Maggie had her back towards Frances. She grabbed a

93

pot holder, jerked the oven door open, pulling out a cake tin. Her jaw was set in a grim line.

'Mum? Is something wrong?'

The clock ticked precious seconds away. Maggie's features smoothed a bit. 'I was a mite worried the crumble might have burnt,' she said. 'That was the last of our sugar, and the shops won't open again until tomorrow.'

Frances breathed in the rich aroma. 'It looks fine, and the smell is heavenly.'

Frances dressed with care. She wanted to look smart, but casual. She'd brushed out the skirt she wore to work, glad her cloche matched the soft lemon of the jumper that went so well with the emerald green of the skirt. She put on ankle socks and her brogues, whistling to bolster up her spirits, as she joined the others.

CHAPTER NINE

*T*hey took the tram up to North Terrace. Frances squeezed in next to her mother. The men had to stand up in the crowded carriage, being jostled from side to side. The air was stale, with that peculiar mix of cold sweat and cheap lavender water that seemed to seep into the very bones of the tram, no matter what. Maggie pinched her nostrils under cover of her handkerchief, but Frances was used to the smell. She held the picnic basket on her lap, clamping its lid shut as hard as she could.

She was glad there was a blanket in Uncle Sal's swag. On a day like this, when Adelaide shone like a jewel, the sky sapphire-blue, the trees emerald, and the stone of the buildings melted in the sunshine to gold and amber, nothing compared to sitting in the grass of the park.

The tram squealed to a stop. Phil took Maggie's arm, helping her off the step in her unfashionably long skirt. Frances handed the picnic basket down to her mother before she hopped off.

On an ordinary weekend, streams of people of all ages

swamped Elder Park. Because today was Good Friday, it was a mere trickle. They should have no trouble finding a nice spot under a tree, close to the grand bandstand that was the central focus of outdoor entertainment in Adelaide since it came over from Scotland thirty years ago.

Frances stole a sideways glance at Uncle Sal and her mother. Uncle Sal was dragging his chain a bit, trying to fool everyone he didn't feel his gammy ankle. She'd have to find a chair for him, and for Maggie as well, so they wouldn't have to squat on the ground. She slowed her pace to match Uncle Sal's steps.

Phil still walked with Maggie, carrying the basket for her.

Maggie looked back over her shoulder at Frances. 'This is nice,' she said. 'I'm glad I let you sway me.' She turned to Phil. 'Do you have anything like this in Melbourne, or is that a stupid question?'

'This park is a corker, but Melbourne does have its attractions, only not as close to everything, and not as homey; maybe because it's that much bigger.'

'Phil, darling!' Miss Bardon's unmistakable voice rang out. 'Over here.'

Frances blinked. For a moment, she thought they'd walked on to a stage set. A huge moss green patio umbrella shaded a cast iron table and six matching chairs, strewn with cushions. Under the table sat two silver plated buckets and a wicker hamper. The table was laid with real china. Any minute now, an army of servants would bear down on them, Frances thought, because there was no way Jack could have set up all this on his own, even with Dolores' help. She suppressed a giggle. How her mum would react to that opulence, given her doubts about the night club crowd?

If her mother found anything out of the ordinary, she hid it well, showing nothing but well-mannered pleasure as Phil introduced her to Jack and Dolores. Frances breathed a sigh of relief.

At Jack's insistence Maggie took the place at the head of the table, with Uncle Sal at the other end. Dolores sat down next to Phil, opposite Jack and Frances.

'Our little offering,' Maggie said, as Phil opened their basket.

'You shouldn't have.' Dolores said. 'We've got pies and salads and a cold turkey.' She gave Maggie a mischievous smile as Phil put the cake tins on the table. 'But I'm glad you brought this. I adore home-made cake. Will you cut me a piece?'

Maggie's baked goods were the first ones to be demolished. Her face glowed with pleasure, and if she had had any misgivings about their hosts, surely she couldn't harbour them any longer, given the easy way she chatted with Dolores.

Frances smiled. They made such an odd couple, the glamorous singer whose skilfully painted face was shaded by a picture hat with a floppy brim, and the plump, middle-aged woman, in her outdated dress and a straw hat that had both been of good quality once but now betrayed their age. But they seemed comfortable enough. Good; it would have been awful if Maggie had objected to Dolores and Jack simply because they belonged to another, more exciting world. She wanted her very much to like them.

~

'That was a beaut.' Uncle Sal wiped his fingers on the linen napkin. 'What do you say, Maggie, shall we go for a walk to aid digestion, before I take you home? The young'uns can do without us.'

Mum held out her hand to Jack. 'In that case, I'll say good-bye now. Don't be too late, Frances.'

'But, Mum, you've hardly been here any time.' She looked at Uncle Sal for support.

He shook his head in a tiny movement. He bent down to Frances, whispering into her ear. 'There's been a theft. Mrs Jacobs's box's gone.'

'Oh no.' A sick feeling crept into her mouth. Uncle Sal dropped a kiss on to her hair and set off after Maggie.

'What's the matter, kiddo? You suddenly look like whitewash.' Jack pulled Frances up off her chair. She offered no resistance, grateful for the warmth of his hand. 'We'll go down to the lake for a bit,' he told Dolores, 'and you can talk to Phil without us being a nuisance. All right, Frances?'

'Sweet.' Dolores only half listened.

'They'll do for a while,' Jack said, as he offered Frances his arm. 'You don't have to tell me what's going on, of course, but if you need someone to listen?'

Frances bit her lip.

'It's okay,' Jack said. 'Whatever it is, it's not worth fretting yourself into a right old state. Most things aren't.'

She kicked at a few pebbles, scaring a couple of lorikeets into screaming flight. He was right, she needed someone to talk to. She'd kept enough bottled up already.

He walked silently beside her. 'It's all so beastly,' she said. 'Why do some people have to be so horrible?'

Jack remained silent, but in a comforting way. They had almost reached the lake.

'Look at all this,' she said, struggling to put her thoughts into words. 'It's all still pretty good, isn't it? No one's got a lot, but then, no one is starving, not with the Salvation Army around, and the food dole, and friends and family pitching in. I can understand someone being maybe hungry or desperate to find the money for the doctor, or to keep the roof over one's head, and stealing from a rich person.' She gulped. 'That'd be awful enough, but I could understand that, when you've got a sick baby or the rent collector knocks on your door with an eviction notice in his hand.'

She turned her head towards Jack. 'You want to know what happened?' She drew in a deep breath. 'Do you remember the greengrocer's I went to? Well, Mrs Jacobs kept a box next to her till. It's for donations, to help pay for funerals, and everyone puts in a few coins if they can.'

Her voice shook. 'It started last year, when a baby died, and the parents didn't have the money to pay for his funeral. They pawned off their kitchen table and chairs and even their china to see him buried properly. So Mrs Jacobs collected money to ensure that doesn't happen again. Now someone's swiped the whole lot. Taken the box and cleared off with it.'

A vein in Jack's throat pulsed.

She sniffed. 'Mum has promised a neighbour she'd go door to door with her, asking people to help out with paying for old Henry Cooke's send off.' Tears formed in her eyes. 'How can anyone steal from the dead?'

'Never mind the dead. It's the living those bastards hurt.' The anger in his eyes died down as quickly as it had flared up. His tone changed back to the relaxed style she was fast becoming used to. He handed her a handkerchief. 'Do you feel better, now that that's off your mind?'

She nodded as she patted her eyes dry. 'I don't normally cry,' she said. 'It's just ...' She stopped herself. She'd almost blurted out what really weighed her down, the fact that she thought she was an accessory to a crime and there was nothing she could do about it.

'Frances?'

He sounded so much like her brother that she had to remind herself that she barely knew him. 'I'm fine,' she said, handing back his handkerchief. 'Thank you for listening.'

'Any time.'

Dolores and Phil sat where the others had left them. He talked in a soft voice, his hand on hers, and she listened with rapt attention.

Frances felt shy again. She tugged at Jack's arm. 'Let's walk the other way,' she said.

'Feel like we're in the way?'

'A little, yes.'

'Stay here,' he said. He strode over to the table, took the rest of the bread and the half-filled bottle of lemonade and said to no one in particular, 'I'll be back in half an hour. Bluey'll be here soon to help pack up.'

She doubted Dolores heard his words, but Phil gave Jack a quick nod.

Jack tore the bread into small pieces. He threw a handful on to the lake, where they floated for a few seconds. The first mallard swam closer, in unhurried circles, until he picked up a morsel of bread.

'Watch,' he said, as the mallard dipped his bill down to gobble faster and faster, while the rest of the brace closed in. A handful of ducklings paddled in their mother's wake as fast as they could.

Frances took some bread and flung it towards them.

'Don't drop anything on the ground,' he said, 'or we'll be ankle-deep in ducks in the flap of a wing.'

She squatted down, crumbled more bread between her fingers. 'You don't mind, do you? Here, ducky.' She rubbed the last crumbs off her fingers, watching the ducklings flap around in search of more. She rose, feeling slightly better.

'Thirsty?'

Her throat was parched. She nodded.

Jack handed her the lemonade bottle. 'We don't have glasses, but will a drinking straw do?' His hand went inside his jacket, producing two paper straws.

'Lovely.' Frances took a long sip before handing the lemonade back. She looked at Jack, shading her face with one hand.

'You sound a lot like my brother, and you look a bit like Rob, too,' she said. 'Or maybe it's the way you can arch just one eyebrow.' She sighed. 'He always did it to annoy me because he could do that and I can't.'

'He's gone, I presume?' Jack twirled the drinking straw with one finger.

'Yes. Rob married a Brisbane girl a couple of years ago, when he went there to take up work as an assistant veterinary. They've got a baby boy already.'

'So, you're Auntie Frances.'

'Too right,' she said, smiling at the thought of her nephew. 'What about you?'

The sun must have dazzled him, because he turned his head away. 'No nieces and nephews,' he said. 'My sister went to live with relatives in New Zealand a while back, and my mother left for home ages ago.'

'England? That must be hard for you, not being able to see her. It must be tough for her as well.' Frances frowned. 'Mum is fretting about Rob and Lucy and the baby being so far away, and that she hasn't seen Uncle Fred since Rob's wedding. I wish I could buy her a train ticket.'

'A real uncle? Or another Sal?' He raised his hand as she glared at him. 'I don't mean to say anything against Sal, Frances. He's a real character. You can count yourself lucky to have him around.'

'We are,' she said. 'I'd be lost without him. He does all kinds of odd jobs around the house, and he watches over Mum, she is such a soft touch when it comes to people in need. Without him, she'd buy pencils and doilies and whatever someone knocking at the door is hawking by the cart-load. We have a drawer-full as it is.'

A frustrated sigh escaped her. 'I know most of them have a tough spin, but we've got our own bills to pay.

There's only so many people I can look after.' She reined herself in. She'd almost blurted out her recent money trouble caused by Mum's generosity.

'Which is where Uncle Sal steps in?' He smiled at her.

She smiled back. 'He does what he can to help me. It's hard enough looking after family and friends.'

'It is. Even if they're far away. So, Uncle Fred is a real uncle? Where is he?'

'They live in Melbourne, although Mum keeps hoping that he and Aunt Millie will come back home to Adelaide, now that Uncle Fred's retired from the force.' She shrugged. 'Well, at least he sent us Phil. Uncle Fred worries about Mum, since Rob left.'

Jack gave her a questioning look. 'He doesn't seem to have too much faith in Uncle Sal's protection.'

'What do you expect? Uncle Sal is half a head shorter than you and a retired music hall entertainer, which, for Uncle Fred, is one step short of being as useless as a hat stand. Uncle Fred stands six feet one in his socks, with shoulders like an ox and a will of granite.' She shook her head. 'Besides, coming from a long line of coppers means you've got a suspicious mind to begin with.'

A slow grin appeared on Jack's face. 'True words. I suspect that we should get going before anybody thinks that something has happened to you.'

CHAPTER TEN

$\mathcal{T}$he umbrella had gone, as had the table, the chairs, and their occupants. A red-haired giant leant against the trunk of a tree, eyes closed.

Jack tapped him on the shoulder. 'Where's Dolores, Bluey?'

The man's eyes snapped open, wide as a child's. 'Home, along with the cove she was with.' He blinked. 'She said it was all right, that she was getting tired of fending off the mozzies. So, I took her and the cove home and then I took the old bus back to get you.'

Frances stepped out from behind Jack's shadow. 'I'll better be going, too,' she said.

'No,' Jack said, holding her back with one hand. 'It's all right, Bluey. The cove's name is Phil, by the way, and he's my guest, the same as Miss Frances here.' He nudged her towards the road. 'Would you mind coming up to the apartment for a bit as well? I'll take you home, but I'd rather make sure Phil's supply of anecdotes hasn't dried up before Dolores has had her fill.'

She hesitated. She'd love to see how the glamorous singer lived, but for a strange reason she didn't want to see how Dolores and Jack lived together. Mum would be horrified if she knew about the irregular situation. She wasn't too sure how she felt about it herself.

Jack raised both eyebrows. 'Don't worry, you'll be as safe as in your brother's hands. I promise.'

On the other hand, seeing that she was his guest, it was only polite to give in to Jack's request. 'I'll come in for a few minutes.' She hoped her voice sounded firm.

'Whatever you wish.' He led her to the car and opened the door for her, motioning to Bluey to climb into the backseat.

'Sorry about that,' Jack said, 'but I need to make sure young Phil can hold his tongue if Dolores has brought out the fizz.'

'But she wouldn't drink while it's still light outside, would she? And on Good Friday, too.'

Jack accelerated. 'That depends on what Phil told her about the war, kiddo, and how good he is at twisting things a bit. Sometimes there's a lot of solace to be found in a glass.'

'What do you mean, twisting things?' She held on to the handle dangling above her as he forced the car around a sharp bend.

Bluey said, 'Steady, Mr Jack. She's a good bus, but you want to go easy on her. Do you want me to take the steering wheel?'

Jack slowed down.

'I don't understand a single word,' Frances said, getting more confused with every minute. 'First you want Phil to meet with Dolores to talk, then you make sure they are uninterrupted, and now you get all nervy and upset because they're alone together too long?' That could be jealousy of course, but she doubted it.

'We're nearly there,' Jack said. 'And yes, I thought it was a godsend, having someone who was with Simon in those last few weeks.' He took one hand off the steering wheel to tap his right temple. 'Someone who's got a bit of action going on in here. The thing is, there's a limit to how long you can spin things out.'

'He's lying to Dolores?'

'If he's the decent bloke I take him for.'

She stared at Jack's calm profile. 'But that's rotten. She trusts him!'

He blew out his breath. 'Frances, you ask anyone who's been there about the war, and he'll clam up or he'll lie the blue out of the sky to you. That's God's honest truth.'

'Oh. I see.' Her voice sounded as small as she felt.

Jack pulled up along the kerb, stopped and cut the engine.

'You must think I'm stupid,' she said.

'No,' he said. 'Only very young. How old are you, by the way?'

'I'm twenty-two.'

'I thought as much. And I'm almost thirty-six.'

They stood at the back of the Top Note. Four steps led down to a basement door. A wall sconce burned already, illuminating the worn concrete.

Jack unlocked the door and pushed it wide open, feeling on the wall for a light switch. She followed him. Solid oak doors led left and right from the hallway. Straight ahead another flight of stairs led to what must be the club.

He stopped three yards short of the stairs and pushed two doors on the right-hand side open to reveal a lift.

She stared at the riches in front of her. The walls of the lift were painted ivory, with gilt mouldings framing them. On the left side, from top to bottom, ran a bevel-edged mirror, next to a row of buttons on a steel panel. Two fold-down chairs upholstered in green velvet completed the picture.

He pressed a button, and the lift doors closed. The ride, though jerky, was short-lived. The doors opened as Jack pushed another button. Soft music flowed from behind one of the three wooden doors that led off the landing. Thick grey carpet covered the floor, silencing their steps.

He rang a door-bell.

'Darlings!' Dolores flung the door wide open. She had changed into flowing pants and a silk kimono more reminiscent of a boudoir. Again, Frances was glad her mother wasn't here. She sometimes had very old-fashioned ideas. Not that she herself wanted to wear daring clothes like that, of course, but still, they were nice to look at. And they suited Dolores. Her pale face was flushed with excitement. 'Do come in.' Dolores swayed, humming in tune with the music.

Jack raised an eyebrow at Frances in a silent question.

'Ten minutes,' she said. 'Mum will be worrying.'

'I'll take you home as soon as we've said hello to Phil. Maybe he wants to leave as well.'

She gave Jack a quick glance under her lashes. Judging by the laughter from what she supposed to be the parlour, Phil was having have a bonzer time, but Jack didn't seem to mind.

'What takes you so long?' Dolores called out.

Jack gave Frances a rueful grin and ushered her inside the apartment.

It was even more elegant than she'd expected, with chrome and glass in abundance. The furniture alone must have cost enough to feed a family for a year. Phil looked very much at ease in these surroundings. He sat in a black, leather wingchair, his hands folded behind his head. A marble ashtray stood next to two half-filled glasses and a wine decanter on a butler's tray table.

Dolores motioned for Frances and Jack to sit down on the settee, before she put a new record on. 'Everyone shush now,' she said, lowering herself on to the second armchair, legs drawn in under her. A rich voice filled the room, singing 'Swing low, sweet chariot,' a song as familiar to Frances as the Lord's Prayer, and yet it was as if she'd never heard it before. She closed her eyes to hide unexpected tears. Someone took her hand and gave it a light squeeze before he let go.

'Dame Nellie Melba,' Dolores said, with the reverence of a student in the presence of a master. 'I've got all her recordings, thanks to darling Jack.' She tilted her head to the side, as if listening to music nobody but she could hear. 'It was when I heard her sing Verdi that I knew I'd never make the big time.' Dolores reached for her glass, watching the ruby-red liquid swirl. 'So here I am, singing my heart out for jokers who couldn't care less about my voice, and a bunch of tarted-up gold-diggers.' She swilled her wine.

'Shh, darling.' Jack moved over to Dolores. He stood behind her armchair, giving her shoulders a gentle massage. 'You're still the biggest attraction in town, and masses of people love you.'

She shook her head. 'You're just saying that to be nice. Or is he, Phil? Frances?'

Phil gave Frances a helpless look. She swallowed. 'I've never heard anyone to rival you, Dolores. Uncle Sal says so too, and he's travelled everywhere. He's toured England and all of the continent before the war, so he knows what he's talking about.' Her glance met Jack's. He gave her a quick nod.

'He's a sweetheart,' Dolores said. 'Promise me you'll bring him along the next time you call on us, won't you?'

'Sure,' said Phil. His teeth gleamed as he smiled at her.

Jack let go off Dolores' shoulders. 'I'm taking Frances home. Care for a ride, Phil?'

'You're not leaving yet, are you, Phil?' Dolores pleaded. 'I've already arranged for supper.'

'How could I say no to a lady?'

'In that case, we'll tell your landlady not to wait for you,' Jack said.

'You must forgive that melodramatic moment upstairs,' Jack said, as soon as they sat in the car, this one a Rover roadster with its canvas-top rolled back.

'Do you mind terribly?'

'Mind what? That Dolores tends to become very emotional and dramatic when she's upset?' Jack shrugged, fingertips drumming on the steering-wheel. 'I can't say about your Uncle Sal, but most artists are a bit highly-strung.'

'I don't mean that,' Frances said. 'There were some men there practically drooling as they ogled her all the time, and of course she'd hate pouring her heart and soul into her art, singing in a what's nothing but a night club after all, instead of an opera house, where she'd belong.' She clapped her hand over her mouth. 'I didn't mean it the way it sounded.'

Jack gave her another inscrutable glance. 'Too right you did, kiddo, and it's true. The Top Note's a decent place, and I keep it clean, with solid fun and good entertainment, but it's nothing but a night joint all right.' He chuckled softly. 'But at least it keeps us all in bread and butter and the best fizz that money can buy.'

'But you do mind about Phil's staying?' She felt her cheeks grow hot, glad Jack couldn't see it in the dark.

'Why should I? Dolores is a grown woman, but if Phil turns out to be less of a gentleman than I take him for, he's in for a fight. One press of a bell, and he'll have half a dozen seasoned soldiers ready to teach him a thing or two.' Jack grinned. 'That is, if he's so lucky. The last leery cove who got a bit of a funny idea got chased by Ginny. That woman's the size of a bantam hen, but strike me pretty if she didn't scare the living daylights out of the joker with her frying-pan.'

'I see,' Frances said, glad for Phil that Jack didn't seem

to be jealous but at the same time puzzled by his cavalier attitude towards Dolores.

He pushed his hat back on his head. 'Ginny Barker's our cook and housekeeper upstairs. She and her husband Archie live in the third apartment.'

'Third apartment?' Now she was even more confused.

Jack pulled over to the side to let another vehicle past. 'That driver's had enough over the eight to make sixteen,' he said. 'See how the car swerves? God help the poor soul who gets in his way.' He eased the Rover back into the middle of the lane.

'I had the whole floor converted when I took over the building,' he said. 'Much easier than in our first digs in Whitmore Square, where Dolores had no dressing-room in her apartment and the poor Barkers had to bed down in a box-room. Archie still swears they didn't mind and that after France, this was princely accommodation, but he lit a dozen candles for the Virgin Mary when first the house in Wellington Square and then this place came up.'

'I can imagine,' she said, the wheels in her head spinning. So, Jack didn't live with Dolores after all. She found herself breathing easier but there were still a few things that confused her.

Not that Jack's and Dolores' private affairs were any of her business, of course. She tried to keep her voice neutral. 'Mr Barker was in the war with you?'

'We all were, Bluey, Danny, Archie and all the rest. Simon, too. Ah, there we are.'

He insisted on walking her to the door. 'I promised I'd deliver you in good time,' he said. 'Barely eight.'

Frances fumbled for the door key. Holding the key in

her left hand, she stretched out the right. 'Thank you for a lovely day.'

Jack took her hand in his, smiling at her. 'Like I said earlier, my pleasure. And don't wait up for Phil. I might join him and Dolores for a bit. If it gets too late, someone'll put him up for the night.'

She turned the key.

'And, Frances?'

'Yes?'

Jack pressed a ten-shilling note into her hand. 'For Henry Cooke's funeral. Give my regards to the widow.'

Frances frowned. 'But—'

'Shush. I like your cloche, by the way. At least you won't block some poor cove's sight with a wagon wheel on your head when we go to the talkies tomorrow.'

'What—'

He interrupted her again. 'I'll pick you up about three? It's Easter Saturday, so all the cafés will be open for business. We'll have some tea, then the pictures. I hope you're not a Rudolph Valentino or Theda Bara admirer. I've had a bellyful of drama today.'

'I like comedies.'

'I knew you had good taste. See you then.'

CHAPTER ELEVEN

aggie and Uncle Sal sat listening to the wireless. A tray with tea things and eggcups complete with shells stood on the side table. Maggie promptly picked it up to take it to the kitchen. 'I didn't feel like tidying today,' she said. 'Did you have a good time, love?'

Frances sank down onto the sofa. 'It was a nice picnic, wasn't it? I wish you'd stayed a bit longer.'

'It was good enough for me, and I really couldn't let Edna and Bertha down.' She sighed. 'I'll go with them to Dobbs' funeral parlour to see if we can come to some arrangement.' She picked the pieces of eggshell out of the cup, avoiding Frances' gaze. 'I wish we—'

'I'm sorry.' Didn't her mother ever get it into her head that they could afford only so much charity? 'Tell Bertha that repaying the rest of the money can wait, but that's all. Anything I can save is for our roof. We need to get it fixed.'

Uncle Sal opened his mouth, but she shook her head.

'You're brilliant, Uncle Sal, but I can't have you climbing up there and trying your hand at tiling.' For a fleeting moment, his jaw set in an obstinate line, but then he nodded at her.

She took Maggie's hand. 'Please tell me you haven't gone and promised her more money.'

'Frances! As if I would do that ever again without asking you.'

Her mother's stricken face was enough to make Frances' conscience twinge a bit. Maggie was too soft-hearted by half, without any business sense.

But at least she had something that might cheer her mother up. She slipped her hand into her skirt pocket to produce the folded bank note. 'With compliments from Jack Sullivan. I hope this helps?'

Maggie's face lit up. 'Ten shillings, and he doesn't even know Bertha. Sal! Can you believe that?'

'I told you White Jack's a decent fellow,' Uncle Sal said. 'There's no more harm in him than in me. If you don't believe my judgment, ask Phil what he thinks of his old war cobber.'

Maggie glanced at the wall clock. 'Where is Phil?'

'Having a good chin-wag, I reckon. Good on him, too. It can be a bit lonely in a strange city, and our Frances won't have much time for him, and neither will Pauline, with her work and all.' He patted Maggie's shoulder. 'Don't fret about that boy, Maggie. You'll see him at breakfast, all bright-eyed and gung-ho.'

At a quarter to three on Saturday, Frances brushed her hair

for the umpteenth time. There was something calming in the motion that helped steady her nerves. If only she knew what best to do. She'd almost confided in Jack yesterday, but somehow that moment had passed. Maybe she should flip a coin to decide.

She formed her lips into a pout to apply her newly acquired lipstick, as raised voices disturbed the peace.

'You should have told me!' Phil said.

She put the lipstick down.

'Told you what?' Uncle Sal sounded irritated.

Frances rushed down, nearly tripping in the process. She pushed the door open. 'What's wrong?'

Three pairs of eyes turned towards her; Maggie's helpless, Uncle Sal's cold, and Phil's angry.

'We were talking about Henry's funeral,' Mum said.

'And?' Frances looked at each one in turn, hoping for an explanation that made sense.

'Phil seems to mind that no one mentioned the funeral fund and the theft of the money to him.' Maggie fiddled with her hair; a sure sign that she was under considerable strain.

'It's nice that you care, but what would telling you have changed, Phil?' Frances said. 'If you want to give a bob or two, you're welcome to. But there's no need to upset Mum. She's been through enough.'

Uncle Sal nodded. 'Do you hear that, boy?'

'I do,' Phil said after an awkward pause. 'Sorry.' He cocked his head. 'The doorbell. Shall I go and answer it?'

'I'll do it.' Frances ran to the front door and flung it open.

'Hello,' Jack said, taking off his hat with a flourish. 'I hope I'm not too early?'

Any thought of acting all grown up and sophisticated, as if a caller was an everyday occurrence in her life, vanished. She grabbed his hands and pulled him inside. His touch felt reassuring. 'Thank goodness you're here.'

Jack stepped into the parlour with the easy confidence of a visitor of long standing. 'Mrs Palmer, nice to see you. Uncle Sal. Phil.'

He inclined his head in a nod. 'Mr Sullivan.'

Maggie sounded surprised. 'How nice of you to drop in. Or were you expected?' Her gaze travelled from Phil to Frances and then to Uncle Sal.

Jack paused. 'I haven't come at a bad moment, have I?'

'Of course not,' Frances said. 'We were discussing a few things with Phil.'

'Nothing too weighty, I hope. Or have you committed a few bloomers already, mate?' Jack grinned.

Phil's face grew sheepish. 'I'm really sorry, Maggie.' Maggie's frown-lines smoothed. The whole atmosphere changed. How did Jack do that? Frances gave him a grateful look.

Uncle Sal's usually twinkling eyes still held their frosty look. 'Not so fast, my boy,' he said to Phil.

A faint tinge crept into Maggie's cheeks. 'It's fine,' she said, 'we'll simply forget everything.' She put a hand on Phil's arm in a conciliatory gesture.

Uncle Sal harrumphed.

'A difference of opinions?' Jack lowered himself on to the edge of the table, hat between his hands.

Uncle Sal looked straight into his eyes. 'Let me ask you this, Jack, my boy, how far back do you and this bird here go?'

'We came home on the same ship, in early 1919, that's all. Why do you want to know?'

Frances leant against the wall, confused.

'Sal?' Maggie's frown returned.

'Don't worry, Maggie, I'm not saying anything. It's just – you can't be too careful these days, who you have under your roof.'

Frances stared at Phil. Surely he would say something?

Instead, Jack broke the silence with a rollicking laugh. 'Uncle Sal, I believe you got the wrong end of the stick. I lay you odds of ten to one our boy here is no crook. Uncle Sal, you had your own police escort to the Top Note. Or who else would a retired police officer like your Fred send to lodge with his sister and niece?'

His teeth flashed in his tanned face as he broke into a wide smile. 'What happened in Melbourne, Phil? Did you get in trouble with the local talent?'

Phil said, 'Something like that. I was working undercover for a bit, until someone tumbled wise, and my boss thought I'd better get a transfer to Adelaide.' He pushed up his shirt sleeve to reveal an angry looking scar that went from his elbow half-way down to his wrist. 'I was lucky enough to get away with my life.'

'But why didn't you say you're a policeman?' Frances said. 'You lied to us. You told Mum you were in the cleaning business. And you broke the law, buying us drinks after six o'clock.'

An ugly thought crept up in her mind. 'Was that your

plan? Trap Jack and Dolores into trusting you and then busting them, if that's the word I'm looking for?'

She felt tears of frustration welling up in her eyes. They'd all been taken in. She blinked back the tears. 'Shall we go now, Jack? He's taking me to the pictures, Mum.'

'And afternoon tea,' Jack said.

Phil had the grace to hang his head. 'I'd have told you soon enough,' he said. 'I wanted everyone to get to know me as Phil the man first, not the police, that's all. Plus, I thought the force might be pretty unpopular with some of your neighbours, what with the beef riot on King William Street back in January, and all that.'

'Fair enough,' Sal said. 'And who'd blame them. Seventeen men in hospital, because those poor blokes didn't take it too well to have to live on old mutton instead of their usual beef? Say what you like but the police shouldn't have fought with those men.'

'I agree,' said Phil. 'I reckon you'll understand why I wasn't too keen on shoving my badge into people's faces.'

'Yes,' Uncle Sal repeated, 'that's fair enough. What do you say, you apologise to Maggie about fibbing to her, and then we shake hands and let the matter drop, eh?'

'Not so fast, Uncle Sal.' Frances walked right up to Phil. 'What about the Top Note and making us all break the law?'

'Breaking the law?' He shook his head. 'Nothing doing, I can't recall anything of that sort. All I remember is going to a club in the company of friends, to listen to some of the best music you can hear from Bananaland to Tassie.'

A smile began to crinkle his eyes. 'I distinctly remember you asking Jack Sullivan here for lemonade, which he not only served but shared with you. If you ask me, it doesn't get more law-abiding than that.'

He held out his hand. 'I'm a boneheaded duffer, and I deserve all the rag you've handed out. Will you please forgive me?'

A wave of relief washed over Frances as she shook his hand.

'Are you ready to go now?' Jack asked as if nothing had happened. 'We'll be back after supper, Mrs Palmer. Oh, and Phil, Dolores comes on stage tonight at nine, and she asked me to invite you and Uncle Sal over. She needs an hour to get ready for her show, so the best time to come and see her would be about six or otherwise closer to midnight. She hopes to see you again soon too, Mrs Palmer.' He inclined his head again and put on his hat at an angle that shaded his eyes.

'I'm coming,' Frances said.

Jack parked the car in front of Balfours', one of Adelaide's most renowned cafés; no half price buns sold before closing time here.

The doorbell dinged as Jack made his way inside, his hand cupping Frances' elbow.

Waitresses bustled about, carrying trays and multi-tiered cake stands to tables where ladies dressed in the latest fashion and, occasionally, an equally well-dressed gentleman fit right in with their surroundings. Urged by Jack, Frances sat down on the edge of an upholstered chair.

Jack was probably known to most of the customers

here. They all looked like they had champagne and cocktails on a regular basis.

He was perfectly at ease. 'Tea or coffee?' he asked. 'Or would you prefer lemonade?'

'Coffee, please.'

He signalled the waitress. 'Coffee and frog cakes for two, please, Miss.'

By the time their order arrived she had relaxed a bit. A look around the room showed her that she and Jack were virtually ignored. Everyone else seemed busy either enjoying their afternoon tea or, judging by the words uttered two tables away, some equally tasty gossip.

Jack leant forward. His elbows rested on the starched linen table cloth. 'One of the councillor's wives,' he said. 'Too bad for her that hat-veil doesn't disguise her voice as well.'

She stifled a giggle. The voice had indeed a cutting quality that made it instantly recognisable.

'That's better, kiddo.' He took his fork and sliced the frog cake in four equal pieces. 'You're not eating,' he said. 'I should have asked you what you'd like.'

'It's fine,' she said, eyeing the fondant-cloaked concoction that had established Balfours' success. 'This frog is almost too pretty to eat. And it seems to grin at me.'

He took her plate and turned it around. 'Now you can't see its grin or the piped-on icing eyes. Or do you expect a bit of sponge cake, jam, and St Patrick's Day green sugar to turn into a prince before our very eyes? Don't you think you'd have to kiss it first?'

'Very funny.' She returned her plate into its original

position before she took her fork and decapitated the frog. It tasted even better than it looked.

Jack gave her a curiously tender look as she scraped the last morsels off the plate, the way he'd look at a puppy, she thought, with a pang. 'How about another cake?' he asked.

'No thanks.' She dabbed her mouth with a snowy napkin. 'Shouldn't we go if we want to catch the afternoon show?'

He glanced at his wristwatch. 'We've got plenty of time left.' He handed her a torn-out newspaper page, listing the movies currently showing.

She handed it back. 'You choose,' she said. 'It's only fair when you're paying.'

'I like anything as long as it hasn't got any leftover vamps from the silent era in it, or the war. What about you?'

'I adore comedies,' Frances said. 'Or a murder mystery or a revue. Anything really, that tells a good story.'

'Do the Marx brothers appeal to you? *Animal Crackers* is on. Or how about *The Benson Murder Case*, with William Powell?'

'I love William Powell.' She put her chin into her hands. 'He appears so – well, not like a film star, but as if he could actually live next door to an ordinary person.'

Jack gave her another of those looks. 'I'm glad to hear you won't swoon over a dark, dashing hero leaping into a burning house to rescue a damsel in distress.'

'I might, if he's had the good sense to call the fire brigade first.' She grinned. 'You'd better not take Pauline to the pictures. She's lost her heart to Ramon Navarro and John Gilbert, in changing order.'

'I'm not interested in taking out Pauline, but thank you for the warning.'

The mocking tone in his voice was obvious. She decided to change the subject. 'It was kind of Dolores to ask Uncle Sal to see her again. He is happy enough at home, but he misses his stage days, or at least, talking to someone who truly understands.' Frances made a sweeping motion with both hands. 'This is all very nice, but it must seem very boring to someone who's performed in so many countries.' She wished she could keep that longing note out of her voice. 'Does Adelaide bore you?'

'It's not exactly a quiet backwater,' Jack said. 'And there's such a thing as too much excitement. Especially these days.' He folded his napkin and put it next to his empty cup. 'Don't worry about your Uncle Sal. He and Dolores will keep each other entertained.'

The Benson Murder Case had Frances hovering on the edge of her seat. Her gaze was glued to the screen. Occasionally she glanced at Jack out of the corner of her eye. He seemed to be enjoying himself as much as she did. Good; she'd feared he'd find her company boring, compared to his usual set.

Ribbons of hot pink and deep purple swirled across the cobalt blue sky as they left the movie theatre. Frances still marvelled at how the amateur detective, Philo Vance, played by suave William Powell, knew that the murderer was five feet, ten-and-a-half inches tall.

Jack pointed upwards. 'Still think it's boring?'

She tilted her head towards the setting sun, basking in what remained of the warmth of the day. 'What's wrong with wanting to see other places? I'd love to travel, although I'd always come back home in the end, like Uncle Sal did. What about you?'

'It's a good place,' Jack said. 'It's big enough to make a decent living, and not big enough to attract the scum you find in the big smoke. It fits my bill.' He pushed his hat far back on his forehead. 'Shall we take a stroll to the lake before I take you home?'

Elder Park teemed with people. It was as if every family who stayed away on Good Friday was trying to make up for it now. Picnic rugs dotted the grass. Boys kicked balls around, girls chased each other while parents enjoyed a brief respite.

Frances dodged a high-flying ball. 'Sorry, Miss,' a gap-toothed boy said in a shaky voice. Frances managed to wag her finger sternly in the culprit's face. Eyes round with relief, the boy ran after the ball.

'He probably expected you to nark him,' Jack said. 'Although, judging by the looks one of the ladies under the tree gave him, he's in for a few stiff words.'

'I hope not,' Frances said. 'He didn't do any harm. If anything, he could do with a bit more attention, if you ask me. That dirt on his neck was grey with age. The shirt was filthy, too.'

'Maybe his people have no running water in the house,' Jack said. 'Or they've got to save their pennies.'

Frances thought about it, before she shook her head.

'No, you can be poor and clean. Or rich and dirty. If nothing else, his mum could scrub the boy's neck right here, in the lake. Beautiful, isn't it? Let's walk around it.'

CHAPTER TWELVE

*J*ack stopped at what had once been a jetty. Strips of wood peeled off the remaining piles. He gave one pile a tentative kick. Bits of wood crumbled into the water.

'This is where the Floating Palais used to be,' Frances said. 'Do you remember it? I went there once, shortly before it closed.'

'Did you enjoy it?'

'Oh yes,' she said, lost for a moment in a happy memory. 'It was my twentieth birthday party, and all those Chinese lanterns sparkled on the water like a million glow-worms. They had a band that played all the latest swing and jazz, and we stayed until long after midnight.'

She paused. Her shoe-tip traced a circle in the sand.

'What a shame you didn't get to go back another time,' Jack said. The Floating Palais had died an ignoble death when it was discovered that, below the waterline, its beauty was built on rotting planks.

'It wouldn't have been the same anyway. Not with the boys gone.'

'The boys?' He shoved his hands in the pockets of his jacket.

She felt the blood rush into her cheeks. 'I shouldn't have said that.'

'Why? What's the big secret? Or am I stepping on someone's toes here?'

'What? No, not me. But I promised Pauline I wouldn't say a word.'

'What's Pauline got to do with that?' Crinkle lines appeared around the corners of his eyes. 'You're beginning to get me all perplexed.'

She let her gaze travel towards a group of mallards making their way to the humans.

'Frances?'

'Promise me she won't lose her job.'

'Why should she? As long as Dolores is happy with Pauline, and she is, she'll stay. Unless ...' Jack cupped Frances' chin with his hand, making her face him. 'She isn't keeping company with the wrong kind of people, is she? Because if she is, she's out. I won't have anything shady going on in the Top Note.'

'What are you talking about?' She raised her head until he let go off her chin.

'Well, whatever is so bad that you can't spit it out?'

'Pauline's got a boyfriend. She's as good as engaged.' Frances twisted a strand of hair. around her finger. 'That is, if Tony can find work in Queensland and manage to save up enough money to come home again.'

'And if she doesn't change her mind. Why the big

secret? Or is there someone else in the picture? She seemed quite taken with Phil, although I fancy she doesn't have much of a chance.'

She stared at him, open-mouthed. 'She wasn't. Or at least, there's nothing in it, she's friendly to everyone. But she told me that you only employ single girls.'

'I solely give work to people who depend on the income, which Pauline does, if my information is correct.'

'Oh yes.' Frances thought of the dingy house she'd visited and shuddered.

He picked up a pebble and flicked it across the water. The stone bounced twice, sending out two sets of ripples that spread until Frances could no longer tell them apart.

'Why did you walk me home when we first met?' The question had niggled on her mind for days, but she hadn't come up with a satisfactory explanation thus far. Annoyingly enough, it wasn't for her charms, she admitted to herself. That much was obvious for anyone who'd seen Dolores.

Jack lowered his eyelids until they half-covered his eyes. 'It was refreshing for once to meet a girl whose beauty owes nothing to art and everything to nature; you don't see a lot of real people in my business; and I needed bread.'

'You've got a housekeeper, so that argument doesn't work, and I'm not beautiful.' She sighed. 'Not like Dolores. She is – what do men say? She's an eyeful.'

'An eyeful,' Jack said, 'and an earful, and most of all, a handful. But,' he flung another pebble, 'so are you. You're way too trusting.'

'I'm not. I told you I can look after myself.'

He turned around, facing her. 'No, you can't. Remember

when we met on a Friday? That's payday for most people, and there you were, striding along, swinging your little bag for every half-baked crook to grab.'

She opened her mouth to protest.

Jack dug his thumbs into his vest pockets. 'I followed you for at least twenty yards, and you didn't notice. You also didn't notice the rat-face who appeared out of an alleyway, making straight for you.'

Something was wrong with her voice, reducing her words to a whisper. 'You're making that up, aren't you?'

'I'm not saying he was after your bag, Frances, I'm merely saying he might've been. Desperate times create desperate folks.'

She suddenly felt faint.

'Frances?' He took her by the shoulders. 'I didn't mean to scare you.' He bent down to pick up a sizable chunk of rock. 'Stick that in your bag on paydays, or something similar – solid, like a half brick, and you can roundhouse any miscreant. Here, let me show you.'

He wrapped the rock in a handkerchief, took her bag, and put the rock inside. Grasping the handle, he swung the bag in a circle before he handed it back to her. 'Your turn,' he said. 'I'll try to grab your bag, and you lash out.'

She took a step back. 'I might hurt you.'

He still smiled at her when his arm shot out. Frances ducked and swung her bag. She half expected to feel it collide with Jack's arm, breaking bones. That rock must have weighed two pounds at least.

He sprang back, the bag missing him by an inch, before he attacked again.

Three more rounds, and her hand trembled. 'Enough?' she asked, sinking on to the grass.

Jack settled next to her. He folded his arms around his legs.

Frances snapped her bag open to inspect its contents. The rock was still tightly wrapped into the handkerchief. The small coin purse she carried and her enamelled powder compact seemed undamaged, as did the artificial silk lining of the bag.

'Can I have my handkerchief back?' he asked.

'And your rock.'

'Keep it,' Jack said. 'Unless you exclusively care for real shiners. Mind you, if you did, you'd need more than a half brick to prevent the bad coves from sticking you up.'

'Oh yeah? Very funny.' Frances said, imitating the menacing growl of the villain in the picture they'd seen. 'Well, I'm not that kind of dame.'

'I'm not joking.'

She pulled her skirt over her knees and hugged them tightly. 'Then stop talking like a gangster in the pictures.'

'Was I? I didn't realise.' His lips twitched. 'One of the hazards of running a night club, I reckon. Some of the punters rub off if one isn't careful.'

Her eyes widened. 'You allow gangsters into the Top Note?'

'Not the heavy talent, if that's what you mean.' He gave her a quick glance as if to gauge her reaction. 'And I've got a clean skin myself. Talk to Phil; he'll have made enquiries about his new mates already if he's worth his pay. Ask him if I've ever taken anyone lakeside.'

The words rang in her ears. Her chest tightened. She could hardly breathe.

He leant back on his elbows, watching Frances under his lashes. 'Disappointed in me? Kiddo, ask the police, it's much better to watch the enemy from within than having them run loose where you can't see them, and like I said, the big fish meet elsewhere.'

He gave her a closer look. 'You're shivering. Does my life repulse you that much? Come on, then. I'll take you home to your mum and Uncle Sal, and I'll drop from your sight.'

He made as if to get up. She grabbed his arm to hold him back. 'It's not that,' she said. 'It's something that you said.' She took a shilling out of her purse and flipped it over on her hand. Heads, she'd confide in Jack, tails, she'd keep quiet. She looked at the coin. Heads.

She ran her tongue over her dry lips. 'You break the law, right?'

'When I have to.'

'But you're still a good man.' She touched his sleeve. 'So, hypothetically, what would you do if you knew that something bad might be planned but you can't tell anyone?'

'That depends. How bad is the bad thing, and why do I have to keep my mouth closed?'

'It's murder,' Frances said, her voice sounding distant in her ears. 'A man might be killed and I can't do anything to save him.' Her lower lip trembled.

'Oh, kiddo.' Jack pulled her close to him and hugged her to his chest. He smelt of spicy after-shave, and comfort. Her pulse slowed down a bit. 'It's all right,' he said, as if calming a child suffering from a nightmare. 'I'm here; we'll take care of it.'

She pressed her head against the rough fabric of his jacket, unwilling to let go. 'It's true,' she said. 'You believe me, don't you?'

'Tell me what's going on,' he said.

'I heard them talk about it, on the phone.' The words came faltering at first, but then they tumbled out, as if they gained a momentum of their own. Frances didn't know if anything she said made sense at all, but she didn't care. She told Jack everything, why she'd listened in on that phone call, and how she'd been unable to shake off the sense of dread.

Her voice began to shake. 'I wanted to believe it's a hoax,' she said, clinging to Jack's sleeve. 'Or maybe that I heard wrong because there was so much crackle and other noise.' She swallowed. 'But it didn't sound like it, and when you started talking about sticking up someone or taking him lakeside, I sort of knew that it's for real.'

'We'll tell Phil about Croaky and his mate.'

'No.' She struggled to free herself. 'Don't you think I haven't thought about it? We can't. He's the police. I'd lose my job for breaking confidentiality, and then how shall I pay the mortgage and the other bills?' She wiped her nose with the back of her hand. 'It wouldn't do any good anyway, because I don't know who the victim is.'

'Then we'll investigate ourselves,' Jack said. 'Or rather, I will. And I'll think of something to pass on that information that leaves you out of it.'

He pulled her off the grass. 'Do you want me to take you out for dinner, or do you want to go home?'

She hesitated.

He stroked her hair. 'How about we get some

sandwiches and eat them here, and then I'll take you home.'

'Yes,' she said, leaning against him for the briefest moment. He pressed her shoulder, unsettling her pulse again. 'Please, Jack.'

~

Frances' nerves still twitched when Jack took her home. 'Would you care to come inside and say hello to everyone?' she asked, not wanting to let him go just yet. She felt safe when he was around; safe, and oddly excited at the same time.

His thumb grazed her cheek. 'Anything to make you happy.'

Maggie's face lit up as Frances ushered Jack into the kitchen.

'You're in time for a cup of tea,' she said. 'The kettle's already on.' She put the pillowcase she was darning into the sewing basket sitting on the floor.

'Do you drink tea at all, Jack, or would you prefer coffee?' Maggie hesitated. 'Otherwise we might have a drop of brandy left.'

'Tea is fine,' Jack said, handing Frances his hat and jacket. 'Uncle Sal and Phil aren't home yet?'

'I didn't expect them to be.' Maggie poured a small amount of water into the teapot, rinsed it and refilled it with boiling water after she'd spooned in tea-leaves from a China caddy. 'Or should I?'

He settled down on to a kitchen chair, crossing his

ankles. 'No reason at all,' he said. 'I'm glad Uncle Sal and Phil are sacrificing their time.'

Maggie's lips twitched. 'From what I've seen of Miss Bardon, they wouldn't consider it a sacrifice.'

Frances set three cups with a wildflower pattern on the table. The sugar bowl didn't match, but it still looked pretty.

'Who was Simon Grant?' she asked as she poured the tea. Jack spooned sugar into the amber brew.

'Dolores' husband,' he said in a matter-of-fact tone. 'They got married on Easter Sunday 1916, with special permission from her father because she was under age.' Jack swirled his tea in the cup to dissolve the sugar. 'We shipped out to France a week after that. She never saw him again.'

Maggie folded her hands around her cup. 'Oh, the poor girl.'

'I was best man at the wedding,' Jack said. 'It took her years to get over it, but she's coped. It's only sometimes that it gets to her this bad; times like Easter, and when she drives around town and sees all those legless or armless men that are begging or hawking on the streets. At least they came home.'

'But she's got you,' Frances said before she could help it. She ought to be ashamed of herself, for envying Dolores.

'I promised Simon I'd take care of Dolores. We all did. But sometimes that isn't enough.' He took a long sip. 'You can imagine how glad I was when Phil walked in.'

'You weren't with Simon when – it happened?'

Jack touched his shoulder. 'I got winged a couple of months earlier, not too bad, but infection set in and they sent me to a British hospital. I recovered in time to be demobbed together with Phil, a couple of weeks after the rest of my mates. That's how we met, although we didn't mingle much onboard the ship. I wasn't overmuch in the mood for company.'

Maggie touched his hand. 'I see. I hope Phil will cheer the poor girl up.'

'But you said all the men in your night club were in the army together,' Frances said, her mind working on something that had been puzzling her for days. 'Surely they must have been able to tell her everything she wants to hear about her husband?'

Maggie shook her head at her daughter. 'That's not the same. To them she'll always be Simon's widow, but for Phil she's a beautiful woman in her own right. She simply happens to have been married to a man he met who died a long time ago.'

Jack pushed his chair back a little, allowing more space for his legs.

'Would it be too much of a liberty to ask for a refill?' His teeth gleamed as he smiled at Maggie. Jack looked perfectly at home in their kitchen, Frances thought, and the way he exchanged glances with her mum hinted at something like mutual understanding or – her eyes narrowed – shared amusement, the way you enjoyed the antics of a puppy.

The legs of her chair scraped over the wooden floor as she got up, hiding a yawn.

Jack treated her to another smile. 'I should be taking myself off,' he said. 'The club will be hopping tonight, and I can't neglect my duties.'

She took the empty cups and placed them on top of the

still dirty crockery in the sink. 'I'll do the dishes,' she said. 'You get a rest, Mum, and I'll see you in the morning.'

'I can spare enough time to help, and I don't want to hear a word of protest.' Jack undid his cufflinks to roll up the sleeves of his shirt. Faint white lines crisscrossed his skin, as if he'd once caught his underarm on barbed wire.

A warmth started to spread inside her as Frances opened the tap to fill the sink and shook some soap flakes from a tin.

Her mother hesitated.

'Off you go, Mum. I'll see Jack out as soon as we're done here.'

Frances wiped the plate with a cloth, rinsed it off again and handed it to Jack. 'The drying rack is on the top shelf, unless you merely want to stand around with that tea towel, looking domesticated.'

'What I did want was to remind you to write down every scrap of information you remember,' he said. 'And to give your mother a break. She looked all in.'

'No wonder,' she said. 'I wish she wouldn't feel obliged to go and sit with everyone who's ill or dying or feeling plain lonely.'

He reached for the last plate. 'I could imagine it's more the theft that is bothering her.'

She lifted a sudsy finger to rub her nose. 'I'd almost forgotten about that.'

'Small wonder.' He dabbed her nose with the tea-towel.

'Dry again.' The dishes done, Jack gave Frances a reassuring smile as she followed him to the door.

'Don't get yourself all worked up,' he said. 'It'll all come right.'

A tear of relief trickled down her cheek. She wasn't alone any more.

CHAPTER THIRTEEN

*A*t breakfast, Uncle Sal greeted Frances, hollow-eyed but chirpy. Phil managed a weak nod. Judging by the greyish tint of his skin and the haste in which he downed his coffee, it had been a long night.

She sat down and filled her cup. 'It looks like you had a bonzer time,' she said to Uncle Sal. 'I didn't even hear you come home.'

Uncle Sal beamed at her. 'I didn't mean to stay out until the wee hours, love, so I'm glad my plodding upstairs didn't wake you.'

His eyes grew soft. 'Would you believe that Dolores wouldn't let me go before she'd heard every bit about my meeting Dame Nellie Melba? What a loss her death was for the world! I'll always cherish the night I spent with the great lady of the opera ...' he added a dramatic pause, 'in the same hotel.' His dark eyes twinkled, his hands punctuated every word with gestures that grew larger by the minute, and Frances had to rescue the toast rack from being flung off the table. Uncle Sal was restored to his former self.

'And what did you think she said then?'

She blinked. Uncle Sal had lost her about halfway through the anecdote. Who did he refer to? Dame Nellie? Dolores? Someone else?

'Well,' she said, playing for time. 'What did she say, Uncle Sal?'

She placed a second piece of toast on her plate and leant forward, the very picture of eager anticipation.

'She said ...' Uncle Sal lowered his voice for the punch line, 'Dame Nellie said to me, "this is not a concert tour, this is a revolving door," because she kept forever saying farewell and hello at the same time.'

'Amazing.' She shook her head, at a loss for what else to say.

'Too right. I wish you'd been there last night. Ah well, there's always another day. And another piece of toast with jam, I hope.'

She set the toast rack and the jam dish down in front of him.

'You must eat something, Phil,' the old man said, eyeing his silent companion.

Phil looked down on his plate. A half-eaten triangle of dry toast sat there next to a mound of eggshell.

'I'm full,' he said. 'You told me to eat your boiled egg as well as mine.'

'I did that? I don't even remember. That's what comes from having your mind on other things.' Uncle Sal dabbed his lips before he folded his napkin. He rubbed his chin to feel the greyish stubble. 'You take it easy here, Phil. You've got plenty of time for your beauty routine later.' He whistled as he limped off to the bathroom.

Frances recognised the melody as one she'd danced to with him at the Top Note. She sang along under her breath. 'Keep on the sunny side ...'

Easter Sunday had always held a special place in Frances' family. Her granny Lowry used to tie dried flowers and leaves on to eggs and steep them in tea or beetroot juice or soaked onion skins to create the most delicate patterns.

Frances and Rob were allowed all over the garden, searching for the eggs before they had the biggest, most sumptuous Easter breakfast ever, with more dishes than the king, or so she thought back then. There was always chocolate and home-made ice cream Frances had helped churn the day before.

Granny Lowry had died right after the war, but the old wooden churn was still in use. Frances and Maggie had spent Saturday morning cranking the handle until eggs, cream, milk, sugar, and a jar of plum preserve came together in mouth-watering richness.

The ice cream would be eaten later, after church and a light lunch. There might be guests to share it with. Maggie had asked Uncle Sal to invite Dolores and Jack, to return their hospitality.

Frances' smile waned at the thought of how the singer would be feeling on Easter Sunday. How awful to wave your new husband good-bye after a few days of bliss, pray for years for his safe return, and then lose him a few weeks before the guns went silent. There was no resurrection for her Simon and the millions of other casualties of the war.

Her thoughts trailed off. Easter was halfway over, and she sat here like a dummy, relying on Jack to help another man in danger. She should have confided in him earlier. Time was getting so short. Icy fingers crawled across her spine. She stared at the wall until her vision went blurry and Maggie called at her to get ready for church.

'I should have worn my flat shoes,' Maggie said as they returned home. 'That was a beautiful sermon, but it's getting a bit hard to stand on these heels for longer than the Lord's Prayer, and it took me much longer in the morning to check the flower arrangements than I'd thought.'

She exchanged the round-toed shoes with their two-inch heels for her worn-down slippers, sighing with obvious relief. 'That's old age for you, dear.'

'Nonsense,' Frances said, flinging her cloche onto its hook. 'It's that cold stone floor and the draught whistling in from under the vestibule doors. All you need is a bit of a rest, while I set up for a cold lunch. I'm also going to take care of our afternoon tea, so for once, you won't have to lift a finger.'

When the sun's rays had slanted enough to cast the outdoor table in a murky shade and still the door bell was silent,

140

Frances felt a stab of disappointment. She had taken such great care with her arrangement, using the embroidered linen napkins and the silver they'd inherited from Granny, because she wanted to do Uncle Sal and her mum proud.

She could have kicked herself. Who was she kidding? As if home-made ice cream, eaten in a rather ordinary home with an ordinary family could hold any attraction for a star like Dolores Bardon. As for Jack – she put a firm rein on her thoughts. It didn't do to get romantic ideas, when he clearly treated her like a kid sister.

She began to stack the plates and cups to carry them inside. The air grew nippy, and the kitchen table would do.

The dishes made a loud clink as Frances put them down on the table. She'd put them in their proper places on the dresser and take out their everyday crockery instead.

She was bringing in the lace-edged table cloth when the first rain drops spattered down, and the doorbell rang.

'I hope I'm not too late?' Dolores held on to the rim of her white picture head with both hands, eyes shining. 'I'd have given you a buzz but you're not on the phone.'

'My darling lady!' Uncle Sal must have been ear-wigging from the parlour, to time his entrance this well. He beat Phil by about ten steps when it came to distance, Frances thought, but at least a mile when it came to style.

Both men had spruced up. Their appearance explained why they'd been so conspicuously missing from the scene ever since they'd finished lunch. Phil had changed into a blue suit with half an inch-wide pinstripes in a slightly darker shade, and the parting of his pomaded hair was as precise as if he'd used a ruler. The leather of his shoes was buffed, but in Frances' mind Phil lacked the easy elegance

141

that was so much a part of Uncle Sal. He looked dignified in his sagging tan cardigan with the balding suede patches on the elbows, let alone the evening dress he displayed now.

Uncle Sal raised Dolores' hand to his lips and swept her into the parlour before Phil could say more than hello.

Frances stepped out the side to look for the car. There was Jack, shutting the door with as much care as if he feared to disturb a baby.

The drizzle seemed to have set in. She decided to wait for him in the doorway. Her heart drummed again her ribs. He might even have some news for her already.

He turned around, and her heart plummeted. It was Bluey.

He took his hat off as soon as he spotted Frances. 'Happy Easter, Miss Frances,' he said.

She struggled to hide her disappointment. 'Happy Easter, Bluey.'

'Mr Jack was busy, so he told me to run along with Miss Dolores.' He turned the hat in his hands, round and round. 'He said to tell you he might be along later, to join Miss Dolores, or else I'll take her home when she's done here.'

The hat came to a standstill. Bluey peered at her. 'I hope that's fine with you, Miss?'

'Sure.' Frances forced herself to sound cheerful. If Jack had found out anything about the jeweller, he couldn't tell her in company anyway.

Bluey nodded and slapped his hat on.

'Wait.' She touched his sleeve. 'Where are you going? You said you might have to bring Dolores home, and we can't phone for you.'

142

'That's sweet, Miss. I'll be sitting in the Ford.'

'Whatever for?' she asked. 'There's more than enough to eat for everyone. If you go straight into the parlour, I'll go and fetch Mum.'

Typically, instead of putting her feet up after lunch, her mother had insisted on dropping in on Bertha with a few scones and a small bowl of ice cream. There was no point in everyone waiting for their guests if she could be fetched from three doors down the block in a tick, she'd said.

Bluey hesitated. Frances gave him a small nudge. 'I insist,' she said. She grabbed her coat and an umbrella and ran out of the door.

Bertha's curtains were drawn, but light fell through a chink. Soft murmurs could be heard.

Frances grasped the door knocker. It seemed more appropriate for a house in mourning to give a muted knock than to ring a bell.

The curtain that covered the glass panel in the front door was pulled aside, and Maggie's head became visible. She raised two fingers, indicating that she'd be home in a couple of minutes. Then the curtain blocked out the outside world again.

When Frances came home, Bluey loomed large and lonely in the kitchen, while animated laughter wafted from the parlour. 'I thought I'd rather wait here, if you don't mind,' he said with a sheepish look on his face.

'Of course it's all right,' she said. 'Oh drat. I forgot to ask Uncle Sal and Phil to lay the table.'

'I'll do it.' Bluey seemed relieved to have something to do other than stand around.

She pointed out the China cupboard and the drawer with the ordinary cutlery – not the silver, not this time. She took the cover off the hot plate and put the kettle on top.

Bluey licked his fingertip and touched the kettle. It sizzled. He pulled back the finger in an instant, shaking the hand. 'She's still burning good and hot. I put her to the boil while you were gone, Miss.'

It was hard to guess how old he was, with his wide impassive face, but Frances took him to be about Jack's age.

He wiped his forehead with a handkerchief. 'The air's getting a bit close. We'll get a thunderstorm all right.' He tapped his left shoulder. 'That bit of shrapnel there's never let me down yet, giving me fair warning.'

'Uncle Sal says the same about his ankle.'

Bluey nodded. 'If he's got some bit of metal stuck in there it would. I reckon it's the magnetism as does it.'

The kettle began to hum. Frances grasped an iron hook and dragged the kettle off the hot plate.

'Let me do that for you, else you'll scald yourself.' He demonstrated surprising dexterity when it came to brewing the tea, Frances thought. Or he'd volunteered because he needed to feel useful to lose his original shyness.

'Thank you,' she said, hoping they wouldn't be interrupted for a bit longer. Bluey was opening up fast, and it was fascinating to watch this heavy-set man bustle around the kitchen.

He caught her look. 'We got the same kind of stove at home,' he said. 'The missus was all set against getting an electric one, what with the bills and the fire hazard and all.'

'That's what Mum said, too, when Dad asked her.' Frances walked to the pantry and took an iced pound cake from a shelf. 'Instead, we got a lovely indoor bathroom, with hot and cold water from the tap. Heaven.'

She cut the cake into generous slabs.

'Hard to remember how we used to fill the tub out of the rain butt. Gosh, did the missus go on when she caught a frog hopping out of it.'

She gulped. 'I would, too.'

He scratched his chin. 'Makes you wonder where it ends with all this change, it does. I reckon that's what went wrong in the first place, us getting a taste of the soft life after the war, and then we got a hankering for more.'

He fished the leaves out of the teapot so they could be used again. 'Mr Jack says, people came to thinking that Australia's roads were paved with gold, but instead they're paved with money borrowed from London.'

'But at least we all have work.'

Bluey puffed out his cheeks. 'Too right, and I wouldn't know where to turn without our old captain. He took us all on he did, no questions asked, and it's a nice cushy billet when all is said and done.'

Someone had turned on the radio in the parlour, drowning out the laughter.

'Yes, ma'am,' Bluey said. 'I wouldn't trade places with any other cove in the whole of South Australia.'

'But you've got so many jobs at the same time,' Frances said. 'You do all kinds of things in the club, you drive the car, do odd jobs, protect Miss Dolores ...'

'That's not hard. And she needs looking after. It ain't only one joker from the big smoke who was after luring her

145

there, to sing for them. Or they're after the bit of blunt they reckon she's made, although Mr Jack's accountant keeps a close eye on that.'

'It would be hard for Mr Jack to let her go.' Frances rearranged the chrysanthemums she'd put in a cut-glass jar as table decoration, hoping to sound casual.

'He wouldn't,' Bluey said, planting his feet wide as if preparing for an attack. 'There's too many bad things going on in the big smoke, and that's where the big clubs are. He's not taking any risk again, not with Miss Dolores. None of us would. It'd be letting Simon down.'

'He must have been a special man.'

'We all looked out for each other in the trenches. Mr Jack'd have skinned us alive otherwise and rightly so.'

'What do you mean,' Frances asked, intrigued, 'that he wouldn't take any risk again? Did something bad happen to Miss Dolores before?' Heavens, she began to sound like a gossip-starved tattle-tale. She rearranged the cake slices, while she thought of an excuse for her curiosity. 'I mean, Mr Jack says that I was in danger of being robbed when we met, but surely he exaggerated.'

Blue frowned, as if weighing things matters in his head before committing to an opinion. 'He might and then he mightn't. Just think of that poor cove that got knocked rotten last night, and that as close to his own doorstep as you like, all for a handful of shiners. As for everything else, you better ask Mr Jack. I've said plenty enough already.'

Frances froze. What did he mean? She really needed to talk to Jack, alone.

The music from the parlour got louder.

'I'll go and get Mum,' she said.

CHAPTER FOURTEEN

She'd barely touched the front door handle when the door swung inwards, knocking into her face.

'I'm sorry, love,' Maggie said. 'Are you all right?'

Frances probed the tip of her nose. 'I'm fine. But where've you been all this time?'

'Mrs Thorpe barged in as I was leaving, and I couldn't subject Bertha to her reminders of the many bereavements she and her family have suffered.' Maggie frowned. 'She does mean well, but frankly, she can be a trial.'

Frances took Maggie's hat and coat and hung them up. 'How awful for Bertha.'

'Hello, Maggie,' Uncle Sal said, poking his head out of the parlour. 'We've been entertaining our lovely guest in your absence.'

A snort escaped Frances. She pretended to cough. The way Phil brought up the rear with a hang-dog face, it was clear to see that Uncle Sal had outshone him. Oh dear!

'I'm so sorry,' Dolores said. 'But I must pop outside and talk to Bluey. He'll be waiting for me in the car.' She crinkled her nose. 'Sal and I got to talking about shows we've seen and there you have it. Or maybe you could run along, Phil, and tell him I'll be a while?'

'There's no need,' Frances said. 'Bluey's in the kitchen, helping me.'

'Good on you. I can't get him to leave his place in the Ford, because he doesn't want to intrude on me, poor darling.' Her voice was not just very clear and mellifluous, it also carried without any effort.

Bluey's face took on a pinkish hue reminiscent of a well-scrubbed piglet as the singer entered the kitchen.

Frances gave him an apologetic look.

Dolores lowered herself with a sweeping motion on to the chair Uncle Sal held out for her. Her eyes wide like a child's, she looked around with open curiosity.

'This is nice,' she said. 'It smells like home.' She accepted a slab of pound cake and topped it with ice cream. Her eyes closed as she tasted the first forkful. 'Wonderful.'

Mum smiled. 'It's an easy recipe.'

Dolores said, 'It's the scents I miss most, the smell of fresh bread or a chicken roasting.'

'But surely you have a kitchen?'

'With all the latest things.' Dolores ate another forkful. 'I've got a coffee percolator, two electroplated chafing dishes, and a bell with which to ring for Ginny. She does all the cooking in her apartment, which is lovely, but it feels more like living in a hotel instead of a real home.'

She broke into raucous laughter. 'Listen to me. I can hardly boil an egg without spoiling it, so I should thank heaven for Ginny. And I do, although sometimes I think I'd rather have settled for something like this. A home, a family of my own ...' Her laughter stopped abruptly. 'Can I have some more of that cake before I make a complete fool of myself?'

~

The rest of the afternoon they steered clear of talking about anything personal. Dolores had regained her composure, but Frances saw Bluey watching her out of the corner of his eyes.

When the clock struck six, Dolores gave a small start. 'The show. I've got to be on stage in two hours, and here I sit, chin-wagging when I should be getting ready.'

'There's plenty time,' Bluey said. 'Mr Jack said not to rush.'

'Plenty of time?' Dolores rolled her eyes. 'What do you men know about how long it takes a girl to make herself presentable? And I did so want to have a chat with darling Frances. Somehow we never find a moment.' She flashed a smile at her. 'Come with me to the club, and we'll talk in the car. Bluey will roll up the glass between the front and back, and we'll be all lovely and private. Please, Fran, it'll be such fun.'

'You do that, love,' Uncle Sal said. 'Phil and I'll clean up this mess. I'll make sure Maggie won't have to lift a finger. Unless Phil needs to run off again?'

'I'm all yours,' Phil said, taking off his jacket.

~

Bluey had returned to his former quietness. His mumbled

thanks for their hospitality were the sole words Frances had heard him say in two hours. He must have made a model soldier, she thought, following orders to the last detail and happy to keep to his place. His stolid presence alone must make anyone feel safe and secure.

Dolores snuggled into her fox-trimmed camelhair coat as she sank into the backseat of the Ford.

'Step on it, will you, Bluey?' She flung her hat on to the passenger seat. 'I hate having to rush before a performance. It makes my voice go all funny if I don't have a quiet sit down before I'm due on stage.'

Maggie hurried out of the door while Bluey was starting the engine.

'Wait,' Dolores said. She rolled down her window. 'Did we forget something?'

Maggie held out a cardboard box. 'I thought you might like some of the cake to take home, and the rest of the ice cream. I've wrapped it in old newspaper to keep it cool on the way.'

Dolores blew her a kiss. 'You're a darling to think of it. Do come by soon, will you?'

'I'll hold the box if you like,' Frances said. 'I wouldn't want to risk the ice cream seeping through on your coat.'

'We'll put it on the floor,' Dolores said, as the car rolled off.

She was easy to talk to, Frances found. Dolores chatted about everything that came into her mind, from fashion – she adored Elsa Schiaparelli and Coco Chanel, she said, laughing off Frances' ignorance of famous names – to memories of growing up in Ballarat. 'We all went to the same school, Simon, Jack, Rachel, and I. Of course, we girls sat in different rooms, and Jack ignored me all those years. I was nobody but the shy girl with the skinned knees who used to tag along with his sister.' She chuckled. 'At least he and Simon didn't pull our hair like the other boys.'

≈

Bluey stopped in front of the Top Note.

'Are we already there?' Dolores lowered both feet on to the ground, offering her hands to Bluey who helped her out of the car, the way Frances had seen in the pictures.

She watched fascinated, remaining seated herself.

Dolores made a quarter turn and stretched out her left hand. 'You'll keep me company a bit longer, I hope? Pauline should be in the club already, and it's so rare for me to have a girl to talk to who doesn't work here.' A wistful note resonated in her voice. She looked a bit forlorn.

It would have been wrong to leave her. 'I'll stay,' Frances said as she picked up the cardboard box from the floor and followed in Dolores' wake.

'Bluey will operate the lift for us. It's his pride and joy, isn't it?' Dolores gave Bluey an impish smile. 'Sometimes I wonder that your wife doesn't complain about being deserted for a metal cage, some pulleys, and a box of tools.'

Jack stood on the landing, catching her last words as he pulled the doors wide open.

'You should be grateful that Bluey keeps everything in prime condition,' he said. 'I can't see you climbing up and down several flights of stairs in those flimsy shoes of yours.'

Dolores threw her head back and laughed as she

showed off her high-heeled, diamante-spangled satin shoes. 'Too right I wouldn't.'

Bluey was already half-way down the stairs, but Frances thought she saw the skin on his neck redden.

'He's a good man, if a bit on the quiet side,' Jack said, catching her glance. 'He used to be our grease-monkey, and he's still the best mechanic I've ever found anywhere.'

His voice appeared calm, but there was a tightness in his jawline Frances hadn't noticed before.

Dolores swept them along. 'Don't tell me you were lying in wait for me because I'm horrendously late,' she said. 'You know how I hate to be rushed. I grow all tense.'

Jack said, 'It's all right. Pauline arrived early, and she'll have set out your creams and potions.'

'That's good,' Dolores said. 'But you missed the most bonzer afternoon. Uncle Sal told me the most engrossing stories you can imagine. And don't get me started on the cake.'

He gave her a forced smile. 'These things happen, but I'm glad you had a good time.'

Frances held out the cardboard box. 'Where shall I put this?'

'Ginny's,' Dolores said. 'I've got the tiniest refrigerator in my apartment, but Ginny's kitchen houses one the size of a small country.' She linked her arm with Jack's. 'I forgot my keys again, but if you open the door for me, I might be nice and let you have what's in the box.'

'I'm intrigued.' He freed himself to take a key-chain out of his pocket and unlock Dolores' door.

'Don't forget to deliver darling Frances back to me,' the singer said, fluttering her fingers.

They walked down to the other end of the corridor. Jack unlocked a door and ushered Frances in.

Her heels clicked on the polished ash floor. An oriental rug, muted with age, covered most of the floor. A built-in window seat made of the same ash was framed by bronze-coloured drapes tied back with simple ribbon.

A water colour hung on one wall, depicting the unloading of a ship in Port Adelaide in broad, confident lines. A mirror on the opposite wall reflected the painting with its bold hues of blue, green, pink, and yellow that, for Frances, were the essence of her city. She ran her fingers over the wooden frame, looking in vain for the painter's signature. The only other pieces of furniture in the long hall were a Victorian walnut chest and a matching coat rack, half hidden in a niche. Two doors were positioned left and right of painting and mirror.

Jack opened the first door on the left. Frances followed him. The kitchen she found herself in came as a surprise. The electric stove was sizable and the enamelled refrigerator took up pride of place. Still, Ginny would find herself hard pressed to prepare big meals on the small workbench or the scrubbed pine table that would sit two at most, let alone wash a mountain of dishes in a sink the size of a toy bath.

'Disappointed?' A bit of the tightness in Jack's face melted away.

'More surprised. I'd have thought a busy cook would need more space. It must be difficult to manage here.'

He leant against the table. 'It serves its purpose. I don't

cook that often, and rustling up an omelette or a steak is no big deal.'

'Your kitchen? I thought this was your housekeeper's apartment.'

He dug his thumbs into his pockets. 'You didn't honestly think I'd waltz into someone else's home without asking, did you?' Jack shook his head. 'And I thought you were brought up nicely.' He was teasing her.

She decided to repay him in kind. 'Maybe it's the company I keep that's rubbing off on me.' She fluttered her lashes at him.

'Maybe.' He opened the refrigerator door. 'Hand me that box, please. What's in it, by the way?'

'Plum ice cream and pound cake. Do you have a cake tin?'

He took the ice cream bowl out of the box, setting it next to a tub of butter. A dozen eggs, a rectangular parcel wrapped in waxed butcher's paper, mustard, a jar of pickles, and bottles of milk and juice barely filled a quarter of the fridge.

The refrigerator door sighed as he closed it. The bread bin, hidden away in a cupboard sitting flush with the stove, contained half a loaf. Jack stowed the cake next to it.

'Would you like coffee?' Without waiting for an answer, he poured a couple of handfuls of coffee beans into a grinder and cranked the handle. The aroma made Frances' mouth water. He filled the percolator with hot water from the tap.

'Can I help?' she asked.

He shook his head. 'Dolores has all we need in her

apartment, but the coffee she makes tastes like she soaked flypaper in it.'

Hissing steam curled up from the percolator. Jack wrapped a tea towel around his hand and lifted the percolator off the stove.

Trying hard not to giggle, Frances trailed him to Dolores' apartment. First Bluey and now Jack, both displaying unexpected domestic traits.

Pauline gaped at her from an adjoining room as Frances entered Dolores' apartment. Pauline was prevented from talking by the bobby-pins she held in her mouth as she tried to put Dolores' heavy tresses up in a loose knot at the nape of the creamy-white neck, with a few tendrils curling down the temples.

Dolores waved at them, her gaze unwavering on the large square-cut mirror that sat on top of a tall dresser. The back of her black satin dress was low-cut, revealing the same creamy white skin until four inches below the shoulder blades. The front of the dress hinted at bare skin, but the fabric fell in soft waves halfway to the waist.

She stretched her neck so Pauline could slide another bobby-pin into the hair-do.

'That'll do, Pauline. You can go now,' Dolores said, adding a few strokes with a black pencil to her brows. 'How do I look, Jack?'

He blew her a kiss. 'You'd outshine the moon if you set your sights on it. Pauline, you can go down if you wish and get something to eat. Now, Dolores, where would you like your coffee?'

'My sitting room, darling. Make it half a thimbleful, and then I need to rest my voice for a few moments.'

Jack briefly rested a hand on Dolores' shoulder. 'I can always have the band playing a couple more tunes without you if you'd like.'

'That's sweet of you, darling, but no,' she said. 'You know as well as I do that once I start that, I'll soon make a habit out of it, because I'm lazy, and before you can snap your fingers I'll get a reputation for being unreliable.' She touched his cheek. 'Now where's my coffee?'

Frances felt self-conscious again as she watched the easy rapport between them. She drank her coffee in slow sips. Dolores gave her a rueful look. 'Can you forgive me for dragging you here and then deserting you straight away? Jack, you'll have Bluey take her home, won't you? I really feel bad about it, but I'm hopeless when it comes to tight schedules.'

'That's all right,' Frances said. 'I've enjoyed it.'

'I'll take her home,' Jack said. 'Bluey's got other things to do.'

'Thanks, darling. And maybe we should give Pauline a tiny pay rise? To show her we appreciate her looking after everything, even if it's not her responsibility?'

'If you wish.'

Dolores bestowed a dazzling smile upon him. 'Can you give the poor girl a few shillings tonight, so she can take her dress to the dry-cleaners first thing in the morning? Or she could drop it off tomorrow night and put it in with my laundry? She got a nasty stain on it when she cleaned up in the powder room downstairs.'

Jack furrowed his brows. 'Why wasn't the room cleaned last night?'

'Darling, how should I know? All I can tell you is that

Pauline looked for something to do while she was waiting for me, and obviously someone had put more powder on to the mirror than on their face. Pauline must have trailed her arm along it because I noticed a long floury streak on her sleeve the second I saw her.'

She paused. 'I don't believe she's got more than two or three dresses, apart from her work uniform, and I'd hate her to have ruined one because she hadn't changed yet.'

A muscle in the right corner of Jack's mouth twitched. 'I'll take care of it. Frances? It's time to go.'

Dolores shut her eyes. 'You're a star.'

CHAPTER FIFTEEN

*J*ack ran down the stairs. Frances followed at a
sedate pace, not quite knowing what to expect.
Something clearly had upset him, and she had
no clue other than that Pauline was somehow involved. She
clenched her hand into a fist. Her palm felt sweaty. She
couldn't imagine picking a fight with Jack, but if Pauline
needed support, she'd be there for her. She quickened her
steps.

Jack pushed the low swing door, that led from the
ground floor hallway to the service rooms of the club, open.
It swung back and forth until Frances stopped it with her
hand. Two men in dress suits made way for her as she
hurried past.

'Sorry,' she said, but she didn't slow down. She didn't
want to lose Jack in this maze of back rooms that, judging
by warring smells and noises, housed kitchen, laundry,
storage, and staff rooms, as well as a rehearsal room for
Dolores and the band.

He headed straight to the powder room.

She followed him inside. He stood in front of the mirror, put on a pair of glacé gloves he had snatched along the way from a cupboard, and ran the tip of his index finger along the inside edges of the frame. Every couple of inches he paused and checked the gloved finger.

'What are you looking for?' Frances asked.

'Spilt powder.' He didn't bother to turn around, taking up his search again.

She moved closer, blowing softly into the corners of the frame. A few particles floated up from the frame. 'I think that's what you're looking for. Though it could be simply dust.'

Jack rubbed his finger along the indicated spot. A few grains of something white clung to the glove. He touched the stuff with his tongue and spat it out. A shutter came down in his eyes.

He turned around on his heels, marching out of the powder room and into a small storage room. 'Bluey?'

The stolid man walked out of the kitchen, a half-eaten cold pie in one hand.

The vein on Jack's left temple pulsed. 'Who was in charge of the cloakroom and ladies' powder room last night, the hours before closing time?'

Bluey tugged on his earlobe. He looked as bemused as she felt, thought Frances. Jack seemed to have forgotten all about her. Whatever it was that had made him angry, it must be bad. The tension around her grew until all her nerves were stretched taut. She stood transfixed, until Bluey said with an air of finality, 'It was Len's turn.'

'Go get him. You can eat on the way.'

159

Bluey crammed the pie in his mouth, exchanging an odd look with Jack. He gave a tiny nod in reply.

'Jack?' She touched his shoulder, to remind him of her presence.

He gave her a distracted glance. 'Give me a few minutes, and then I'll take you home.'

'Do you want me to wait outside?'

'It might be better, kiddo. This could get ugly, and it's got nothing to do with you.' The ghost of his usual smile hovered on his lips. 'Or your friend Pauline, in case you're wondering. I can promise you that much.'

She stared at the ground. Part of her wanted to leave, but somehow, she couldn't. She'd trusted him, now he needed to trust her. If not ... She moved back against the wall where a battered wardrobe cast her in shadow. The words came out timid, not as strong as she'd intended. 'I'd rather stay.'

Jack took off his gloves and slapped them together in the palm of his left hand. They sounded like a whip. 'It's up to you. I wouldn't blame you for leaving.'

Bluey frog-marched a man into the room. Frances recognised him as one of the men she had passed earlier. His square forehead glistened, his porky stubs of fingers clenched and unclenched. Part of his left ring finger was missing.

'Take a seat, Len,' Jack said, leaning against the edge of the table. 'I have a few questions.'

Len's Adam's apple bobbed up and down. 'I've done nothing wrong, boss.'

'Right-ho.' Jack's smile left his eyes cold. He reminded Frances of a cat letting a mouse get away for fun, before pouncing. 'No worries, then. Take a load off your legs.'

Len plonked down onto a wooden chair, resting his fists on his fleshy thighs. Bluey moved behind the chair.

Frances tried to shrink back further into the shadow.

Len slid his tongue over his upper lip. 'Sweet,' he said, his voice coarse. He swallowed. 'Fire away, boss.'

Jack's gaze travelled along the ceiling. 'Oh yeah, Len, last night. Pretty busy, wasn't it? Punters floating in and out of the club, till the small hours.'

'Yeah?'

Jack waved the soiled glove in the air. 'Couldn't be bothered with a bit of mop and tidy-up, some of us.'

'I never.' Len's upper lip stuck out. 'I did them powder rooms as soon as I could, like always. Till midnight it was Anna's job anyway, popping out of her cubicle and giving it a seeing-to whenever the room was empty. You know you don't want us men to go in there while there's still customers around.'

Jack nodded slowly. 'Maybe you did the room a bit early and someone popped in there after Anna'd gone and while you were handing over the last couple of coats and stuff?'

Len moistened his lips again. His Adam's apple bobbed harder. 'Could be. I got but two eyes, boss.'

Frances didn't see where this was leading, but why Jack had warned her away was beyond her.

He ignored her completely, while he continued his interrogation. 'And maybe some sheila went in there while her gentleman friend hung around outside, making sure she had a bit of privacy?'

Len's shoulders stiffened. 'No harm in that.'

161

Jack's smile had a reptilian quality. 'None whatsoever. Unless, of course, the gentleman happened to have given the lady a little something she'd rather not share.' He gave Bluey a nod.

Bluey grabbed Len's shoulder, pulling him off his chair. Len winced. Frances pressed her knuckles against her mouth to stifle any sound.

'Who was it, Len?' Jack asked. 'Who was that obliging gentleman, and how much did he pay you to look the other way?'

Len twisted in Bluey's grip. 'You're bloody breaking my arm, mate.' The veins in his throat protruded. 'I didn't mean no harm, I swear.'

Jack slid off the table. His fist slammed into Len's nose. A crunch, and then blood spurted from Len's nostrils, the only colour in his white face.

'The name, Len.' Jack's voice was low.

Len spat out. His saliva was mixed with red streaks. Bluey pressed harder on Len's shoulder. The injured man howled.

'Whitey,' he gasped. 'It was Whitey Morgan. What's it to you anyway, boss?' Blood dripped onto the floor.

Frances felt bile rising in the throat. She closed her eyes, fighting it down.

'You know the rules, Len.' Jack sounded calm. 'No drugs in my club, no pimping, no hawking any other illicit wares than a couple of drinks.'

'Those sheilas were gagging for the snow, boss.' Len's speech was slurred.

Frances opened her eyes.

A red trickle ran unhindered into Len's mouth. 'If I'd

stopped him, they'd have screeched the place into the ground, and then you'd have had the cops busting us.'

'You don't listen, Len. No drugs, not for anyone. Who were the girls?'

Bluey gave Len's shoulder another hard squeeze.

'One of them used to wait tables on the Floating Palais.' His pupils dilated. 'Her girl-friend said they had something to celebrate and wanted to spend a bit out of the petty cash. That's all I heard, boss, I swear.'

'Let him go, Bluey.'

Len slumped forward. One hand gingerly touched his nose, the other clutched his shoulder.

'I'm blimmin' hurting, boss.'

'Bluey will take you to Doctor Lum Yow. He can stick a bit of plaster on your nose and give you a bottle of his tonic for your shoulder. Bluey, make sure he doesn't wet himself in the car.'

Bluey gave Len a slap on his sound shoulder. 'I'll better walk him up to North Terrace. Our mate here looks a mite pale, as if he could do with a bit of air.'

'The Chinese quack? I don't want any of his foreign poison, for Pete's sake.'

'Suit yourself.' Jack motioned for Frances to follow him. She hesitated before she stepped out of the shadow, avoiding Len's gaze. Her hand hurt. She stared at it. Deep marks ringed one finger. She must have bitten it without feeling it.

Jack took her arm. 'I'll see you later, Bluey.'

Len grasped Jack's sleeve. 'What about me, boss? I could work in the kitchen tonight, swap with Davey, if you want me to.'

Jack let go of Frances as he peeled Len's fingers off his sleeve with obvious distaste. She held her breath. Surely, he wouldn't hit the man again? No, he said, 'Bluey will help you gather your stuff. You're out.'

Len began to wheedle. 'But I need this job, Jack. You're not gonna give me the spear over one bloomer? Not after everything we've been through.'

'Give him a fiver out of the petty cash, Bluey. For old times' sake. And then get him out of my sight.'

Flecks of red covered Jack's hand. He caught Frances staring at it. 'I told you it could get ugly,' he said with a curious undertone.

She nodded without looking up.

He stopped in front of the car. 'I never said I'm a nice man, Frances. If you don't like what you see, that's too bad. But at least I'm not pretending.' He raised her chin with two fingers. 'What would you have me do? Let that miserable swine get away with letting drug dealers take over my club? They're worse than killers, that lot. They destroy the soul along with the body.'

She dug her teeth into her upper lip. 'I know.'

'I didn't hurt Len much, although it was tempting.' A tear must have rolled down Frances' cheek, because Jack dabbed at something with his handkerchief.

'I wanted the names, kiddo. There was no easier way to get at them.'

She swallowed, hearing the crunching noise again in her mind, and Jack's relaxed voice. 'It's just – you enjoyed hurting him.' She shivered.

'No. But I won't lose any sleep over Len's little aches. I'll always take steps to stop bad people from muscling in on my club, my friends, and my city.' He paused long enough for his words to sink in, before he asked, 'Ready to go home?'

She struggled to give him a smile. 'Yes.' They fell silent.

~

'It was simply that I didn't expect that,' Frances said on the way home, before the trench between them turned into an unbridgeable abyss. 'The violence and the blood, I mean.'

'I wish you hadn't seen it.'

'No, it's all right.' She rubbed her forehead, struggling to sort out things for herself. 'I'm not that naïve not to see that Len got off lightly. It just takes some time to understand.' She swallowed. 'I think that's what Mum was afraid of, the seedy sides of ...' She broke off.

'The seedy sides of people like me? You don't have to be embarrassed. Like I said, I break the law, and I'm not ashamed of that, but I also won't go past the line I've drawn for myself.'

His mouth tightened. 'I can understand if your mum wants to keep you away from folks like Dolores and me. On the other hand, like I said, I'd be grateful if you spend a bit of time with Dolores, away from the club. She needs girlfriends.'

'I won't desert her,' she said, hoping for a light tone that would make everything between them all right again. 'But I don't see why she would need me. She must have friends by the wagon load.'

'Admirers, sure,' Jack said with a hint of mockery. 'And

jokers who hope her magic will rub off on them. But most females don't take to her.'

'Jealousy, because she's so stunning.' Well, at least she didn't envy her the beauty.

'You'd know more about competition between girls than I.' His smile helped ease the lump that still sat in her stomach.

He honked at a man who'd pushed his billy-cart on to the road. The Rover swerved. The traffic was unusually heavy, with cars piled high with families, dogs, and stacks of baggage.

'It seems like the rest of Adelaide is making the most of Easter,' he said. 'What about you?'

She paused. 'I'm not sure,' she said. 'Part of me is happy, with all the fun we've had, but only when I manage to forget that awful phone call.' She hugged her arms to her chest. 'Have you ever felt some menace that made your hair bristle?' She shook herself. 'I'm being fanciful.'

'No,' Jack said. 'It would be more surprising if you'd feel all chipper after the series of frights you've had over the last week. Seeing me punching the living daylights out of Len wouldn't have helped.'

'One hit,' she corrected him. 'And he deserved it.'

'Too right he did, and more than that.'

'But what about the other man? The one with the drugs?'

'Whitey Morgan?' Jack's mouth curled into a grim smile. 'I've got friends in certain places who'll be pleased to have an idea where to look for the snow that's been falling out of the clouds recently.' His grip on the steering wheel relaxed. 'Your friend, Pauline, has earned a pay rise all right.'

'I'm glad. How much more will you give her?'

'Why? Do you suspect me of short-changing my staff?'

'Not you,' she said. 'But I do hope it'll be enough for her and her mum to get out of that dreadful hovel they've shifted to.'

'Is it that bad? None of my employees is seriously hurting for money.'

'Pauline was without work for over two months, and her mother's been unable to earn money for even longer because she had an accident. If it hadn't been for Dolores, they'd be desperate.'

'Pauline's a good kid,' Jack said. 'She cheers Dolores up no end, and she is smart enough to be quiet when Dolores needs a rest.' He drummed his fingertips on the steering wheel. 'I'll see what we can do. I own a bit of property, mostly to house my staff. Maybe there's something going. If Pauline and her mum want it.'

'They would. It must be horrible for them, in that crude place.'

'You're still looking fit to faint,' Jack said as they turned on to Grenfell Street. 'If I present you to your mother and Uncle Sal in this state, they'll never let you go out with any of us again.'

'I'm all right, simply tired.'

He eased the Rover around, heading back towards the city.

'Where are we going?' She sat up in alarm.

'I'll take you to a restaurant. That's what I should have done in the first place. What you need is a steak, followed by coffee and a medicinal brandy.' He indicated the glove box. 'I've got a flask in there, for emergencies. You don't want to trust on anyone selling you decent stuff, not these days. There's too many sly-groggers around, hawking pink-eye and snake-juice.'

He was serious. Frances pressed her lips together to stifle a giggle. Instead, it turned into a snort. Jack gave a sigh of long-suffering patience. The snort became a hoot.

He signalled the driver behind him to overtake as he pulled the Rover over to the kerb. 'Put your head between your knees and breathe in as deeply as you can,' he said, unscrewing the leather-covered brandy flask. He poured an inch of brandy into the lid that doubled as a cup. 'You've had a bit of a shock, but you don't want to become hysterical.'

That did it. She clapped a hand over her mouth, but this time she couldn't help it. She broke into laughter. 'Stop that,' she said between guffaws. 'You're doing that on purpose, aren't you?'

'Doing what?'

'Sitting here acting all concerned like a card-carrying member of the temperance movement, warning me away from sly-groggers, and then hand me a drink.'

'Who better than me?' He patted her back. 'Drink up, like a good girl. There's a decent place to eat a couple yards further down. We can walk from here.'

The liquor filled France's throat with a comforting warmth rather than burning with the fire she'd expected. She caught a drop running down the outside of the cup with her fingertip and licked it off. 'Nice,' she said.

'Imported all the way from France for this occasion.'

Jack took the cup and screwed it back on again. 'Any of the locally distilled stuff and you understand why our American friends call it rot-gut. Feeling better?'

She fanned her face. 'Apart from the fact that it's getting quite warm, yes.' Her right foot wobbled as she stepped out of the car and onto the sidewalk.

Jack steadied her. She leant in to him, breathing in his comforting after-shave. His lips were tantalisingly close for a moment. Their gaze met, as Jack pulled a few inches away, with an unreadable expression in his eyes.

'Maybe that dose was a bit much,' he said, stroking his chin. 'I keep on forgetting you aren't used to anything stronger than lemonade.'

She shook off his arm. 'I happen to like it.' She tried to look down her nose at him, a feat that was somehow hampered by the fact that Jack was taller than she. Still, he seemed to get the message because he gave her one of his slow smiles and said, 'It was a compliment, believe it or not. Anyway, how about we postpone any discussion until we're inside?'

He led her to a corner table at the window. A mere third of the seats in the restaurant were taken, ensuring them of quick service as well as privacy.

The menu came on embossed paper, tucked into a leather-bound cover. At first glance it appeared very impressive, until Frances noticed the cracks in the leather and how the ink on the menu had become faint. The waitresses had seen better days too. The one strolling over to them, a professional smile frozen on to her face, clung to her past prime with the aid of a thick veneer of talcum powder that clogged every fold and wrinkle.

'Are you ready to order, Frances? Or do you trust me to do it?'

She put down the menu. She'd been too busy trying to clear her head to take in what was on offer. 'Yes please. You do it.'

'We'll both have the beef steak, medium rare, with chips, and pumpkin, a bottle of iced water and coffee for two, please.' He smiled at the waitress.

'Sweet.' The woman swayed her hips a little bit wider as she walked away from their table.

Jack leant towards Frances. 'Does that suit you?'

'Very much,' she said, feeling a rush of self-consciousness. 'I'm not used to dining out.'

'That's easy to change.'

She found herself tucking in with relish, that awkward moment between them firmly behind her.

He watched her with obvious approval. 'You have recovered.'

'Perfectly. I hadn't realised I was that hungry.' She put knife and fork down onto her empty plate and reached for the napkin.

Jack took the coffeepot off the hot plate and poured them both another cup.

She spooned sugar into her cup, added some milk and stirred. 'I almost forgot, over everything else that's been going on, do you have any idea who the man might be? You know, the one Croaky talked about?'

She had lowered her voice to make sure no one could overhear, but still she couldn't bring herself to express herself more clearly.

Jack folded his napkin and laid it across his plate. 'It's possible,' he said, pushing the plate aside.

Frances leant forward on her elbows. 'Then we can tell him to be careful, can't we?' She felt as if a heavy weight that nearly crushed her had been lifted off. 'I knew it. Oh Jack, you're wonderful.'

A nerve on his lower jaw twitched. 'Don't put too much trust in me, kiddo.'

She put her left hand on his. 'Do you have his address? Please,' she gave his fingers a squeeze. 'Will you go there tonight to warn him? Or give him a buzz on the phone?'

His fingers stiffened under her touch. 'You don't understand, Frances. If I'm right, it's too late.'

Her mouth formed a circle but no sound came out.

'I may be wrong.' Jack put a few coins for their meal on the saucer. He helped her up. 'Come on, we'll talk about it somewhere else.'

CHAPTER SIXTEEN

*F*rances kept silent on the way home. Thoughts were running through her head, fragmented like splintered glass, each painful and disturbing, but without forming a recognisable structure.

'It's a case for the police,' Jack said as he took the key out of the ignition.

'No.'

'Are you sure? I'll come up with something that leaves you out of it, if you want to. I could easily have overheard something in the club.' He steered her towards the door. She fumbled in her bag for the door key. Her hand shook so hard she dropped the key into one of the planters that flanked the entrance.

He parted the chrysanthemums, retrieved the key and opened the door for her.

The house smelt of polish, beeswax, fried bacon, and sanity. Frances took a deep breath, letting the sense of home embrace her until she felt safe again.

Jack stood next to her. His lids were lowered, giving him

that deceptively sleepy expression again. He watched her in the detached yet intense way a doctor watched a critical patient. 'We need to talk.'

'But not in the house,' she said, her voice catching in her throat. 'We'll sit in the garden. I don't want anyone to hear us.' And she didn't want to bring anything awful into her home. She couldn't explain, but saying things out loud made them more real in a way, and her home was used to shared laughter and happiness. She wouldn't have it violated.

She held her shoulders as stiffly as possible, as if bracing herself for a physical blow. Jack knocked on to the parlour door as they walked past, opened it wide enough to peek inside the room and say hello to Maggie and Uncle Sal.

She went ahead. Already contours were becoming blurred outside. Another half hour and the sky would be inky, smudged with grey smoke and studded with the glimmer of stars.

A storm lantern hung under the eave. Jack took it down to light the thick candle inside. He pulled out a chair for Frances, perching on the edge of the table himself.

He felt like a stranger as he loomed there, cold and intimidating. She hugged her arms to her chest.

He slid off the table and pulled out another chair for himself. 'What do you want me to do?' He sounded weary. 'Forget the whole business? I will, if you're sure that's what you want.' He raked his hand through his hair. He'd left his hat in the car, Frances realised. That was the single sign of distraction he'd shown.

But then he was used to things like this. Her chest

tightened. The glimpse she'd had this afternoon of his life behind the glittering façade had shaken her more than she'd thought. She wondered fleetingly if Phil would break someone's nose without flinching. He probably would. She shivered.

'Well?' Jack's gaze held hers. 'It's up to you. If you think you can live with letting someone get away with murder—' He shrugged. 'It's your decision.'

She winced.

Jack pulled her close. She sank against his shoulder.

He smoothed back her hair. 'It's all right, kiddo. We couldn't have prevented it. Believe me, if someone wants you dead you haven't got the chance of a three-legged horse in the Melbourne Cup.'

A sob escaped her throat.

'It could be a different man. I swear, Frances, there's nothing we could have done.'

'It's all my fault. We could have warned him if I'd told you early enough.'

'And what would have happened then, even if we'd alarmed every man in the city? How do you prevent being coshed from behind as you climb into your car or shot when you come out of the door?' He rocked her gently.

She shook her head. Her cheek rubbed against the fabric of his jacket. 'There must have been something we could have done.'

'There wasn't. Believe me.' Jack put one hand on the nape of her neck. She lifted her head off his shoulder and sat up straight.

He said, 'Even if there had been anything, we'd have got it wrong. They changed the time frame, didn't they?'

'Yes.' She stared into the crescent of light cast by the storm lantern. 'Or maybe – I don't know. I thought he said, after Easter, but the line crackled and snapped the way it sometimes does long-distance.'

She twisted a strand of hair around her finger and tugged it hard.

'Easy.' Jack's face was almost completely in the shade. She sensed, more than she saw, the sympathy in his face. He must have been a good man to have around in the trenches. No wonder he'd been made captain, as young as he was. Dolores and the rest of the staff trusted him blindly. Even that wretched Len had believed Jack would let him get off with a slap on the wrist and chuckle. It was generous of Jack to spare the man a fiver. At least he had some means until he found another job. If he found one.

She pressed her knuckle into her eyes. Work was too precious. She couldn't have risked her employment by going to the police. 'They wouldn't have believed my story anyway.'

'The coppers? No.'

Frances realised she'd spoken her thoughts out aloud.

'And now it's too late. Water under the bridge.' Her voice sounded insincere in her own ears. No. It was time she did the right thing. She couldn't bring the man back to life, but she owed him that much. She dug her nails into her palm until it hurt. She had ignored the painful truth for too long already. 'Jack? If I keep quiet about Croaky and the other man, I'm shielding a killer.' Salty tears slid down the back of her throat. 'I'm no better than Len.'

He took the storm lantern and set it on the table. Light

fell on to his face. Her eyes searched his for the contempt he must feel for her. Instead she saw nothing but kindness.

'You're nothing like Len,' he said. 'He deliberately chose to aid and abet drug dealers. You, on the other hand, haven't committed any crime. All you worry about is taking care of your family.' He touched her cheek. 'I might've done the same.'

'Maybe that's what Len was trying to do.'

'No. There is no excuse for him. None.' His hand slammed down on the table, making the storm lantern jerk. He got up and walked a few steps away, turning his back to her. 'If it hadn't been for his wife and baby, a broken nose would be the least of his concerns.'

She stared, wide-eyed.

He turned to face her. 'We wouldn't have taken him lakeside, if that's what you're thinking.' Cold fury resonated in his voice. 'But Bluey and I would have given him a hiding he'd never forget.'

'Why? Couldn't you have handed him over to the police?'

'On what evidence? My insight into his shifty little mind?' a shadow flitted over Jack's face. It could have been the light cast by the lantern, but it made Frances tense even more. He went on, 'Having the police sniffing around for drugs isn't good for business either, and I won't have the Top Note tainted with a snowy-white brush. Or Dolores.'

Her jaw dropped.

'Don't get any wrong ideas, kiddo. Dolores may act a bit spoilt, but she's the most innocent soul I've met in the whole bloody business, and there's nothing I wouldn't do for her. I owe her more than I can repay.'

He pushed his hands into his pockets, gaze fixed on the stars.

His voice was so low Frances had to strain to hear as he began to talk. 'It happened a few years after the war,' he said, still not looking at her. 'Most of us struggled to adjust. Nothing was the way we'd left it, neither places nor people.' He paused. 'We were, all of us, injured, some on the outside, all on the inside.'

The pain in his voice made her ache for him.

'Dolores was shattered. It took her a while to get back on her feet after Simon's death, so I stuck it out in Ballarat for a bit, to look after her and my kid sister Rachel, until she convinced me that I'd done my bit. All I needed to do was to find them an apartment in Sydney, she said, and everything would turn out all right.' He pulled one hand out of the pocket to rub his neck. 'It sounded like a great idea all right, to let them go to the big city, because Dolores wanted to study music, and Rachel planned on taking up photography. Mother was all for it, she was already chafing at the bit to return home and tough it out in England with her husband.'

'What happened?' The words were out before she knew it. She hadn't meant to interrupt him.

He looked at her as if he'd just remembered her presence. She got up and walked over to him, to lessen the sudden distance between them. Two steps away from him she stopped, waiting for a sign, but he gave her none. She returned to her chair.

The muscles in his face worked. 'I waved Mother and my stepfather goodbye when they sailed and dutifully chaperoned the girls to an endless parade of the gay,

177

reckless parties everybody seemed to be having. When I'd had my fill, I asked Bluey to keep as close an eye on them as he could. Then I chucked in my engineering job at the roadworks and set off inland to try my hand at fossicking.'

'Did you get lucky?' Frances interrupted him, not so much because she wanted to hear the answer – she could guess well enough – but because he felt so far away from her.

He moved a step closer. 'Did I strike gold, you mean? Oh yes, in a small enough way. I had gathered enough experience, digging trenches, to know what to do with a shovel and a pickaxe, and I'd dabbled a bit in geology at uni. It was bloody lonely though, but that suited me well enough. And I knew the girls would get through their allowance fast. Including my darling mother. They all liked their bit of fun. So, I knew all along I'd better make some serious money while it was good.'

He rubbed his neck again. 'I'd dig a bit, go to Perth, hand my finds over to an assayer and send a postal note, transferring money to the girls. That's how Dolores knew where to find me when the bastards got to Rachel.'

Frances' mouth went dry. 'What do you mean?'

'I told you about the parties, didn't I? Some of them were incredibly hot. We'd all been through hell, and everybody got that sense that time was running out. People began to cram more into their remaining hours, more laughter, more excitement, more fun, more love, more pain. All fuelled by drink and drugs, to mask the stench of fear and loneliness.'

He took a wallet out of his jacket, flicking it open and flung it to Frances. 'That's Rachel.' The photograph was small, maybe two by three inches, but it showed every exquisite detail of the girl's oval face. Her brows were very dark and straight under her fair hair that she wore bobbed short enough for the tips to grace her cheek. Her mouth was generous and curved upwards, and she had the same look in her eyes as Jack.

'She's gorgeous,' Frances said. 'She and Dolores must have turned heads everywhere.'

'Yes,' Jack said, the pain naked in his face. 'I shouldn't have left her. I should've seen how vulnerable she was. She always had this intense hunger for life, and adventure, and when she fell in love with the wrong guy, there was no holding her back. Dolores didn't know until Rachel's boyfriend tried to get to her hooked on snow, too. Thank heavens she's got her head screwed on right. She begged me to come home straight away.'

Tears stung in Frances' eyes. She wiped them away. Poor Rachel, she thought, and poor Jack. 'Why would anyone give his girlfriend drugs?'

'Money. First what the girls could pay for the snow, and then what others would pay for the girls.'

The implication sank in with the force of a hammer. 'Oh my God.'

'I shouldn't have told you that,' he said. 'I keep forgetting how young you are.'

'Poor Rachel,' she said. 'What did you do?'

'Salvaged whatever I could. She was in a pretty bad shape for a while, and she fought me with every breath, but we did it. I took her to my mother's cousin in New Zealand, and she's been there ever since. She's fine now. Not much temptation out there on a sheep station, only peace and solitude, and half a dozen people watching over her.'

'What happened to her boyfriend?'

'His sins caught up with him. Last I heard he was rotting in jail.' A grim smile appeared on Jack's face. 'He got caught trying to sell his wares to the wrong person.'

She had a hunch. 'Did you have anything to do with it?'

'Rachel's my sister. I protect my own people.'

'Was Dolores never – tempted?' Frances hoped she didn't sound as disturbed as she was.

'I don't know, and I didn't ask. All I know is that without her, Rachel might as well be dead.' He gave her an appraising look. 'I told you I owe her. Especially since she came within a hair of having to appear as a witness against the boyfriend, which would have damaged her reputation without a hope of repair. Nobody's got a longer memory and a filthier mind-set than those who were most properly brought-up.'

'But you didn't go back to your dig.'

He stared at the sky. 'You need to know when to walk away. There's only so much solitude I could take, and I'd had my fair share. That's when I came to Adelaide.'

'With Dolores?' That came out wrong. Her cheeks grew warm.

'Sure. I couldn't leave her behind and have one of the thugs who were in the cocaine racket take revenge on her, could I?' Jack folded his hands behind his neck. 'Apart from the fact that I promised Simon I'd look after her, and she's a jolly talented singer. She'd had enough training to make it on any stage, so I built up the Top Note around her talents.'

He must have taken a small army along. Bluey and the

Barkers had all along been part of the set-up from what she'd gathered, doing odd jobs first for Jack's mother, then for Rachel and Dolores. Frances was impressed at how he'd managed to support them all.

'I thought they'd be protected enough.' Jack seemed to marvel at his own naivety. 'There was always someone, except when the girls went out to meet friends or go to a fashionable club. They couldn't very well have a chauffeur or housekeeper trailing after them, could they?' He shook his head. 'You don't notice if anyone's getting hooked on something until they're pretty far gone. Otherwise Bluey would have taken the fellow apart before he could get to Rachel. Or I would.'

Frances felt sick inside, sick and numb at the same time, as if her mind had put up a barrier to keep thefts, drugs, and murder at a safe distance from her.

'You look as if you're close to fainting,' Jack said. 'I shouldn't have told you this, but I thought it might help you understand.'

She pulled her feet up on to the seat, hugging her knees to her. She stared at his calm face. 'Have you often hurt people?'

'When I had to. Do you want me to go?'

'No.' She lowered her feet to the ground and sat up straight. 'At least – I don't think so. But, Jack? What shall I do?'

He sat forward in his chair. 'What advice would your father have given? Or your brother?'

She paused. She could hear the blood pounding in her ears. The night seemed to have swallowed any sound apart from Jack's soft breath and her heart beating. 'They'd have told me that I'd need to do something. Standing by, letting bad things happen, makes you guilty as well. That's what my dad used to tell us.' Her voice took on a high pitch. 'And he was talking about pilfered sweets or someone riding the tram without a ticket.' Her hand trembled as she touched his sleeve. 'But how can I be sure we're talking about the same victim? You haven't told me anything.'

'Fair enough,' he said. 'Here's what I know. On Good Friday, some shopkeepers used the public holiday to get a few things done in their shops, book keeping, or a stock-take, or other chores that needed to be done outside shop hours. Among them was a jeweller, who was rumoured to keep his most precious pieces in a safe in his house in Glenelg, taking them to his shop by appointment only.'

Frances' stomach lurched.

'He'd set up such an appointment for yesterday morning, with a person unknown. When he left his house to walk to his car, someone struck him from behind repeatedly, with enough force to split his skull.'

'Oh my God,' she whispered.

'The police found an empty jeweller's tray, covered in black velvet, half buried under the body.' Jack rubbed his chin. 'There's one thing, though. During the last year, there've been a number of stick-ups, involving jewellers. That's safer than a bank job. Loot's easy to carry, easy to sell, and there are no guards to deal with. I'd have said it's another of those, gone wrong, if you hadn't overheard that phone call.'

Her heart beat faster. She pressed her hand on her ribs to prevent it from bursting out of her chest.

Jack stood up and put both hands on her shoulders. 'You could talk to Phil about Croaky, kiddo.'

'No.' She shook her head wildly. 'He's with the police and he'd have to write a report. I'd lose my job, and we'd all be on the street. Or else he'd lie for me, and how can I trust him, if he's corrupt enough to do that?' She looked straight into Jack's eyes. 'There must be another way, and right now you're the only one I trust.'

'Although I'm a lawbreaker?'

'Uncle Sal says you're an honest crook. That's true, isn't it?'

Jack's eyes softened. 'Good girl,' he said. 'Here's what you can do tomorrow ...'

CHAPTER SEVENTEEN

*J*ack's plan had sounded so simple. All Frances had to do was figure out where she'd put the plugs to get the required connection.

She eyed the switchboard wearily. She'd been busy all morning, moving the plugs in a hectic dance dictated by speed, speed, speed. Now, that Easter was but a fading memory, it felt as if the whole country wanted to catch up on the telephone with whatever deal or dream needed pursuing, and every second call involved her switchboard, leaving her hardly a moment to think. Cold sweat trickled down her armpits. She must figure it out before it was too late. Think, she told herself as she eyed the switchboard. She thought back. She'd accepted the call from the operator, Clara had left, and she'd plugged the jacks in – where?

A tap on her shoulder made her start.

'I have talked to the General Postmaster,' Mr Gibbons said. 'The powers that be have decided, for economy's sake, not to hire a new girl. Instead we will make up a roster dividing up the hours in question among existing staff.

'I did wonder, under these circumstances, if you are still willing to put your name down for a few extra hours again? I realise you've done more than enough already, filling in, but still.'

'I'm glad to help, and of course I can do with some extra shillings, but if there is someone else who really needs the hours, don't mind me.'

Mr Gibbons pulled out a handkerchief and blew his nose. 'Well,' he said, 'Clara's wee brother is poorly and needs to see the doctor every couple of days.'

'She'll need every penny, then,' Frances said. 'Don't worry about my family. We've got a new lodger now, so we're all right.'

'Good. But there is one more thing. I understand it is none of my affair,' he said with an apologetic note in his voice, 'but I did know your father very well indeed, and I feel it is my duty to tell you that certain, ahem, things have come to my ears.'

She kept an eye on the switchboard, hoping he'd get to the point. 'Yes?'

'There's been talk, I'm afraid, about a certain person paying attention to you; a gentleman whose business is not quite reputable, if the rumours are true.'

Frances swivelled around, ignoring the blinking light. 'You're talking about Jack Sullivan.'

His worry lines deepened as he nodded.

'But ...' She paused. 'What about him? He's an old war mate of our lodger, Mr Anderson, who happens to have transferred from the Melbourne police. He invited Mr

Anderson and my family to a picnic so they could share memories of friends they'd left behind.'

Unexpected anger rose in her. 'If there's anything wrong with that, feel free to tell me. And if there's anything specific that should make Mr Sullivan unfit for my mother's company, I'd like to know.' She took a deep breath.

'It's not the gentleman himself who attracts criticism, my dear, but his line of business. But if he's an old friend of this Mr Anderson, that's different. Be glad, Frances, that you're too young to remember much about the war. Those were terrible days, terrible.'

'You lost someone? I'm so sorry.'

'My son. Eddy had just turned eighteen.' Mr Gibbons took off his spectacles and blinked helplessly. 'All you get is a letter, telling you that your boy won't come home.' The poor man.

'Mr Gibbons?'

'Yes, my dear?'

'If you'd like me to, I could ask Mr Sullivan if he can find someone who's been in the war with your son.'

'Gallipoli,' Mr Gibbons said. 'Eddy served on the peninsula. And, Frances?'

'Yes, Mr Gibbons?'

'Thank you.'

The light no longer blinked. Frances rubbed her temples. What a small place Adelaide was! How often had she been out with Jack? Well, once would probably have been enough to set vicious tongues in motion. She put the headset on and concentrated on the task at hand. By the end of her shift her throat felt parched and her eyes smarted, and still she couldn't pinpoint the exact spot on the switchboard. But at least she'd narrowed it down to a few possibilities. That was the good news. The bad news was, those few plugs serviced over a hundred phone lines.

She massaged her right shoulder. It hurt, from carrying a shoulder bag containing the iron horseshoe Jack had given her instead of a half-brick. It made a good weapon, but it also weighed a ton.

She let herself out the back door. Her throat felt even worse than before, because she hadn't had a drink all day. She slid a hand into her skirt pocket. This once the spare pennies she kept there wouldn't end up in a beggar's bowl but in the nearest café.

This was a far cry from Balfours, Frances thought as she took in the peeling paint on the wall and the lack of lighting. Most of the light bulbs in the two fly-dirt spotted chandeliers were burnt out, but then the place was cheap.

She ordered a pot of tea from the placid waitress who stared at her with a puzzled expression. She gave Frances another close look as she brought the tea. It was unsettling, but at least the tea was hot and strong and Frances' tongue no longer stuck to the roof of her mouth.

She cradled the half empty cup in her hand. Two other tables were taken, one by two elderly nurses and the table next to hers by two men. They didn't give her as much as a glance. She planted her elbows on the table and looked out of the window, trying again to remember what the operator on the other end had said. She reached out for the cup as her elbow slipped and her handbag fell off the table.

'Bother,' she said under her breath as she bent down to pick it up.

'The job came off without a hitch,' she heard a man as she crouched half under the table. 'But I swear, mate, next time I'll do it lakeside.'

Frances let out a startled shriek. That voice, she knew that voice. And those words! Look at them, her head told her, look at Croaky, but her body wouldn't listen. Blind panic engulfed her. She grabbed her bag, righted herself and fumbled for her money. She put two pennies on the table, keeping her face turned away from the other table.

'Hey, you there,' the voice said in a harsh manner, and she heard a chair scrape over the floorboards.

'Now I know you.' The waitress put a hand on her hip, shielding Frances from view. 'You're a switchboard operator, right? You used to work with my cousin, Gussie.' The bell on the counter rang. 'Coming,' she yelled, as she turned around at snail's pace.

Stumbling, Frances fled into the daylight. Her blood pounded in her ears. She looked frantically around her. If the man really was Croaky, talking about a murder, and he'd heard her shrieking, he might go after her. Or he'd go after her mum and Uncle Sal. She couldn't go home. He might follow her there. She couldn't go back to the telephone exchange either, because then he'd know for sure that she worked there.

She dashed across the road and around the corner to seek refuge in the O'Leary's shop. The small part of her that wasn't numb with fear listened out for pursuing footsteps, but none came. She breathed more normal now, as she regained her composure. She needed to get a grip on her imagination.

She pushed the shop door open.

'Frances, my dear.' Tilda peered at her with short-sighted eyes. 'What a nice surprise. How can I help you?' She gave her a closer look. 'Are you all right, love?'

Everything was as it should be. A huge wave of relief flooded over Frances. She thought quickly. No need to alarm the old dear, and there was something she'd wanted to buy anyway. She held up her shaking hands. 'Gloves,' she said. 'I can't wear these old things with my gorgeous new dress, can I?'

Tilda gave her a sly glance as she took one of Frances' hands in hers, fingering the darned spots. 'Lovely stitches, really well concealed,' she said. 'But these are things to wear to work and not for an evening in the Top Note.' She moved her head closer to Frances. 'Tell me, my dear, is the club really that fast? I've never been to a night club, but one does hear such exciting stories.'

'Much exaggerated. Don't pay them any heed,' an amused voice said behind Frances' back. 'My mother's debutante balls were a much hotter affair from what I've been told.'

'Jack!' Frances gave a start. 'My goodness, you frightened me half to death. What are you doing here?'

'Hoping for an introduction.' His teeth flashed as he winked at her.

'Of course.' Frances said, feeling weak with relief.

Whatever happened, he'd promised to keep her safe. 'Jack Sullivan, I'd like you to meet Tilda O'Leary.'

Jack bent over Tilda's hand. 'My pleasure.'

Tilda's left hand fluttered to her chest. A flush crept into her cheeks. 'Is there anything I can help you with?'

He treated her to one of his most charming smiles. 'I saw Frances enter and thought I'd take her home when she's done with her shopping.'

'How nice.' Tilda had a speculative gleam in her eyes.

Frances could see her cheeks turn pink in the small mirror on the counter.

Tilda bent down to retrieve an outsized hat box overflowing with gloves. 'We've tried to peg them together,' she said, beaming at Jack. 'There is always the odd one whose match simply won't be found. But at least these should all be the right size for you, Frances.'

Frances rummaged in the box. Most gloves were cotton or silk in a state of disrepair. Those she cast aside on a growing pile on the counter. She had almost reached the bottom when Jack pulled something smooth and shiny out of the box. 'How about these? They are the same shade as your frock,' he said.

She pulled off her own gloves and jammed them carelessly into her handbag. She slid on one glove, admiring the suppleness of the leather.

She glanced at the price tag. Sometimes Tilda's and Martha's spidery writing was hard to decipher. This looked like one and sixpence. Frances put the gloves on the counter and took her purse out of her bag.

'My treat,' Jack said. 'Since I found them.'

'No. I'll pay for them myself. You've already spoiled all of us too much.'

'Are you sure? All right.' Jack inclined his head an inch. 'Goodbye, Miss O'Leary. If you care to drop by, there's always a table waiting for you and your sister in my club. Tell the doorman I invited you.'

'Oh, my goodness!' Tilda clapped her hand over her mouth.

Frances glanced around as casually as she could when they left the shop. No, she couldn't see anyone lurking around. She had been starting at shadows.

She pushed back a lock that had escaped from the grip of a hair pin during her dash from the café. At least Tilda hadn't noticed how flustered she'd been. Jack's invitation had distracted her.

'You didn't make fun of Tilda, did you?' Frances blurted out as Jack ushered her to his car.

'Why should I?'

'Because she isn't exactly your style of costumer. A prim elderly spinster like her would stick out ...' she searched for the right words, 'like a withered flower in a bouquet of orchids.'

He arched one eyebrow. 'Charmingly put. I hadn't thought you to be snobbish.'

'I'm not. I only said—'

'You said that the old girl is too long in the tooth and too plain to enjoy a few hours of sinful decadence?'

'I wouldn't want Tilda and Martha's feelings to get hurt, that's all. They're sweet.'

'That's nice of you, but I promise, if they care to visit, we'll take good care of the old girls. But I didn't come here to talk to you about the club.'

'No.' Her heart sank as he led her to his car.

Jack steered towards the park.

The setting sun sent out pink and orange ribbons that mirrored each other on the glassy surface of the lake. Most families had left for home by now, but a few courting couples and a group of boys playing ball seemed intent to stay.

Jack strolled to the water's edge and unrolled a rug he'd taken out of the car. He spread it out and motioned to Frances. She sat and pulled her legs up beside her.

'What did you find out?' His voice was soft. 'Don't worry, we're out of earshot. And if you could bring yourself to smile at me, no one will pay us any attention. People tend to respect lovers' privacy,' he said. Her pulse quickened. She shifted her gaze away.

She'd considered telling him about the incident in the café, but honestly, what was there to tell? That she began to see Croaky lurking everywhere? And anyway, she wasn't keen on confessing she'd been too scared to even look at the men before she fled.

'You don't have to blush.' He lifted her chin with his thumb. 'Well, did you manage to remember?'

She grasped his hand and held it away from her face.

'No. It's been too long ago, and I didn't really pay attention. You don't, after a while. You hear the number, plug in, and switch off.' His hand felt warm and solid in hers. 'The best I could come up with is that it's somewhere in the Whitmore Square area. And the operator on the other end works a switchboard somewhere in Melbourne. They get shifted around a bit.' She broke off. 'That's not a lot of help.'

'Melbourne,' he repeated. 'That fits. That and Sydney is where you find the real talent. Or at least used to. Not too many thugs I've heard of here who'd be willing to risk a Kathleen Mulvaney for a handful of diamonds.'

'A what?'

'It means going to jail for a long, long time.' He hugged his knees to his chest. 'Around Whitmore Square is where you find a couple of hotels and apartment blocks, if you're not too discerning. I own a couple properties around there.'

He pushed his hat back until it barely shaded his eyes. 'It wasn't a hotel, was it? There can't be too many private lines in that area. I'll tell Bluey to work his contacts. He still lives in one half of our house.'

Frances opened her mouth to protest.

Jack said, 'I'll tell him that it looks like some blokes who're bad news are muscling in. He understands. And don't worry about him. Bluey's smart and he's tough.'

'All right,' she said after a moment's consideration. She liked Bluey. 'I'd better go now. Mum will be waiting for me.'

'Fine. I'll take you home, kiddo, and then I've got to get back to the club.' He got up, pulling her off the ground as well. 'You haven't asked for a name. But maybe you've read the paper.'

She shook her head. She didn't have to rely on the

press. Theft and robbery had been on the increase all over Australia since the depression began, but murders were still something that happened elsewhere. Having one committed here, in one of the best suburbs of Adelaide, was a sensation. Every operator she'd talked to today had discussed it with ghoulish relish, until she was fit to scream.

Jack handed her a folded newspaper cut-out that she studied in the car on the way home.

The Advertiser had a photograph of the dead man, peering self-consciously into the camera. The picture had been taken when Michael Petty opened his new store in Rundle Street. His hairline was receding, the well-cut suit couldn't hide a slight spread around the waist, but there was nothing that distinguished him from any number of middle-aged business men. Certainly nothing in the picture hinted at his violent end.

Frances read the copy. Petty had been a tireless benefactor, it said, of causes close to his heart, from soup kitchens and orphanages run by the Catholic Church, to hefty donations for the opera. He was mourned by his wife, his staff – he owned two stores in the end – and everyone who'd been touched by his generosity and kind-heartedness.

She read this last bit out aloud. Jack chuckled. 'Nice obituary,' he said. 'I met the bloke a couple of times, and he was a strong supporter of the arts back then, especially when they appeared on stage with scanty clothing and not much more talent.'

'You've got half-naked dancers in the Top Note?' She spluttered. If her mum heard that she'd never let her go there again.

194

The clutch groaned as he changed gears. 'I've got to have Bluey take a geek at the car,' he said. 'No, not the Top Note, and you shouldn't know about those things anyway, or at least not admit it in public.'

The corners of his mouth curled up. 'With us, it's high class or nothing, which you should have noticed, kiddo. Petty used to frequent the Floating Palais. I don't know where he went when it closed. Not to us, although he did take a shine to Dolores a few years ago. But she wouldn't give him the time of day.'

He shook his head in slow motion. 'There was no harm in him, though. He was the kind of man who hopes that the gleam of his money counteracts his personal dullness.'

'Oops.' Frances said, struggling to picture the flamboyant Dolores with the man in the photograph.

'He married a waitress who combined tinsel prettiness with the hardness of diamonds.'

'You seem to have known her well.' Her voice came out scratchy.

'No, but it doesn't take long to recognise the type. I only went to the Floating Palais to take Dolores home. The owner had tried to lure her away from me while I was in New Zealand to see Rachel and arrange a few things.'

'Dolores wouldn't leave you, would she?' Inexplicably, Frances felt exasperated for his sake.

'She'd said she'd give it a try, see how his band worked out, and her show.' He snorted. 'She'd never have lasted longer than six months, with the kind of clientele he encouraged. They treated her like one of their fancy girls. But Bluey soon put them right.'

He pulled up in front of the house and walked around

the car to open the door for her. 'Say hello to everyone from me. I've got to go.'

'Sure. And thank you, Jack.'

'I'll call on you if I hear anything. Otherwise, you know where to find me.'

She nodded, faintly disappointed.

Jack said, 'Do you always cover the same shift?'

'This fortnight, yes.'

'And you've got the week-end off?'

'I'm working on Saturday, but I've got Sunday and Monday.' She wondered where this was leading to.

'Right. If I don't see you before then, I'll pick you up Saturday night. Dinner and the pictures, and if you're not tired, we'll watch Dolores' new show. If she's happy with the rehearsals, that is.'

'She's got a new show?'

'A couple of Bessie Smith songs and some Cole Porter. I remember you like to dance.' Without waiting for a reply, Jack touched her cheek lightly and climbed into the car.

Frances floated into the kitchen where Maggie gave her a peculiar look. 'You're home late.'

'Jack and I went for a walk.'

Maggie raised her eyebrows in silence.

'Is anything wrong?' Frances asked.

Maggie grabbed a spoon and stirred her soup so hard, the liquid splashed over her hand. 'Ouch.'

'Well?'

'People are talking.'

Frances groaned.

'I don't want you to get hurt. Or to gain a bad reputation.'

'I thought you liked Jack and Dolores.'

Maggie rinsed off her hand, turning her back to Frances. 'They're charming people, and I understand how attractive that can be to a young girl. But this won't last. You have to stick to your own kind.'

'Is that what Uncle Sal thinks, too?'

'He's an old man, love, and they make him feel young again. But it's different for you.'

'I'm not listening to this.' Frances ran out of the room, barreling into Uncle Sal.

'Steady there, sweetheart,' he said.

'Sorry. Did you hear us?'

'Does it matter?'

He clasped her elbow and led her gently back into the kitchen. Maggie sat slumped at the table, bright red spots on her cheeks.

Uncle Sal and Frances sat down with her. Frances took her hands.

'I'm sorry I got upset, but there is nothing to worry about.'

Maggie stared at their clasped hands.

'Sal?'

'Frances is right, Maggie. There's no harm in her having fun, and White Jack Sullivan knows too right that he'll have me to answer to if he gets any funny ideas, which he won't.'

'But the neighbours ...'

'Let them flap their tongues. Although after everything

Jack has done for them, they'd better keep their nasty little ideas to themselves.'

He patted Frances' and Maggie's hands. 'All good?'

Maggie gave him a forced smile. 'I'm sorry I've been foolish. Now, shall we eat? Then we can have a nice quiet evening, like we used to.'

Frances pulled a face. 'I told Pauline I'd see her for a bit.'

She could see that Maggie was hurt. 'Only for a short while, and then we'll listen to the wireless together.'

Pauline flew out of the door as soon as Frances arrived at the doorstep. She grabbed her by the elbow and led her down the street.

'You sly girl,' she said. 'I couldn't believe my eyes when you waltzed into the room.'

'Dolores invited me.'

'Into Mr Jack's apartment?'

Frances' cheeks grew hot. 'Can you say that a bit louder? There might be someone in Sturt Street who hasn't heard you. And where are we going?'

'Mum's home, and I wanted to be the first to hear everything.'

'There's nothing to hear.'

Pauline boxed Frances' arm.

'Honestly.'

'If you say so.' Pauline pouted, but turned around with Frances. They walked back to Pauline's place in a silence that grew heavier with each step.

The squalor of the parlour did nothing to lift up Frances' spirits, especially when an inner voice told her that she couldn't fool anyone, except herself. She could have screamed.

Ruth clattered in, bath towels in her hands, and greeted Frances with a kiss. 'Put these over your knees before you turn to ice.'

Frances hugged her with all her might.

'You are pleased to see me.' Ruth winked at her. 'And now I want to hear all about your goings on.'

'It's nothing. Dolores and Jack are just being nice to me, because of Uncle Sal and Phil.'

Ruth's face fell. Pauline shook her glossy head. 'You're not fooling anyone. Mr Jack has never had eyes for anyone else but Miss Bardon, and now it's you he's traipsing around with.'

'Traipsing around?' Ruth struggled to hide laughter.

'She was in his apartment.'

'It was the kitchen, and he made coffee for Dolores.'

'Has he kissed you yet? I bet it's divine when his lips meet yours in a moment of passion.' Pauline's eyes took on the faraway look she had copied from Nancy Pickford.

Frances threw off the towel as she got up.

'This isn't funny. If you both want to know the truth, he treats me like a puppy, or a much younger sister. And if you go on spreading rumours, Mum will get even more upset, and all the fun will be spoilt for all of us.'

'I'm sorry if I got it wrong.' Ruth motioned Pauline over. 'Pauline, you need to apologise too. Now.'

Pauline pouted.

'Pauline.'

'I'm sorry. It would've been so nice, my best friend and my boss. Useful, too. You wouldn't consider maybe kissing him once, so he would love to give me another pay-rise?'

Frances' mouth fell open.

'That's what gave us the wrong impression,' Ruth said. 'First thing there's you together one evening, and the next thing Pauline gets more money.'

'Because Dolores asked him to.'

Pauline shrugged. 'Maybe it's better this way. At least you won't start bossing me around then, if Mr Jack is not your beau.'

Frances picked up the towel and slapped Pauline with it, causing them all to break into a fit of the giggles.

CHAPTER EIGHTEEN

*J*ack waited for her on Thursday, outside the exchange.

Frances slowed down her steps. She didn't want him to get the impression she'd missed him, especially after all those hard times everybody'd given her.

And she hadn't, at least not that much, she told herself; what she had probably missed most these last days was the feeling of security he gave her, and the luxuries Jack surrounded her with. Although Phil was doing his best to make up for it. He'd bought a car of his own, a Ford Model T that had belonged to an old farmer.

The Ford had suffered a couple of knocks and bumps on unsealed roads, but Phil planned to straighten it out over the weekend, with Uncle Sal as enthusiastic assistant. The car itself had been given a thorough check by Bluey, and Frances had twice been transported in the cabin. Strange; Phil didn't seem to spend any time with Dolores at all, but she didn't ask. He had as much the right to privacy as she did.

'You're looking very nice,' Jack said, as she approached him. 'There's something different about you.' He let his gaze travel over her. 'You've changed your hair style.'

She touched her loose curls. 'It was Pauline's idea.'

'She's got talent.' Small crinkle lines fanned out from the corner of his eyes. 'I hoped to be here a bit earlier, but I had to sort out a few fishy bills. I reckon your boss has already left?'

'Mr Gibbons? He's still inside, locking up. Why?'

'I've got a few names for him.' Jack handed her a slip of paper. 'If he wants to talk about the peninsula, these are the men he needs.'

She dashed back inside, praying Mr Gibbons hadn't left through the post office exit. No, there he was, bent over the small safe hidden behind a wall panel.

'Mr Gibbons?' she said.

The steel cassette containing money, stamps, and money orders clattered to the floor. Mr Gibbons swung around, pressing his body against the wall. He wiped his brow when he saw Frances.

'I'm sorry if I've startled you, sir,' she said, holding out the slip of paper. 'This is for you. Jack Sullivan says these men might be useful.'

Mr Gibbons picked up the cassette. 'I'm not usually that easy to scare, my dear,' he said, 'but crime's getting worse and worse each day.'

An icy lump formed in her stomach. 'I understand. Goodnight, Mr Gibbons.'

She slipped away, leaving him staring at the paper.

～

'That was kind of you,' she said.

Jack shrugged. 'You've seen with Dolores, the worst is the not knowing. The mind can deal with facts, however painful, but if all you're left with is your imagination, it breaks you.' He ushered her into the car. 'How's Phil, by the way? We haven't seen hide nor hair from him the whole week.'

'Busy, I reckon.' She opened her handbag, pretending to search for something. Phil had been busy, granted, but he'd also spent most of his evenings sitting in the parlour with them after he'd finished tinkering with the car once it got dark. On second thought, wasn't there something forced about his cheerfulness? She hadn't really paid attention. It was hard enough to hide her own growing worries from her family. She even resorted to taking different routes to the tram in the morning to feel safer.

'Your uncle Sal sent Dolores flowers, by the way. And you don't have to be embarrassed because Phil had other things to do than to hang around a girl. Either he'll be back or he won't. If not, he's not a great loss.'

He whistled a few soft notes. 'Stardust'; Dolores had sung that song, that first night at the club.

The whistling broke off. 'What's wrong with your friend Pauline, by the way? She burst into tears twice yesterday, because she forgot to put sugar into Dolores' tea.'

She hesitated. 'She's a bit upset, that's all.'

'About what? That I can't offer her an apartmentt? I'd have done it, but we had to put up Len's wife and the baby somewhere. You can't have an infant in a homeless shelter.'

'Len's wife?' Her sympathy was awakened.

'The bastard blamed the whole shebang on her when

he staggered home, stinking of snake-poison and raring to take his misery out on someone. He'd have knocked her around if Bluey hadn't had the foresight to send one of the boys along in case it got ugly.'

Oh no. 'Where's Len now?'

'He won't come within a mile of her without invitation if he values his skin.' He gave a snort of disgust. 'I should have known. Artful Dodger, we called him in France, though there was nothing artful about his dodging out of any sticky situation. If it hadn't been for his late brother-in-law's sake, he'd never made it past the back door of the Top Note. So, if it's about the apartment, it's too bad for Pauline, but there are lots of folks out there who had a thinner time than she.'

'It's Tony,' she said, after a short discussion with herself. She shouldn't have given in to Pauline's badgering, but how could she say no to her best friend? Even if that friend might think too much of Frances' influence. 'She told me yesterday. He sent her a letter.'

'He dumped her? Poor kid. That's not what you want to find out through the post.'

'He hasn't dumped her. He'd never do that, at least not in this shabby way.'

'What is it then? Is he ill?'

'No,' Frances said, 'but he's not coming home yet. He's saved a couple of quid, and now he's had another job offer, laying bricks in Fremantle.'

'But instead of this news being the good oil it smells rancid to her?'

'Pauline's afraid he likes being on the road so much he won't be able to settle down again. It happens. Her dad doesn't write anymore, and her mum thinks he's gone bush.'

'How long has he been carrying his swag?'

'Tony? Since October, but Mr Meara left almost two years ago, since they laid him off at the brick works. Tony worked there too, after he lost his job as a technical draughtsman, but they dismissed the older men first.'

'That's bad.' Jack sounded genuinely sorry.

'I told Pauline not to worry, but she misses Tony so much.'

'She's been hiding that pretty well from what I've seen at the club.'

That remark stung. 'She wouldn't look twice at any other man if Tony were around.'

'Maybe,' Jack said. 'All I can say is, the poor bloke's tramping all over the country to make a few honest shillings, and if his girl is losing faith in him, she'd better cut loose or else have it out with him. It's not fair to string him along.'

Something in his voice made her drop the subject.

Phil and Uncle Sal were working outside as they arrived. A pile of picket railings leant against the house wall. Uncle Sal steadied a post while Phil forced the nails out with a crowbar.

'Nice work,' said Jack.

Phil paused, righted himself and rolled his shoulders back and forth. 'Yeah. Maggie is letting me put up a shelter in the back for my Ford.' He wiped the sweat off his forehead. 'This fence was made to last until kingdom come. It's a pity to take it down but there's no other way to get the old bus up the back.'

'What brings you here, Jack?' Uncle Sal still held on to the post, his feet planted in a wide stance to keep his balance.

'I wanted a quick word with Phil.' The men exchanged an inscrutable glance.

'Let's sit on the back porch,' Phil said. 'I could do with a breather.' Jack followed him, hands in his pockets, motioning Frances to follow.

She gave Uncle Sal a questioning look.

'You go, and I'll bring glasses and a water jug,' he said. 'If they want to be private, they'll tell you.'

Phil squatted on the steps that led from the porch to the garden, facing Jack. Jack perched on the edge of the table. Phil's face brightened as he saw Frances. 'We've saved the chairs for you and Sal. Where is he?'

'He won't be long.'

Phil gave Jack a questioning glance.

'There's nothing I want to say that Frances can't hear,' Jack said. 'I was wondering how you've settled in, that's all.'

'I'm sweet,' Phil said.

'Working which beat?' The tension was almost palpable. Frances shot tiny glances from one man to the other.

After an agonising moment, Phil answered. 'The big stuff.'

'Right-oh.' Jack studied his fingernails. They were square cut and blunt, with a few blue paint speckles marking them. Strange. 'Ever heard of Whitey Morgan?'

A quick gleam came into Phil's eyes. 'I might have.'

'That's what I thought. In case you want to meet up, he's rumoured to have taken a fancy to fresh air lately, hanging around the aerodrome in the Barossa Valley on certain mornings. Like Wednesdays and Fridays.'

Frances caught her breath. Jack gave Phil a nod and said, 'I've got to go. Shall I give your regards to Dolores or do you want me to keep my mouth shut about seeing you?'

Phil cleared his throat. 'Tell her I'll be around as soon as I can. If she still wants me to.'

Something had changed. The air between the men felt less charged. 'I'll go and help Mum,' Frances said, relieved. 'Goodbye, Jack.'

'Bye, kiddo. Well, Phil, did we come up as clean?'

Frances stopped in the doorway and turned around to face the men. What were they talking about?

'Clean enough to hide in a cloud of snow, and with a halo of gold,' Phil said. 'You'd have done the same.'

'You bet,' Jack said, 'but I wouldn't have done any courting before checking. You'd better make up for it to Dolores.'

He clutched Phil's outstretched hand and squeezed it until his knuckles went white, a friendly smile frozen on to his face.

Frances went inside.

The next day she used her lunch break to study the phone register. If only she could remember that number. Her finger traced the row of entries. How could it have grown that long so quickly? There couldn't be that many rich people in Adelaide, the way things had gone from bad to worse in a tail-shake.

Frances tapped her toes on the floor. It must be nice to have your own phone. Dolores had one, on her own private line, Jack had one, and then there was the line for the Top Note. She'd written down the numbers in her small notebook. Usually she jotted down shopping lists in there, and prices of things she'd bought, to keep track of expenses.

She'd learned that the hard way last year, when she gave in to impulse and bought the gramophone for the parlour, to find that her mum had dipped into their savings to lend two quid to a neighbour who'd lost his job. That month she'd had to ask for an extension to pay the electricity bill.

She sighed. She pushed the notebook aside and concentrated on the register again.

When the lights began to blink, she was almost grateful. At least the work would distract her. She swallowed the last bit of the sandwich she'd nibbled on while studying the register and switched on her headset.

CHAPTER NINETEEN

*H*er shift was over. Frances sat down in the staff room to change her shoes. She'd taken her ankle straps along in a brown bag. The brogues she wore were sturdy enough for walking to work and back home, but who could tell if Jack was waiting again with his car? Or Phil, for that matter.

She lifted her left foot, admiring the silvery sheen of the ankle-straps. They made her look much more grown-up. The brogues resembled school uniform shoes.

She strolled over to the back door and peered through its glass panel. One lonely car, but this one was occupied by an elderly man. That didn't have to mean anything. Phil, for example, preferred to park on the other side of the building, right in front of the public entrance. Maybe she should have a quick peek around the corner. If she wanted to, she could always change back into her walking shoes.

Frances almost slipped on the envelope as she stepped forward to crane her neck to survey the cars sitting at the kerb. She bent to pick it up. The flap gaped open, and the edge of a small cardboard book stuck out. The envelope was unsullied. It must have been dropped a short time ago.

She turned it in her hands. There was no address, nothing to indicate who it belonged to. She took out the book, hoping for more information.

'Oh no.' Inside the book, a signed piece of paper had been tucked away, with what looked like a grocery list. Frances groaned. Some woman had lost her precious food dole book, with the food chit for one adult and three children. Almost fourteen bob's worth of food, and the owner wouldn't be able to claim it. Worst of all, she'd need that book to get it signed again, tomorrow at ten o'clock, or she'd have to go without for a whole week.

Frances surveyed the road again, hoping to see the woman returning, but she was all alone.

Her stomach tensed. Where was Jack when she needed him? And this was urgent. As much as the thought of venturing out alone still scared her, she really had no choice. That book and the paper needed to be returned, at once. She stuffed them into her handbag, took out her brogues and put them on the ground. Hopping on her left foot, she undid the strap of her good shoe, took it off, holding it in one hand and slipped into a brogue, before she repeated the process, all the while clutching her shoulder bag to her chest.

Frances set off at a clipping pace. At least the name Alice Kaye and address were inscribed in the book, so all she had to do was to find out where she needed to go. She'd have to take the tram and ask the driver where to get off, because she wasn't familiar with the area.

She broke her stride. Maybe she should also ask the

trammie what sort of area it was. There were a few places in Adelaide where a girl in her right mind shouldn't go. But what choice did she have? She needed to return the book and the chit straight away, or the woman and her children would go hungry. She pushed ahead, glad she had a couple of hours of daylight left, and that there were people milling around. Surely nothing bad could happen to her in a crowd.

The trammie told her to get off halfway along O'Connell Street and look out for a boarded-up house on the left. There she'd have to turn left, walk a couple hundred yards, and turn into an alleyway.

He sounded cheerful giving these instructions. Frances spirits rose. Anything that didn't involve Hindley Street or Sturt Street with its ladies of the evening should be safe for a girl on her own, and she was far enough from the phone exchange that no one would know her here, especially with her cloche pulled deep over her face. She hopped off the tram and walked on.

She found the address without much trouble. The Kaye's house itself was shabby, with paint peeling off the weatherboard, but the straggly lawn was cut and the cracked window pane shone. Someone took care of their home. Frances rang the doorbell, but the only answer was silence.

The woman had probably walked home, saving the thruppence tram fare. More, if she had her children with her. Heaven knew then when she might turn up.

'Can I help you, Miss?' A care-worn woman struggled with a pram. A toddler sat in front, giving Frances a grin that revealed all his five teeth. Sucking noises behind him told her that there was another child in the pram.

'Are you Mrs Kaye?'

'No, love.' The woman rocked the pram, beaming at her baby. 'But if it's her jam you're after, I got some of me own left.' She leant over the pram, hefting a box that she'd kept wedged in between the children. 'I got marmalade and strawberry. Goes down a real treat, it does.'

She practically thrust a jar into Frances' hands. 'Home-made, after me gran's recipe, and you won't find any better.' A crooked smile revealed gappy teeth, although she couldn't be much over thirty. 'For you it's fourpence, love.'

Frances hadn't the heart to say no. She handed over the money.

'Now love, is there anything else you were wanting?' The woman rocked the pram harder as the baby began to wail. 'Only I got this lot here to feed their tea.' She ruffled the toddler's hair. He stuck his thumb into his mouth and sucked as if to prove his mother's point.

'I need to return something Mrs Kaye has lost.'

'Somethin' important?' The baby fell quiet.

'Her food dole book.'

'Blimey! I reckon you better not hand that to anyone, love. There's folks as'd love to get one and claim what isn't theirs.' The woman shook her head, clucking her tongue. 'Not that I'd blame them, when your kids are all hollow inside and bawling for food.'

'But Mrs Kaye isn't home,' Frances said, 'and I can't wait too much longer.'

'Slide it under her door. I'll pop around later and tell Alice you were here in case she don't bother to look down. It won't be nicked. Alice and the littlees are on their own now her old man's taken off. You know what blokes are like when it gets bad.' She gave her the kind of conspiratorial look that implied a bond between them.

Frances found herself nodding. She slipped the resealed envelope under the door.

The woman grunted as she swung the pram around. 'You want more jam, you ask for Hattie. You'll find me the next street down towards Whitmore Square. You can't miss it, with the bits of scrap metal in front.' She smiled again. 'Mustn't grumble, eh? Them older kids are that good, collecting tins and stuff to sell, or it'd be burning Collingwood Coke instead of good wood for us.'

'Whitmore Square? There's a tram stop, isn't there?' Frances asked on impulse. Jack and Dolores used to live there, didn't they? And the phone call had been made to somewhere around there. Curiosity struggled with fear. If it was far, she wouldn't go there. If, on the other hand, it was close by, it couldn't hurt looking, if simply to prove to herself she wasn't such a bad coward after all.

'Aye, love, and it won't be longer than traipsing back the other way. You walk straight down here, and then it's right and right again, and you'll be there in a twinkle.'

Frances rearranged the contents of her bags before she set off. She'd rather not put the jam in with her shoes and risk breaking the jar, messing everything up.

With a sense of triumph, she located a string bag that her mum had purchased from an old lady, hawking doilies, potholders, and these bags from door to door. She'd put it inside her bag, to please her mother, although she got exasperated with Maggie's generous use of her hard-earned pennies when it came to the flood of people who sold everything from wire-pegs to patented candle-holders that fell apart if you breathed on them. That much she knew from experience. They had three at home.

The jam jar went into the string bag.

She almost stumbled over a pair of legs. A scrawny man sat on the ground, a saxophone cradled in his arms. He didn't look up as he lifted it and began to play. A beggar's bowl sat next to him, an itinerant musician's license pinned to it. The notice had faded in the harsh sunlight. It dated from Christmas and was issued in Sydney. Its validity had long expired.

She fumbled in her purse. The jam jar hit her hip. She put the jar into the bowl, laying a penny on top.

The music followed her as she hurried down the sidewalk, sweet and melancholy, echoing her mood. The houses were bigger now than the ones she had passed a few minutes ago, but there, women had sat on their porch, brushing carrots or peeling potatoes, and children ran around, squealing. This area was almost deserted.

She clutched her bag tighter, almost wishing she'd resisted the impulse to walk to Whitmore Square. It was stupid to have come here, on the odd chance of finding out more about Jack's and Dolores' past. She tried to picture their house in her mind. The singer would have chosen a modern building, all sharp angles and metal framed windows, Frances thought, considering Dolores' taste for fashionable opulence. But she couldn't picture Jack in a flashy house.

There was something restrained about him. His clothes were well-made and clearly expensive but also unobtrusive, his shoes shone with polish instead of having that brand-new sheen, and the bits of furniture she'd seen were comfortable rather than impressive; pieces you'd inherit rather than find on Rundle Street.

If she was honest with herself, she had also, for a wild moment, harboured the idea that one of the buildings would trigger something, so she could impress Jack after all. She'd copied the addresses of all the houses with private phone lines on Whitmore Square into her notebook. They alone filled a page, and she hadn't even started on the adjoining streets.

The absence of human noise began to prey on her nerves. It shouldn't be this quiet, she thought, not in this fashion. It was as if a blanket pressed down on her, blocking every sound. The loudest noise she could hear was the shuffle of her soles and her irregular breathing.

Frances paused. To the left and right of her the houses were boarded up, crude planks nailed upon every opening in a slapdash fashion. She began to whistle under her breath, to give herself courage, as she marched towards the nearest tram stop, her gaze straight ahead.

She only heard the soft steps behind as the other

person drew almost level with her. She walked faster. The steps became faster too.

'Hello my pretty.' A rasping male voice, mocking and menacing.

Without looking back, Frances ran.

Laughter filled the air.

Frances tried to fight her rising fear. If only she could get to the tram stop. She glanced around her. There must be other people, surely. Her breath got ragged as she stumbled on. The blood pounded too loud in her ears to hear if the man still followed her.

Something touched her arm. Frances swung her bags wildly. Fear blurred her vision.

'Miss Frances?' a familiar voice said, comforting in its very ordinariness.

'Bluey!' Her knees gave in. She dropped the bags and collapsed into his arms.

'It's all right,' he said, steadying her. He peered over her shoulder. 'You're safe now, Miss. No one will bother you, not with me around.'

His open face took on an air of watchfulness. 'Mind, what are you doing here, Miss? This is not the sort of place you should be on your own.'

He picked up her bags with one hand. 'You look all in. What you need is a bit of a sit-down. Come along, and the wife will make you a good strong cuppa, and then I'll take you wherever you want to go.'

He held her by the elbow, to propel her forwards. A hazy thought pierced its way through the fog in her mind. 'Bluey?'

'Yes?'

216

'I don't know your name. The real one. I can't very well call your wife Mrs Bluey, can I?' This was bizarre, she thought, as soon as the words had escaped her mouth. She must still be rattled.

Bluey gave her a little smile. The creases on his forehead smoothed. 'It's Barney Fitzpatrick, Miss, but my old mum's the only one who calls me that.' He touched his carroty hair. 'With my thatch, I've been nicknamed Bluey since I was in short trousers.' He slowed down. 'It's not much further now. The bad bits stretch until the next street, around the corner we go, and then it's as nice a neighbourhood as you could wish.'

He was right. Turning the corner took them into another world, one with well-tended flower beds and bits of lawn to the front of the buildings that clustered around the square. Frances breathed easier.

Bluey took her to a semi-detached, two-storey Victorian house, built of bluestone, with brick mouldings around the door and window frames. He let go off her elbow to take a key out of his pocket.

The yeasty smell of fresh bread enveloped them as Bluey opened the front door.

'Daddy!' A boy of maybe three flung himself at Bluey who caught him in his outstretched arms and threw him up in the air, catching him with ease. The boy squealed with delight.

'That's enough, Bobby.' The stern voice from the kitchen made Bobby giggle. Bluey's lips curled into a wide grin as he put down his son. He gave him a pat on the bottom. 'Run to your Mum and tell her we've got company.'

217

Bobby's mouth formed a circle as he noticed Frances. He stepped back until he was half hidden by his dad.

'Hello, Bobby,' she said.

The boy stuck his head out, turtle-fashion, and stared at her.

'Now, what's going on there?' A young woman came out of what must be the kitchen at the back. She pushed back a dark curl that fell into her eyes. Flour stuck to her arms and her cheeks. Bluey's grin got even wider. 'Hello, sweetheart. I brought some company. Marie, this is Miss Frances.'

His wife gave him a gentle nudge to get out of her way as he gave her a one-armed hug. She turned towards Frances and gave her an appraising glance before smiling at her disarmingly. 'You'll excuse my appearance, Miss. It's baking day, as you can see.'

Frances felt herself returning the smile. 'Call me Frances, please. I hope you don't think it's terribly rude to barge in like this.'

'I found her half a mile toward the Sturt Street end.' Bluey said. 'Some joker'd frightened her badly and I thought a nice cup of tea might set her to rights, Marie.'

'You poor thing,' Marie said, marching them all into the airy, gleaming kitchen. 'Things are getting so bad I don't fancy going that direction myself any longer.'

She rinsed off her hands and arms under the warm water tap, wiping them dry on her pinny.

'Don't stand there like a big lump,' she said to Bluey. 'Put the kettle on, and then we'll all have a scone. They're just cooling. Bobby, you can help Daddy put them on a plate.' She pressed a hand into her back, stretching herself, before she pulled out two chairs for herself and for Frances.

Frances took in the scene with delight. Marie Fitzpatrick barely came up to her husband's chin, but the chain of command was clear. She was very pretty, very efficient, and very pregnant.

Marie wiggled around a bit. 'That's better. This one is getting pretty lively these days.' She patted her swollen belly. 'But enough about that. What in the name of all that's holy were you doing in that forsaken part of town?'

The hollow feeling in Frances' stomach returned. 'A lady dropped her food dole book. She doesn't live too far from here, so I took it to her house. I was trying to find the tram stop at the Square.' Her hands began to shake. 'It was all right at first, but then everything was deserted and felt all wrong, and then a man began to whisper to me. He was breathing down my back, and I was so scared I ran.'

Marie patted Frances' hand. 'No wonder you were frightened. Lucky you ran into my Bluey. There are some nasty people out there.' Bobby toddled over to her and leant against her knees. She pressed him to her.

Frances swallowed. 'It was stupid, but that voice behind me really put the wind up me.'

'No. I'd have run myself. It used to be quite a nice neighbourhood down there, but with so many factories closed down, the steady folks had to leave, and those who are left ...' She left the sentence unfinished, with a meaningful glance at her son.

Bluey put cups full of steaming tea in front of them. A plateful of scones followed. They were warm to the touch, strawberry jam melting into them.

Marie broke off a piece, blew on it, and popped it into Bobby's wide-open mouth.

'When Daddy's had his cuppa you can go and play trains with him while I have a chat with the lady.' She cocked her head to one side, like a watchful bird. 'That is, if you don't mind sitting with me for a bit, Frances. It's nice to have someone new for company.' She bit into a scone, catching the oozing jam with the tip of her tongue.

Frances cradled her cup of tea. She glanced out of the window. Nearly dark; she needed to get home before Maggie sent out a search party.

'Ten minutes,' Marie said, sending Bluey off with a nod. 'You must think me very nosey, but you see, I've heard a fair bit about you.' She touched her belly again. 'And I do miss the Top Note. Much as I love my family, it can be a fair cow sitting here, moping while all the fun's there.'

'You've heard about me?' Frances' curiosity was piqued.

'I sure did.' Deep dimples appeared in Marie's face. 'And about Salvatore the Magnificent. My, I'd love to meet him. Dad didn't like it a bit, but Mum took me along to the music hall when I was a young girl, and we went every day for a week because she wanted to see him. He really was something.' She shook her head, as if she was lost in admiration. 'I nearly fainted when he threw his knives at the girl, and his juggling act ... It made me feel fourteen again, to hear Bluey and Mr Jack talk about him. I wish I'd been there.'

'I'll tell him,' Frances said. 'Better still, why don't you and Bluey come and visit us? Uncle Sal'd love to meet you too, I'm sure.'

Marie pulled a face. 'I don't think I'll be going anywhere soon.' She sucked in her breath.

Frances tensed. Marie couldn't have her baby now, could she?

Her panic must have been clear to see, because Marie said, 'Don't look so scared,' as she relaxed again. 'I've got a fortnight to go. If not, well, I used to be a nurse during the war, and the club's only a phone call away. So's the hospital. But let's talk about nicer things.'

'Do you mind a brief stop at the Top Note?' Bluey sounded apologetic as they set off in the Ford. 'I'm supposed to report back to Mr Jack.'

'I could take the tram. I've caused you enough trouble already,' Frances said, trying to ignore the lingering unease.

Bluey shook his head. 'Mr Jack will have my hide if I let you run around on your own in the dark, and if he doesn't, my Marie will.' A tender tone crept into his voice.

'She's lovely,' Frances said. 'And so's Bobby.'

Bluey beamed. 'I knew she was the one for me as soon as she told me in the veteran's hospital to stop being a waste of space and straighten myself out. Pretty as a picture, she was, and brave enough to have tackled Jerry single-handedly.' He chuckled. 'One cove got some silly ideas, and don't you know, she beaned him with a chamber pot and then she spent half the day nursing his swollen head.'

Frances laughed. She could picture that easily. 'How long have you been married?'

'Going on eleven years. The new baby will be number three. Sophie, our oldest, is spending the holidays with her nana and poppa up in Tassie, to give Marie a bit of a breather.'

He rubbed his neck with the left hand, the right gripping the steering wheel.

'Should you be working nights? It must be hard on Marie and the kids.'

Bluey shook his head. 'They're used to it. I usually have a kip when Bobby's having his nap and Sophie's at school. Weeknights, Mr Jack sends me home around midnight, now I don't have to drive Miss Dolores home to Wellington Square anymore.'

'Wellington Square? Didn't she and Jack use to live in your house?'

Bluey braked hard as a shadow streaked out of a doorway. 'Blimmin' dog,' he muttered. 'No, they lived in the other half next door. Mr Jack bought the place when we settled in Adelaide, and had the other one converted into apartments. Then he got hold of a place in North Adelaide, right before Bobby came along, but it got a bit much for Miss Dolores to be shuttled back and forth in the dead of the night, so he had the apartments over the club kitted out to suit them.'

Bluey chuckled. 'You should've seen the state they were in. They hadn't been cleaned since Queen Victoria was on the throne, I can tell you. But it's easier for everyone now, and now the whole staff can keep an eye out for anyone shifty trying his luck with Miss Dolores.' Bluey rubbed his cheek. 'And it's not as if Mr Jack needed a family home, after all.'

Their arrival at the Top Note prevented him from further revelations. Frances swallowed her frustration.

Bluey leant over to her. 'Are you sure you want to wait in the car?'

'Yes,' she said.

'No,' someone else said in the same instant. 'It's not the done thing for a young lady to be seen in front of a night club, waiting for someone. Come inside for a few minutes, kiddo.'

CHAPTER TWENTY

*J*ack took Frances straight up to his apartment.
Soft music filtered through from Dolores'
side. Frances strained her ears. She caught a
few words in a foreign language.

'Verdi,' Jack said. 'Dame Nelly Melba singing arias from
La Traviata.'

She found herself in a large drawing room. Mahogany
bookcases covered two of the walls floor to ceiling. Leather-
bound volumes jostled each other on half of the shelves.
The others displayed various bits of colourful pottery, glass
vases and bottles glowing like jewels, and silver ornaments.

They all had two things in common, Frances noticed.
They were beautiful and old.

Jack sat down on a leather armchair. Its colour echoed
the melted toffee of the rich wood the occasional tables
were made of.

Bluey settled on the desk chair, facing Jack.

Frances looked around. A painting caught her eye. It
reminded her of the one in the hallway she'd admired

before. This one showed a scene at the beach by sundown, with a lone sunbather packing up for the day. The raven-haired girl was shown from afar, and she had her back turned to the viewer. Two seagulls feasted on the remains of a fish, while the surf foamed white on a turbulent sea. Frances drank in the details.

There was nothing extraordinary about the picture, but that was partly its appeal, she decided. That and the vibrancy of the rich hues of pink and blue and gold the artist had chosen, and its simplicity. She moved closer. Again, she couldn't find a signature, but whoever the artist was, he had talent. She could almost hear the screech of the seagulls.

A shrill ring brought Frances back to earth.

'Yes,' she heard Jack answer the telephone. 'Is that you, Marie? Sure, I'll send him on his way.'

'The baby?' Anxiety, mixed with excitement, was written large on Bluey's face.

Jack grinned. 'Off you go, and don't forget to pick up the doctor. Marie's already phoned him.' He gave Bluey a smack on the back. 'Don't you dare show your mug here until Marie's getting fed up with you getting under her feet.'

Bluey was out of the door without so much as a by-your-leave.

'Good luck,' Frances called after him.

Jack laughed. 'Marie'll be fine. It's him we'll need the doctor for. He's apt to go to pieces where she is involved. But enough of that. What did you do around Whitmore Square? Playing detective?'

Her cheeks began to burn. 'I only wanted to have a

quick squiz.' She thrust her notebook towards Jack. 'I've written down the numbers of private lines and the address.'

'And did any of them ring a bell? Or did you expect to find a hand-written sign in a window, advertising rooms with a phone for travelling crims?'

She stared at her shoes.

Jack lifted her chin with his fingertips, looking at her with something like brotherly concern. 'Frances, you're a good girl, but please, keep away from places like Sturt Street. Or take someone else along, if you run off on an errand of mercy. The next time Bluey might not be around.'

'How could I tell anyone? And how was I to know there's something wrong with the neighbourhood, if you used to live there yourself.'

'Point taken. Would you like something to drink?'

She shook her head. 'I need to get home, or Mum and Uncle Sal will be all over the place. I should've been back ages ago.'

'You should,' Jack said. 'Lucky for you that Bluey phoned me after he'd picked you up, so I could tell them.'

'You did? How?'

Jack pointed at the wall-telephone.

'But we don't have a phone,' Frances said.

'You do, now.'

'That's impossible. We can't afford it.'

'You can't afford not to. Don't raise your hackles.' He put a finger on her lips. She caught her breath. 'How do you think Phil is going to be able to keep in touch with his superiors? Crooks don't keep to normal work hours. He needs lodgings where he can be called out. The expense won't fall on you, if that's what you're afraid of.'

He handed back her notebook. 'You'll find a pen on the desk, next to an address book with your phone number. You'll want to write it down.' Jack's lips curled up fleetingly. 'I'll get some coffee. Are you sure you don't want anything? Water, maybe, or lemonade?'

'Coffee would be nice.' She flicked through Jack's address book. He'd listed two Andersons, but no Phil.

'It's under P,' Jack said, as he put a filled cup next to her on the blotter. 'P for Palmer

They drank in companionable silence. Frances screwed the top back on to Jack's pen when she remembered something.

'Did Bluey mention Michael Petty's name?'

Jack perched on the edge of the desk. She could feel his breath on her hair.

'I told you he'd work his contacts.' He looked at her, unblinkingly. 'I thought that's what you wanted. I haven't mentioned your name, if that's what you're concerned about.'

She broke the eye contact and nodded.

'He wouldn't blab, kiddo. Don't make the mistake of underestimating Bluey. There's a lot more going on in his head than most people credit him for. They see a burly, blank-faced cove who's driving Dolores around or tinkering with cars.' He chuckled. 'Don't tell me you didn't fall for it.'

'He's very much a family man, isn't he?'

'The most married man I've ever seen. But now, back to business. Bluey's done what we should have done first, which is ask ourselves a few questions and take it from there.'

By now she should have gotten used to that sense of

confusion that settled on her thick like dust on a windowsill. 'Like what?' she asked.

'Like, who gains? The police think it's tied to those other stick-ups that have been reported in the papers over the last year, but we know they were used as a cover, right? This was premeditated murder.' Jack slid off the desk, pulled open a drawer and unscrewed the pen.

'The widow goes on top of the list.' His handwriting was neat, with the letters leaning a fraction to the right. Frances peered over his shoulder. 'She stands to inherit, she's been said to have been well acquainted, once upon a time, with a man who used to work as muscle for high-ranking gangsters in Melbourne, and it's reasonable that she knew her hubby'd be carrying those baubles.'

'You believe she's behind it?' Frances' heart beat drummed in her ears.

'Not that fast, Frances.' He scribbled down more names. 'Second, we have the business partner, recently acquired to help set up shops in Perth. He's invested heavily in gold and silver mines and might find himself a wee bit cash strapped. It could also be that, as a partner, he's in for a nice share of the stock.'

'Have you heard of him before?' She leant closer to Jack.

'With every successful man, you'll hear rumours about dodgy deals, unless the money is old enough to have lost that kind of whiff and acquires respectability by dint of its antiquity.' He pushed back a strand of hair that had fallen on to his forehead. Frances was glad he didn't go in for the oily pomade most men used on their hair. Jack went on. 'Third, the employees. They could have helped themselves to some of the stuff in the shop and needed to cover up the theft. Petty was sure to have noticed if his jewellery went walkabout.'

He sounded like someone out of a talkie, which suited Frances. It blurred the ugly reality. 'Let me have a look.' She angled for the list.

Jack brought his hand down on hers. 'We haven't finished yet.'

'But there are no more names.'

'Because we don't have them yet, Frances. Think about it. Who is the mysterious client who arranged to see Petty's most precious jewels? From what Bluey and I've heard, he or she hasn't come forward yet.' He arched his eyebrow and gave her a meaningful glance.

Her lips twitched.

'What's so funny?'

'You are. I mean, not you personally, but right now all you need is a moustache, a monocle and a haughty stare to be William Powell as Philo Vance.'

'I shouldn't have taken you to see *The Benson Murder Case*. It's given you strange ideas.'

She ignored this remark, instead snatching the list. 'What shall we do now?'

'We'll pose as customers. You could ring up the shop, and arrange an appointment for us to look at their finest selection.'

'And then?' Frances pursed her lips. 'Will you twirl your moustache and announce to the world the game's up?'

'What is it with you and your moustache?'

'It's not mine. I don't have one.' She giggled. A belated reaction to the earlier fright, she decided. She needed to calm down, or Jack would think her demented, or worse, childish.

He shook his head at her and smiled. 'The point is to get them to talk. Even if you don't recognise a voice, we might get an idea about their true feelings.'

'That might work,' she agreed, sobering up. 'But who are you buying expensive things for? I don't want to have any more talk.'

'Don't worry. It's going to be a surprise present for Dolores, and you are tagging along to help me pick something. It's not going to harm her reputation, and it is common knowledge that she adores jewels. You've seen her diamonds.'

'They're real?' Her eyes widened. 'But she's wearing them everywhere, day and night. She probably even wears them to bed.'

His lips twitched. 'I wouldn't know that bit, but they're real enough. Why do you think I've got a man watching over her from a respectful distance wherever she goes? And yes, I've tried to convince her it's risky to flaunt riches like that, but those diamonds make her happy.' He gave her a quick glance. 'Maybe Phil can get her to see sense. If he's coming back to visit her at all.'

He pulled her up. 'I hope your mum will have some supper left for you. It's been a tiring day for you. Or shall we see what Ginny's got to offer?'

She stifled a yawn.

'Another time, then,' he said, deciding for her.

For once, Jack drove her home without a detour. She struggled to keep her eyes open. How strange to think his working day had barely begun. Their worlds couldn't be more different, she thought with a stab of regret.

The streetlights cast searching fingers over his face. The houses lay dark, huddling closer in the glare of the headlights. A few solitary lamps shone.

They were home at last.

Jack pressed a piece of paper into Frances' hand. 'My private number, and Bluey's and the Top Note. Call me when you've set up an appointment with Petty's.'

'Don't you want to come in for a moment?' She tried to hide her disappointment.

'I've got to change the roster to replace Bluey.' He stroked her cheek with two fingers. 'And I'll need to be home when he calls with good news. Marie doesn't shilly-shally when it comes to having her babies.'

Frances sneaked inside and felt for the light switch on the wall. She intended to creep quietly upstairs, but unfortunately things had changed since she went to work that very morning. Three steps away from the flight of stairs, her head bumped against a heavy object, dislodging something that struck her on the shoulder.

She yelped. Her probing fingers found the object that had collided with her shoulder. A telephone receiver. She managed to put it back into its cradle without switching on the light.

She paused to listen. Everything was quiet. It must be

much later that she'd thought. Rubbing her still smarting head, she clambered up the stairs and went to sleep with teeth unbrushed, wishing for once the bathroom weren't located next to the bedrooms, with the pipes gurgling like a waterfall.

～

The alarm sprang to life hours too early for her liking. The same went for her family. A cheerful voice rang out loud enough to disturb sleepers on the other side of town.

Frances snatched her dressing gown from its hook and wrapped herself in it as tightly as she could as she dragged herself to the bathroom.

'Right-ho,' she heard Phil shout. 'Sweet. The chemmy parlor, eh? Illicit gambling?'

She opened the cold water tap, splashing herself with a vengeance.

～

Phil made a dash for the door as she came downstairs.

'Bye, Frances,' he called out, slapping his hat on at a rakish angle. 'See you tonight.'

She slumped at the kitchen table. Maggie hummed to herself as she toasted bread for Uncle Sal.

'Morning, my darling,' Maggie said. 'Sorry I didn't wait up for you.'

'I didn't intend to stay out that late.' Frances shifted on her seat. She slid a piece of toast from Uncle Sal's plate onto hers. He looked as peaky as she felt, the poor darling.

She reached for the butter knife when she remembered something. 'Do you know, Uncle Sal, that I met Bluey's wife, Marie? She is so nice, and she remembers you being on stage. Her mother was smitten with you, from what Marie says.'

'Don't be silly,' Uncle Sal said, but his shoulders straightened and his eyes lit up.

'It's true. I said you'd love to meet her.'

'What an interesting day you must have had.' Maggie cracked two eggs into a bowl, added a splash of milk and whisked the mixture.

'And what about you? Getting a telephone without bothering to tell me, you sly creatures.'

'We only found out when the workmen knocked on the door, didn't we? When Phil ordered the phone to be put in he was told it might take up to a fortnight.' Maggie poured the egg mixture into a sizzling pan.

Uncle Sal winked at Frances. 'Someone must have pulled a few strings to move us up on the list.'

'Probably the police chief,' Frances said. 'Although, judging by the noise Phil made on the phone, he could simply stick his head out of the window and yell.'

Uncle Sal chuckled. 'If the other bloke wasn't deaf before, he'll be deaf now.'

Maggie stirred the scrambled egg. 'That's unfair,' she said. 'When Jack rang yesterday to say that you'd be delayed, he had to repeat his words twice, to make himself heard. You of all people should know how noisy the lines can be.' She set three plates out and divided the egg equally.

Frances had just taken the first forkful when Uncle Sal

233

asked, 'What did you do anyway? We couldn't quite make out where you were.'

The scrambled egg went down the wrong way. She coughed and sputtered. Maggie patted her back. Uncle Sal handed her a glass of water.

She took a big gulp. 'I found a food dole book for a woman with three kids.' She cleared her throat again. 'I had to take it to her place, didn't I?' She looked at her mother for support. 'If I had known we'd got a telephone, I'd have given you a buzz.'

'Phil wanted it to be a surprise,' Maggie said. 'I thought I'll put a notebook on the side table in the parlour, where we can log the calls we make?'

Frances pushed back her chair. 'That's a good idea. I'll make sure we pay our fair share.' She blew Maggie and Uncle Sal a kiss. 'I've got to run.'

CHAPTER TWENTY-ONE

*T*he air had a decided nip to it. She opened her handbag to take out her old gloves, locating the first one straight away. But the second one wasn't there. Drat; she must have dropped it when she tried on the kid gloves, but, and this thought cheered her a bit, Martha or Tilda would have found it. She'd pop over to the shop after work.

Leaves crunched under her soles. Curls of smoke drifted from the chimneys. Frances shook a few leaves off an overhanging branch to watch them drift to the ground in a lazy spiral. She felt self-conscious, going to work wearing her good tweed skirt that flared out below the knee and the matching jacket. But, after all, they might go to Petty's today, and she had to look the part.

It took all her courage to place the call for an appointment during her lunch time.

She didn't dare lock the door, but instead she'd settled for the next best thing and blocked it with a chair. The door could still be pushed open, but it would be noisy enough for her to be warned so she could disconnect. If Mr Gibbons or anyone else for that matter inquired why the chair wasn't in its usual place, she'd claim she'd seen a mouse clamber on top of the tall filing cabinet next to the door and climbed on the chair to investigate.

Five minutes later she placed another private call. Jack picked up after two rings.

She said, 'Quick, I can't talk long. Today, at a quarter to five. I said it's for Miss Bardon and that you're solely interested in the most expensive pieces. The girl said they couldn't have the merchandise in store any earlier.' She glanced around her, lowering her voice further. 'Don't pick me up here. There's enough talk already. I'll meet you outside Balfours' café. I finish at four. Bye.'

'Got it,' Jack said before he rang off.

In double-time she tore off her headset and dashed over to the door. She put the chair back in its usual place, took out her sandwich and bit into it. Being on edge always made her hungry, and right now she was starving. She wished she had enough time left to go and retrieve her glove now. Or, she made a calculation in her head, she could run there after work and hope she'd still be in time for her date with Jack.

'Frances, what a lovely surprise.' Martha beamed at her short-sightedly. 'Tilda's been as giddy as a school girl ever since your charming Mr Sullivan invited us to the club,' she twittered. 'Do you think it would be too naughty if we went, my dear? It must be utterly thrilling.'

'Tell me in time, and we could make up a group with Mum and Uncle Sal.' Frances felt herself warm to the idea. Jack was right. Why shouldn't the sisters have a good time?

'I'm sorry I can't stay longer,' she said, 'because I'm in a bit of a rush and I only wanted to see if you've picked up my glove, but I'll come back another day, so we can make plans.'

Martha's face glowed with pleasure. 'That'd be lovely, my dear. I'll go and get it for you.' She bustled away, her heels clip-clopping on the wooden floorboards.

Frances barely had time to glance around before Martha returned and handed her the missing glove. 'Now you can run along and meet your young man, Frances.' She beamed at her. 'Before I forget, did the other man, now what was his name, find Maggie all right? He was so keen to get in touch after all these years. I think it's always so nice to catch up with old family friends.'

Frances' heart missed a beat. 'What man?'

'Why, the gentleman who saw you leaving the shop with Mr Sullivan. Bit of a rough voice. He came in to ask your name, and when I told him, he said he knew you straight away from your family likeness, although you wouldn't remember him after all those years. Funny, isn't it, how small the world can be?' Martha peered at her with sudden worry. 'Are you unwell, love? You're as pale as a sheet.'

237

Frances shook her head, forcing herself to breath normally. 'I'm fine. I'll be back soon.'

~

Outside, she stretched out a hand against the wall to steady herself. She stumbled more than she walked as she headed to Balfours to meet Jack. He was the only one who could help her.

He was already waiting, pretending to be window-shopping at a man's outfitters. As she approached him, he nodded towards the display. 'I quite fancy the purple dressing gown with the yellow pinstripe. It would go particularly well with the artificial silk pyjamas in that astonishing shade of pink.'

'Jack, please! I've got to talk to you.' She grasped his sleeve, to reassure herself of his presence.

'What's the matter?' he asked, the smile wiped from his face. He took her arm. 'Steady, kiddo. We can either sit in the café and you tell me what's bothering you, or we'll talk in the car.'

'The car,' she said.

'Right. We've got Danny with us today, acting as chauffeur. Take a deep breath. Whatever it is, I'll take care of it.' Jack gave her an appraising glance. 'You look very smart, every inch the companion of a successful business man like me.'

He looked the part too, thought Frances with the small part of her brain that wasn't paralysed. He was very flash with his starched shirt and silk vest in dove grey, dark grey suit and heavy golden cufflinks. The tie pin was inset with three sparkling gems glowing in a rich burgundy.

Jack stripped off his leather gloves and lifted his hand up to the light. His little finger sported a matching signet ring. 'Pretty impressive, huh?'

'Very,' Frances said, feeling herself calm down.

'They're all family heirlooms on my mother's side, except for the wristwatch,' Jack said, keeping up the light tone. 'It's a bit too ostentatious for my liking, but in grandfather's day that was considered very restrained. It should make me look like someone who's willing to drop a bundle on jewellery, I hope.'

Danny opened the car door for her. He lifted his black cap. She hardly recognised the wiry waiter in the blue uniform with satin lapels.

She plumped down on to the back seat, hugging her arms to her chest.

'Frances?'

'He knows who I am,' she said. It came out as a whisper.

'Who does?'

'Croaky. At least I think it's him. I heard a man talking about the job. I thought I recognised the voice, and shrieked, and then the waitress asked me if I worked at the phone exchange. I panicked and ran away without getting a proper look at him, to Martha and Tilda's when you met me, and I was so sure no one had followed me, that I thought I made a mistake.'

Her voice shook. 'Jack, Martha says a man came in and asked who I was, a man with a rough voice. She told him my name and about my family and where I live.'

He stretched out his arm and pulled her close. She

sank against his chest. 'Don't be frightened,' he said, with an edge to his voice. 'We'll get Croaky, you'll see, and I'll keep you and your family safe. I promise. We'll keep a watch on your house. He won't get you, or your mum, or Uncle Sal. Do you believe me?' He pressed a kiss on her hair.

'Yes.' She opened her bag to fumble for her handkerchief.

'Are you feeling strong enough to follow through with our plan?'

She forced down the lump in her throat. 'Yes.' Even with Jack at her side, she knew she wouldn't feel safe as long as Croaky was free.

'Good girl. How about putting your handbag with the other stuff in the front? Something heavy is poking in my ribs.'

He handed the bag to Danny who wedged it in between a beribboned perfume bottle and a teddy bear.

Frances leant forward and stroked the bear's head, glad about the comfort it gave her to touch these very ordinary things. It made the dread she'd felt earlier less real somehow. 'I haven't even asked about the baby. Boy or girl?'

'A strapping, seven-pound girl. Bluey says she doesn't have a single hair on her head, but apart from that she's the spitting image of Marie, and they're both doing great.'

'I bet he's besotted. Do they have a name yet?'

'I haven't asked. I talked for less than a minute with Bluey.'

'I'd like to get the baby a present,' Frances said. 'Would you mind taking it along if I drop it off at the club?'

'I'd be delighted, if you promise me not to go out alone.'

Jack gave Danny a signal. 'Wait for us here, right outside the shop window. I want them to be able to see you.'

Danny nodded. He slumped back in the seat, eyes watchful. That was all it took to make him appear meaner and shiftier, the kind of man who knew how to fight. It was all very trust-inspiring.

'Mr Sullivan and company? We have an appointment.' The man must be the manager or the new partner, Frances thought. His dark, heavily pomaded hair was parted with precision, his moustache trimmed to a pencil-thin line, curling up half an inch at the end, and his manicured fingernails gleamed.

Jack handed his hat to a girl in a smart black suit. Everything in Petty's whispered money and discretion, from the deep, oblong, glass cases to the sofas upholstered in black velvet and the black and white tiled floor. Floor-length mirrors could be wheeled where needed, and chintz curtains hung ready to create privacy.

'Randolph Walker, at your service.' The man's face seemed to be frozen in a perpetual half-smile that allowed a glimpse of the gold molar in his lower jaw. 'What can we do for you?'

Jack stripped off his gloves, putting them on a marble counter. 'As Miss Palmer told your staff, we are exclusively interested in the best.' Frances had never heard him use this haughty drawl before.

'I don't know if you're an Adelaide man yourself ...' Jack went on.

Did she imagine it or was that a faint sneer on Walker's face? 'Sydney. I'm the original cornstalk, born and bred in New South Wales.'

'Right,' Jack said. 'Well, in case you haven't been around long, you may not have heard of Miss Bardon, the star attraction of my establishment. I want to get her something that complements her beauty.'

'And the lady likes?'

Jack addressed Frances. 'Didn't you tell them?' He faced Walker again. 'Miss Bardon wears diamonds, diamonds, and rubies, in the style of,' he fluttered his hand in a languid gesture, 'Cartier or Tiffany. She loves her jewellery modern, but sophisticated. That's why we're here. I was told Petty's should be the first place to go to.'

'Indeed. We have prepared a selection of necklaces, bracelets, and earrings.'

Jack nudged Frances forward. 'The young lady is a close friend of Miss Bardon's and as such, knows her taste better than I do.'

Mr Walker acknowledged her with a tiny nod. 'If you'll follow me? We don't have that kind of merchandise on display, as you can imagine. We keep it in a safe.'

'Very wise. By the way, my condolences to the loss of your employer.'

'It was a terrible shock, I'm not ashamed to admit. Things like that,' he sounded as if he had tasted something bad, 'you don't expect them to happen in a nice suburb. But, alas, life goes on.'

He led them into a room of generous proportions. Four club chairs sat around a low glass table. A stack of magazines awaited perusal. Two chairs flanked a dresser, with an oval mirror on top.

A golden-haired woman, dressed in tight-fitting black stood staring into the mirror. Her heavily powdered face was tight, and she flinched when Walker's glance met hers in the mirror.

'Mrs Petty?' Jack lifted her hand to his lips. 'My deepest sympathy.'

'Thank you, Mr Sullivan.' She gave him a wan smile that left her eyes as cold as a glacier. Frances received the barest glance which she returned with more civility than she felt.

Mr Walker said, 'Mrs Petty has offered to show you the most suitable pieces, in case you'd prefer to see them modelled.'

Jack's drawl became melting. 'I wouldn't have dared to ask. If you're sure it's not too painful.' He drew out a chair for the widow, clasped both of her hands and made her sit down.

Frances sat down too, positioning herself so she could watch in the mirror without appearing to do so.

'It's what Michael would have wanted.' Mrs Petty dabbed at her kohl-lined eyes with a wisp of a handkerchief. 'You may not remember him, Mr Sullivan, but he was a great admirer of Dolores Bardon. Me too, of course.' She lowered the dry handkerchief.

Jack gave the widow's hands a tender squeeze before he released them. 'It's Jack to you, and although I can't say I remember Mr Petty, I sure haven't forgotten you, Madam.'

'Call me Ella-Mae.' A white hand fluttered to her throat. Frances was reminded of a third-rate silent picture actress.

Mr Walker cleared his throat as he lowered two satin-covered trays on to the dresser. Ella-Mae opened a dresser drawer and took out another tray. Mr Walker stiffened.

Jack lifted a necklace in form of a white-gold snake biting its own tail. Diamonds studded its back, the eyes were made of rubies.

Ella-Mae draped it around her neck. She leant closer to Jack. 'Do you like it? We've also got the matching bangle.'

His eyes were fixed on her throat. She practically drooled as she slid on the bangle and dangled her wrist under Jack's nose. Frances sat up straighter, trying to read Jack's expression.

He gazed at the widow. 'What a crime.' Ella-Mae's eyes flickered for the barest moment. Mr Walker sucked in his breath with a hiss. Even Frances felt a stab of unease at Jack's tasteless remark.

Jack traced the snake's head on Ella-Mae's wrist with a fingertip. 'A crime, to let another woman have these pieces. They were made for you.'

'What about this one?' Ella-Mae pointed out a necklace made of a strand of interwoven filigree leaves, leading to a cluster of diamonds forming a rose.

Frances heard another sharp intake of breath. She lowered her lids and glanced at Mr Walker. He stood motionless, arms at his side, hands clenching and unclenching.

Raised voices from the sales room announced more customers. Frances sank deeper into her chair, trying to catch a few words. No, they were too muffled by the door to be audible.

Jack moved his left hand over Ella-Mae's to let her

admire his ring, scraping his watch hard over the bangle in the process.

'How stupid of me,' he said, still gazing into the widow's eyes. 'My dear, would you be an angel and fetch my gloves? I forgot them on the marble counter.'

Frances slipped out of the room before Mr Walker could interfere.

The male shop assistant was busy singing the praises of a silver hip flask, while the girl rang up the till for an elderly lady.

Frances retrieved the gloves, thankful they still sat on the counter, and ambled around, examining the rings in the case next to the silver flasks. No. The voice was all wrong for Croaky's boss. The man on the phone had sounded flatter, more nasal, and without the slight stutter the shop assistant displayed.

Jack got up as she entered the room, kissing Ella-Mae's hands once more, whispering a few words as he raised his head. Her smile was strained.

So was Mr Walker's as they took their leave. He shook Jack's and Frances' hands, saying Petty's would be delighted to hear from them once Jack had made up his mind. His voice sounded smooth, but Frances saw the tendons in his throat tighten as he stared at Ella-Mae with barely concealed fury.

CHAPTER TWENTY-TWO

'Where do you want to go now, boss? Home?'
Danny asked as they got into the car.

'No. Take us to the next expensive jeweller's, please. I told Mrs Petty that I'd arranged to see some more before I decided. We'd better keep up appearances.'

At the next store, they simply did a quick tour of the sales room before Jack ushered Frances out again. They were walking. He'd sent Danny away, to pick up Dolores' seamstress and deliver her to the apartment. Frances experienced a pang of envy. Diamonds, a chauffeur, beautiful dresses, and, on top of that, Jack to fulfill her every wish – that lady had it all. Then she remembered Dolores' face when she spoke of Simon, and the envy disappeared like mist in the sun.

'That was a big sigh,' Jack said.

'Yes. None of the men was the one I heard, I'd swear to that. That was a complete failure.'

'Don't say that.' His arm shot out between her and an

old man pushing a billy-cart stacked high with sacks of kindling. 'We learned a lot.'

'Like what? That dear Ella-Mae isn't overwhelmed with grief. Her hankie was dry. And that she's got expensive tastes?'

'Interesting, isn't it?' He shoved his hands into his pockets. 'She didn't mourn her husband, as you said yourself, but her hands were icy, her pulse in her neck twitched, and under those thick layers of paint she had black circles under her eyes. She's afraid of something.'

'Or someone.' She mentioned the hate-filled glare Ella-Mae had received from Randolph Walker.

'Or someone. Can you walk to the club in these heels, or shall we take the tram? I can't wait to get home and change. This collar's so stiff it's killing me.'

She winced.

He made a rueful grimace. 'Sorry, wrong choice of words, kiddo. But I swear I'll always keep you safe, no matter what it takes.'

Frances nibbled a biscuit while she waited in Jack's drawing room. She didn't mind being here on her own, because it gave her the opportunity to explore without appearing nosy.

She turned her back on the alluring painting, or else she'd still be engrossed in it when Jack had finished changing his shirt. Instead, she studied the book shelves.

The books covered a wide range, from popular detective fiction to classic novels, philosophy, art, and poetry. Cracks in their spines showed they had been read a lot. She tilted her head to the right, to decipher the faded title of a particularly hard-worn book.

'Don't squint,' Jack said, putting a hand on her shoulder. He opened the book case door and pulled out the volume. '*The Great Gatsby*,' he said. 'Wonderful book. If you want to, you can read it, but it's not a story to be emulated.'

'Uncle Sal has got a copy.'

'He would.' He put it back on to the shelf and motioned to her to sit down.

'What do you think Ella-Mae's afraid of?' she asked.

'It could be a few things. What is interesting is that she admitted she'd been to the Top Note recently, with a girlfriend to accompany her.'

'What's so astonishing about that?'

'My sweet, the Ella-Maes of this world don't have many girlfriends except for their own kind, and they'd rather stay at home than be seen without a swain by their side. Plus, she told me she usually frequents the Ginger Cat which is renowned for its spicy entertainment and colourful clientele.'

Frances was puzzled. 'Well?'

'She also said the visit wasn't planned, because they'd intended to go away for a few days.'

'Maybe her friend wanted to go to the Top Note.'

'True, but still interesting.' He rubbed his chin. 'Another possibility is that her old boyfriend is back in town, and she didn't want to see him or be seen with him in a club frequented by the criminal element.'

'Do you know the man?' She hoped he'd say no. She didn't want Jack to be acquainted with a real gangster.

'It's more a case of I know of him. But I'd recognise his pretty face if that's what you mean. And no, we're not going to look for him in any of the places where you find the bigger fish. It's too dangerous.'

Her pulse faltered. 'You believe that he and Ella-Mae are behind the murder.'

'It is possible. Or maybe she blabbed to him about when her husband would carry the most valuable of his jewels, and he thought it'd be nice to nick the stuff and have a rich widow as his best girl. That would make me twitchy too, in her shoes.'

Oh yes. 'It's too bad we can't prove it.'

'Kiddo, we can't prove anything. We don't need to. All we have to do is put a name on the culprit.'

'Then he'll break down and confess?'

'Then I'll tell Phil that due to a certain conversation I happened to overhear in the club, he might want to have a good look at certain people. That's called acting on information received, in official jargon.' He paused. 'The police know their job, Frances, once they're on the right trail. They'll find plenty enough evidence.'

He gave her shoulder a light squeeze. 'As soon as Phil claps the killer in irons, we'll break open a bottle of French champagne that sailed home with me in 1919. Until then, I'll have one of my men watching your home and your back, when you're out. And, Frances?'

'Yes?'

'Don't forget I'm taking you out to the pictures tomorrow night. If it's all right with you, we can say hello to Bluey's and Marie's newest addition first?'

Her mind raced. 'I'd like that,' she said, 'and I'd love to

see the baby, if Marie's up to it.' Could she finish a pair of baby bootees by tomorrow night if she took everything along to the telephone exchange? She did have a foolproof pattern that she'd used when her nephew was born. Now where had she put it?

~

The wool was not as soft as she'd liked, because she had to make do with the leftover material from Uncle Sal's scarf and a bit of yellow wool her mum had used for Frances' winter jumper, but the result was better than expected.

She hummed to herself as she put the finishing touches on the second bootee, all the while keeping a watchful eye on both the for once silent switchboard and the clock. The needles clicked in a steady rhythm that only changed when Frances dropped the needles to take a bite of her banana. After all, it was her lunch break.

Two knit, two purl, two knit, two purl – she held the bootee up to the light, admiring its regular stitches. Two knit, two purl – the door was jerked open, making her drop the needles. Several stitches slipped off. Frances jumped off her chair.

'You've got to help me!'

'Pauline?' Frances picked up her knitting and put it aside to sort out later. She hugged her wailing friend, fear rising in her. Pauline had never barged in on her at work. She made her sit down. 'You wait here while I get us a cup of tea and then you can tell me.'

Pauline's lips quivered. Fresh tears welled up in her already red-rimmed eyes.

Frances found a few biscuits to go with what was left in the tea pot. She groaned. A few weeks ago, she'd wished for a bit more excitement in her humdrum routine. Well, now she had a bellyful.

Pauline took her cup with shaking hands, spilling a few drops on her coral dress. Her head was hatless, her usually carefully arranged hair hung limp.

Frances perched on the edge of her chair, waiting for Pauline to break the silence.

'It's Tony.'

Frances clapped her hand over her mouth, dreading what was to come.

'I did what you and Miss Bardon told me, write him a letter asking if he wants to be rid of me. How could I ever be so stupid?' A sob escaped her throat.

'Oh Pauline.'

A new wail erupted. 'What am I going to do now?'

Frances' heart went out to her friend. This was all Jack's fault. He'd put the idea of confrontation in her mind, and now Pauline had lost Tony.

'You'll forget him,' she said, swallowing a big lump in her throat. 'If he prefers his swag to settling down, it's too bad for him. Why, you're so pretty you can have any man you want.'

Pauline's eyes grew round. 'What are you talking about?'

'What are you talking about, yourself?'

'Tony, of course.'

'But you just told me that he broke off with you.'

'Broke off with me?' Pauline nearly shrieked. 'He wouldn't do such a thing.'

Frances wiped her forehead, all the while watching the switchboard. Two minutes until her lunch break ended. It had been ominously quiet all day; this couldn't last. 'Tell me again, Pauline, before I get all muddled, but this time from the beginning.'

'I tried to keep a brave front, I really did, but Miss Bardon noticed and she asked what was wrong.' She sniffed. 'Then I told her all about Tony, and how clever he is, with his technical draughtman's skills and his brick making and bricklaying, and like you, she said I should write to him.'

Frances held up a hand as the switchboard sprang to life. 'Give me a moment.' She grabbed her headset and answered the call.

For once, the connection came through as smoothly as she could wish for. She turned her attention back to her friend.

Pauline hadn't written straight away, because she'd struggled to find the right words. 'Miss Bardon came and told me that there might be some part-time work needing to be done on the building. She wanted a few changes to her apartment, and Mr Jack owns a couple other places that need looking after. So, she said if Tony should happen to be around, he and Mr Jack could have a word.'

Frances moved to the edge of her chair, waiting for the pieces to fall into place. 'And?'

Pauline clutched the neckline of her dress, twisting it. 'I wrote to him, four days ago, and now he's sent a telegram. Mum nearly fainted when the postman knocked on the door. She thought it was a rent collector, and that we'd be thrown out of the house because the rent money had gone astray again.' Frances gave her an encouraging nod.

Pauline's lower lip trembled. 'Oh Frances, he's coming home on the next train, and he wants to get married if he gets the job.'

'But that's what you wanted.'

'I know. But not that fast. I don't want to mope around at home and be a good little wife when it's so much fun working for Miss Bardon.' She pouted like a small girl who'd been denied a sweet.

Honestly, Frances thought, it could be very trying to be Pauline's friend. All that fuss about nothing. She rolled her eyes. 'Tony wouldn't make you quit.'

'No, but Mr Jack will. You said yourself, he solely keeps staff when they're the breadwinner.' She twisted the neckline of her dress harder. 'You of all people should understand. Remember when Tony and I first walked out together and his mate George was sweet on you? You told him that night at the Floating Palais you didn't want to get married too young and give up your pay-check. And he could have supported a family, easy.'

Frances' cheeks grew warm. She'd forgotten all about smooth-talking George. She didn't even remember his face, although at that time she had felt very flattered by his attention.

She shrugged off the memory. 'Why don't you talk to Miss Bardon first? I can't imagine Jack making you go if Dolores wants you to stay.'

Pauline's face lightened up. 'That's true. He does everything she wants.' She slid off the chair and straightened her neckline. 'I'll talk to Miss Bardon.'

She gave Frances a questioning look. 'You might tackle Mr Jack.'

Frances picked up the knitting, hoping her face didn't turn crimson. 'Again? Why?'

'He listens to you.'

Frances knitted the final row and sighed. The switchboard blinked again and again, lighting up like a Christmas tree. 'But this is the last time, all right? I can't always beg him for a favour for you.'

'You're a star, Frances. I knew you'd do this for me.' Pauline blew her a kiss and made for the door.

'Pauline?' Frances said, with a wicked grin. 'One last thing. Your lipstick's on crooked.'

CHAPTER TWENTY-THREE

*J*ack leant against the bonnet of the Rover as Frances walked out on to the street. His hat was pulled down to his brows, to shade his eyes from the glaring sun. He gave her a small salute.

She waved back and hurried over to him.

'Hello kiddo,' he said. 'There's no need to rush.'

'But you said we'll go and see Marie and the baby.' She pulled the bootees out of her handbag. Lacking wrapping paper, she'd bludged an old handkerchief of Uncle Sal's and tied the bootees up in it, like a miniature swag.

'We still don't have to rush. They won't be going anywhere soon.'

The baby was indeed hairless, Frances had to admit, as she said hello to little Sally Fitzpatrick.

Marie looked exhausted but happy as she swayed back and forth in the rocking chair Bluey had put on the back

255

porch. Bobby doodled with crayon stubs on paper scraps, and Bluey bustled about, tending to his wife. Before Frances could as much as ask after Marie's well-being, he'd already wrapped her in an old paisley shawl, put a knee-rug over her legs and swathed Sally in another baby blanket, because he'd felt a chill just now, when the sun clouded over.

Marie's smile became a trifle strained as she tried to get a word in.

Jack said to Bluey,' Come on and let the girls have a chin-wag while we have a quick word.'

Marie expelled her breath as the men went inside. 'Bless his heart, but the poor lamb is driving me crazy. Jack'll sort him out, though.'

'Is Bluey always this clucky?' It was impossible to be shy around Marie.

'Good heavens, no, I couldn't stand it. It's only for the first couple of days that he decides the baby and I are made of china.' She cradled Sally in the crook of her arm. 'Bluey's mum lost two, so I don't blame him.' A dimple appeared in her left cheek. 'It's better than having a useless article on your hands who couldn't tell one end of a bairn from the other.'

Frances nestled her gift out of her bag.

'Now look at these bootees.' Marie gave her a swift hug with her free arm. 'They're lovely. Bluey!'

The men rushed back. Marie said, 'See what Frances made for the baby.'

A slow grin split Bluey's face. 'Sweet,' he said. 'But don't you think you need a bit of a nap, love, while I get tea on?'

'Lovely.' Marie's lids drooped. 'Let me feed Miss Sally

first. Sorry I'm not better company, Frances. We'll have a good old chat the next time.'

'I'm so glad I could see you and the baby,' she said. 'My sister-in-law didn't feel up to visitors for a whole fortnight after my nephew was born.'

'Not me, I'm strong as a cart-horse. Mind, Len's wife was the same.' She shook her head in resignation. 'Plain daft, throwing away the best job he'd ever find. It's not as if he'd pilfered a bob or two from the petty cash, is it? I feel sorry for the wife and the kids, though.'

She dropped a kiss on Sally's forehead. The baby began to make snuffling noises.

Jack raised an eyebrow. He motioned Bluey closer, whispering in his ear and receiving a nod in return.

'What was that all about?' Frances waited until they sat in the Rover. Jack pressed the pedal down.

'A hunch,' he said. 'And a bit of a change of heart. Nothing like a happy family to appeal to your better self.'

She pursed her lips. If Jack wanted to talk in riddles, let him do so.

'You're quiet,' he said. 'Still scared?'

'No; not with you around. But I had a busy day.' She glanced at him. His features were blank, and his hands rested lightly to the steering-wheel.

'Can I ask you something? Hypothetically?'

'Ask away.'

'It's about Pauline. Again.'

'What has she done now?'

She poured out the story. Jack listened with something approaching mirth. Then his lips began to move, until he broke into a laugh. 'Tell her, as long as Dolores wants her, she'll have a job. Even if it's for entertainment purposes alone.'

'Very funny.'

'Come on, kiddo, you could barely keep a straight face yourself. We deserve a bit of a laugh after all this drama lately.'

Jack stopped to let a young woman cross the road. With one hand she dragged a toddler, with the other she clutched a bawling baby that sat on her hip as she stumbled headlong without so much as a glance at the traffic.

The woman couldn't be much older than Frances, but she already had a defeated air. Frances nodded at the retreating threesome. 'Can you blame Pauline for not wanting to rush into marriage and motherhood?'

'No,' Jack said. 'But the last I remember she was teary-eyed because she wanted to settle down.'

There was some truth in that, but she leaped to Pauline's defense. 'There is a difference between wanting to get married straight away and plain being sure it's going to happen one day.'

'True,' Jack said, 'but enough said about Pauline.'

She played with the clasp of her handbag. 'Except that it is very nice of you to offer Tony the chance of a job.'

'I wouldn't, if I didn't need someone with experience to look after our property. Some of the houses need repairs or don't have indoor plumbing yet which needs to be fixed.' He gave her a slanted grin. 'I'm not doing it out of charity, kiddo. I'm a businessman, which reminds me, I'll need to replace Len. That shouldn't be too hard. Most of his shifts he worked the cloakroom and the door.'

'What's going to happen to his family? I know you've put them up, to get them away from him. But what if he comes back?'

'He already has.' Jack's grip on the steering wheel tightened. 'Bluey's heard from the wife. He's going to pay them a visit as soon as Ginny comes to sit with Marie for a while.'

'You're not going to kick them out!' She stared at his impassive profile.

'I won't have to. Len knows it's no use pushing his luck. They'll probably return to their old lodgings and hope for the best.'

'But how can Len pay the rent? That fiver you gave him won't last forever.'

'Which is why Bluey's going to see them and have a little chat. If Len plays his cards right, he might find himself back on the straight and narrow again instead of heading for jail.' Jack's expression darkened. 'I'd hate to see that family of his ending up in a tin humpy somewhere while he's serving time. Mind you, he would have had it coming a long time.'

Her head began to spin. 'You're going to take him back after all?'

'Like hell I am!' He gave her a quick glance. 'Sorry. But, no. If Len as much as sets one foot in the Top Note he'll find himself singing the whole scale of regret.' His voice calmed down. 'There's a job going at an abattoir that's managed by one of our old mates. The stink and filth should be right up his street.'

Jack parked the car a block away from the movie theatre. The show was not due to start for another half hour, but people were already flocking to the entrance, happy to escape their dreary existence for a few hours. Everybody was penny-pinched, but the movie theatres were always full.

A Raggedy Ann leant against the wall of a shop building, about thirty yards from the movie theatre, playing her violin soft enough not to risk being called a nuisance. Her eyes were closed, and she swayed gently; not in rhythm with the music, but like someone faint with hunger.

Frances fished for a penny. Jack took a five-shilling note, folded it and waited for the music to stop. The Raggedy Ann opened her eyes and lowered the bow. Jack pressed the money into her hands, inclining his head an inch before he strode on without looking back.

They were shown to a row of seats up a flight of stairs covered in plush, pale blue wool carpet. Frances' shoes sank into the thick material. It looked wonderful, but she couldn't imagine how the staff cleaned it, when so many muddy boots dragged over it and refreshments tended to be spilt.

This whole upper part of the theatre was much roomier

than the cheaper seats below that Frances was used to. Jack led her to two seats that could be curtained off. At the other end of the row, someone had already done that, and the giggling behind the curtain hinted at a lover's tryst. To her own embarrassment, her cheeks began to burn.

Jack leant back into his seat, crossing his legs. 'Don't worry,' he said. 'I thought we could do with some privacy to talk during the newsreel and the Three Stooges. It's the same one we saw last time, so we won't miss out on anything.'

'Good.' She did not intend to let anything distract her during the main act, a comedy called *Young Man of Manhattan*, with Claudette Colbert, one of her favourite actresses.

Thinking of the enchanting Miss Colbert made her think of Dolores. She put her hand on Jack's sleeve as the lights went out. 'What is going to happen when Dolores hears that you went to Petty's to buy her a present? Can you turn up empty-handed without having to tell her the truth? Because she will hear of it, believe you me.'

'I'll tell her I was sent by a friend who wants to stay anonymous, and that he plans it to be a surprise for his best girl.' His features softened. 'Dolores has got a weakness for lovers, as you've seen.'

'I hope she'll find happiness again.' Especially if it was with someone like Phil.

'Now you're getting sentimental.' He crossed his legs and dug his thumbs into his vest pocket. 'She loved Simon dearly, but I've always asked myself if part of the allure is that they never had to deal with the small nuisances of married life. No fight over bills, or being late for supper.'

'That doesn't sound very nice.'

'But it's true.' He gave her an odd look. 'My old man used to annoy the heck out of my mother with his drinking and gambling, until he finally jumped a rattler and rode off into the night when I was eight. She divorced him for desertion after the appropriate amount of time, mightily relieved that Australia offered her at least that luxury.'

'Your poor mum!'

'On the contrary, she was happy to be shot of him. She'd have left him if she'd been able to put her hands on the money for a second-class cabin for us on a steamer back to England.' He stroked his chin. 'No steerage berth for my darling mother. Her motto is, do things in style or don't do them at all.'

He drummed a tattoo on his right thigh. 'Mind you, when she went back to Blighty, with my stepfather, a few years ago she knew that the party was over. Times are bad in England, but she's been toughing it out ever since.'

'She must have felt awful about Rachel,' she said before she could help herself.

His fingers dug into his thigh. 'No. I never told her the whole sorry story. There was no need to upset her. All my mother knows is, that Rachel went to New Zealand for a change of scenery.'

'I'm sorry.' She tried to shrink into her seat.

His fingers relaxed. 'It's all right. As I said, it'll all come right again in the end.'

The Three Stooges came on, provoking gales of laughter with their slapstick routine.

Frances fidgeted in her seat. It was good to know that

Jack didn't mind her blunder, but it didn't ease her apprehension.

It had nothing to do with him or his family, though. She felt like she'd overlooked something, and it had to do with Ella-Mae Petty and Randolph Walker.

She let her mind trail back. She had to hand it to Ella-Mae; the pretty widow had certainly known how to get Jack's attention. Mr Walker hadn't seemed to mind her using her charms though, at least not in the beginning.

She furrowed her brows. When did his behaviour change? He had introduced them, put down the trays and then he'd stepped back, watching from afar. Ella-Mae had put on the snake bangle, and the atmosphere had changed.

She sat up in her seat. The snake necklace and bangle hadn't been on one of the trays that Walker had carried; they'd been on the one Ella-Mae had produced. Maybe he'd suspected her of stealing jewellery her late husband kept at home, and the snake necklace and bangle confirmed his suspicions?

No. That was ridiculous. But there was something going on, if only she could figure it out.

One of the Three Stooges slipped on a bar of soap, provoking an uproar in the audience.

She pulled on Jack's sleeve.

'Yes?' he said, but she had to guess with all the noise.

She waited until there was a lull before she tried again and whispered into his ear, 'Maybe I'm fanciful, but I think there's something seriously wrong going on at Petty's.'

'There is,' he said. He pushed back his sleeve, tapping his finger on the glass of his watch. 'Look at this.'

'I can't see anything. It's too dark.'

'That's the point, there is nothing to see,' he said. 'Not a scratch from when I scraped it badly over the diamond encrusted back of Ella-Mae's snake bracelet.' He let the sleeve fall over his wrist again. 'In case you don't know, diamonds have the distinction of being hard enough to cut through glass – which in this case they haven't.'

Her pulse quickened. 'What does that mean?'

'It's paste. What Ella-Mae was showing me were excellent pieces of jewellery, but they were fakes.'

'No wonder she was twitchy, trying to sell them to you.'

'I don't think so. Did you see her face as she put those pieces on? She lusted after them with a passion I can't imagine her having for imitation diamonds. Which means, she didn't know what they were.'

Frances nibbled her cheek as she digested this information. She still didn't see clear, unless ... 'He did. Mr Walker knew. That's why he glared at her like that.' Frances shivered. 'She must have decided she'd take the jewellery out simply to be able to wear it for a little while.'

CHAPTER TWENTY-FOUR

*T*he Three Stooges finished to thundering applause. The screen went black. Downstairs, a queue formed in front of the refreshment stand. This way the young men could treat their girls without spending more than a few pennies. Some of these girls might never have been taken out for frog cakes at Balfours' or illicit champagne in a night club, because the nice boys couldn't afford it and the ones who could usually weren't nice.

How easily one got used to the good life, Frances thought with something resembling regret. She'd miss being driven around town and taken for nice meals once Michael Petty's murderer had been found. She rested her chin on her knuckles, propping her elbows up on her knees. Most of all she'd miss Jack, even though she knew she wasn't anyone special for him; unfortunately, he treated her almost the same way as Pauline, or Marie.

He touched her shoulder. 'Would you like a refreshment before the main picture begins?'

'No, thanks. I hate it when people rustle with wrapping

paper or suck boiled sweets when I'm watching,' she said. 'It wasn't too bad with silent pictures, but sometimes you can't hear what's being said for all the noise. But if you want to have something, I don't mind.'

He shook his head. The big screen flickered to life again, and Frances became enthralled with the story of best friends Ann and Puff, who tried everything to get their reporter boyfriends to pay them attention in fast-paced Manhattan.

She drank it all in. The skyscrapers, the neon lights, the hustle and bustle in the streets, and of course clever, clever Ann played by the luminous Miss Colbert. To admire the hats and dresses was a treat. It must be wonderful to live in a place like New York.

A loud cough came from the curtained off box, and broke the spell. When she cast a swift glance around under her lashes, she saw Jack look at her with an inscrutable expression. She sank deeper into her seat, concentrating on Ann's adventures again.

They were among the last to stroll out into the night. The streetlamps threw passing people into bright relief. The leafy trees that lined many of Adelaide's wide streets were painted with golden stripes from the lamps, making the dark spaces in between even darker.

A man barrelled out of a house. He smelt of unwashed skin and booze. Jack pulled Frances closer, but the man bumped hard into her shoulder, making her stumble. She winced as her ankle twisted with a crunching noise.

'Hey, watch it, mate,' Jack called out to the retreating man, at the same time putting an arm around Frances' shoulder to support her as she touched her ankle. 'Are you all right, kiddo?'

'I'm not sure,' she said. 'I can move the foot, but it hurts.'

'At least it's not broken, but we don't want to do any more damage. Shall I carry you or would you rather stay here while I fetch the car?'

'I'll wait here.' Frances grimaced as she put her weight onto the sore foot, but the pain was bearable. If only the heel hadn't come lose. She'd ruin her new stockings if she had to take off her shoes.

'I'll do a bit of window shopping while you're gone,' she said, with more conviction than she felt. 'The light's still on in the shop, so nothing can happen.'

'Good girl.' Jack brushed her cheek before he hurried away.

Frances hobbled over to The China Gift Store. She peered into the window. The shop was owned by a Chinese lady, and it stocked the most luxurious kimonos and silk undergarments as well as household linens, crockery, and spiderweb-thin lace as trimming that could transform an old sacking into a blouse fit for a ball.

She rested her fingertips on the window pane. A garnet kimono caught her attention, with its embroidered birds and flowers in all hues of the rainbow. Frances squinted but she couldn't read the price tag.

'Well, strike me dead.' The blurred image of a stocky man appeared in the window. She couldn't see his face which was cast in shadow by the hat he wore, but his croaking, nasal voice implied that he leered at her. The voice! Help, she tried to shout, but no sound came out.

He moved closer, blocking the shop door. Her whole body went rigid with fear. Where was Jack?

'What's a pretty sheila like you doin' here all on her lonesome?'

Perspiration beaded Frances' forehead.

'No need to be shy, my pretty.' He was close enough for her to smell his sweat. She nearly gagged.

'I can show you a good time, have a drink or two, take a stroll lakeside, and if you're nice to me, we'll get you that fancy underwear all right, first thing tomorrow morning. How d'you like that?' His breath ruffled her hair.

Her heart beat loud enough to be heard a mile away.

Another shadow appeared. A hand clamped down on her tormenter's arm, twisting it behind his back.

'She doesn't like it at all,' a smooth voice said. Jack! Frances pressed her hand to her heart to slow down its beating.

He said, 'The lady's with me, and you'd better remember that if you value your bones.'

The man drew in his breath through clenched teeth. 'Right,' he said.

Jack gave his arm another tug before he released the man. 'Off with you,' he said, in an unruffled manner. The man looked first at Jack, then at Frances. 'Bloody hell.' The sulky expression in his face changed to white-hot fury.

Jack met his gaze with a cold smile.

The man turned on his heels and swaggered off, as if to show he didn't care.

She bit on her knuckles to refrain from sobbing.

He clasped both her shoulders. 'I'm here,' he said. 'I won't let anything bad happen to you, sweetheart.' She began to shake.

His eyes narrowed. 'Did that bastard touch you?'

She shook even harder. 'No,' she whispered. 'But, oh, Jack ...'

'Yes?'

'The voice. It was the same voice. That was Croaky.' Tears welled up in her eyes. 'It was when he said he'd take me lakeside. He recognised me, didn't he?' Her knees buckled under her.

Jack lifted her up with one swift movement and carried her ten steps to the car. He closed the door behind her and walked over to the driver's side. He revved up the engine as soon as the motor came to life.

'Where are we going?' she asked.

'Following our man. We need to make sure Croaky won't bother you again.' His voice became gentle. 'Unless you're too shaken.'

'No. It was only the shock, and that I couldn't run away, and I didn't know where you were.'

Jack peered out of the front window. 'Over there,' he said. 'He's hot-footing it into that alley. Makes me wonder why he's in such a hurry.'

'He knows who you are,' she said. 'You could see it in his face.'

'Am I that scary?'

She attempted to smile.

He braked. 'It's too narrow down there for the Rover,' he said. 'I'll have to follow Croaky on foot. Lock the doors from inside, Frances. Can you drive? No? Well, if I'm not back in ten minutes, wait until a respectable looking person walks by, roll down the window and send them to get Bluey.'

He pressed a handful of coins into her hand. 'Give a bob to the messenger, and promise him the rest as soon as he returns with Bluey.' He threw the door shut and rushed off.

She locked the Rover from inside. The fear came back to haunt her. What if Croaky cut through another back alley and found her here? He might smash in the window to get at her. She slid down on the seat as far as she could.

The silence grew thicker. The street was deserted. She could have been the last person left in the world. A weapon; she needed a weapon. She felt around in the glove compartment. Her fingers touched a cloth-wrapped bundle. She pulled it out, uncovering a spanner and a monkey-wrench. Their solid weight comforted her as she put them into her handbag.

How quiet it was, she thought. Too quiet. Shouldn't Jack be back by now? A distant scream broke the silence. She couldn't tell if it was male or female, or human at all, but what if it was Jack?

She fumbled with the lock, jerked the door open and stumbled onto the pavement. A stab of pain shot through her ankle. She ignored it as she limped into the dark alley. The ubiquitous streetlights that made Australia the most modern country in the world had not made it this far. The thin sliver of the moon made a feeble attempt to relieve the dark grey of the night.

She glanced around. The houses closed in on the alley, with barely enough space in between for a man to squeeze through, and solid brick walls enclosed the rear end of the properties.

She limped on. There must be a light somewhere, or voices, or, best of all, Jack's comforting presence that would end all her fears. But she didn't know where to find him. Her ankle throbbed. She paused two steps away from the last house.

A cat sat in a half-opened window. It gave her a disinterested stare as she heard the voice again. It said, 'You looking for anything in particular?'

'Could be.' The answer was barely audible, but Frances felt it in her bones it was Jack. Her inside knotted up.

'Don't get cocky with me.' A slapping noise, followed by a long silence.

She sank on to her knees and crawled under the window, thanking heaven for the large bottlebrush planted at the right distance from the house wall for her to hide behind.

The cat jumped down next to her, brushing its tail along her knees. A second scream made Frances flinch and the cat hiss; another feline, she thought with a small part of her brain. That must be what had startled her earlier.

Croaky went on, 'Maybe I'll ask you to be my guest while I go fetch your girlfriend. Took me long enough to find her, so how 'bout she and I have a bit of fun together.'

'I thought I saw something venomous crawling inside the house.' Jack's speech was slightly slurred. 'A big snake, that's what brought me here.'

'Get up,' the other one yelled, only to lower his voice again. 'You think you're so smart, White Jack Sullivan, eh? Tell you what, I'll phone the boss, and then you and I will take a nice trip to Lake Torrens, and tomorrow there'll be another floater fished out of the water. Your sheila can wait.'

Frances bit her knuckle to prevent herself from crying out. She needed to think, and quick, or Croaky would kill Jack, and then he'd come looking for her.

Jack asked, 'Who is your boss? If you condemn a man to death it's fair to let him know who's the judge and the jury.'

The pause lasted long enough for Frances to hear her own heartbeat. 'You met his brother, that's all I'll say.'

'Randolph Walker? I thought as much when I saw his weasel-face.'

Another slapping sound. 'Enough,' Croaky said. Frances heard a telephone being dialled. 'It's me, boss. Yeah, I know I shouldn't call. Yeah, White Jack's here. Sure, Lake Torrens. Meet me there in half an hour.'

She crouched deeper as she opened her handbag open to get at her weapons. A tall figure emerged from the entrance; Jack. A second figure followed, poking something into the other man's back.

The cat jumped into the bottlebrush, snapping a twig.

Croaky swivelled around, pistol pointing away from Jack.

'Duck,' Frances yelled, letting the spanner, the monkey-wrench and the horseshoe she'd taken out of her bag fly in rapid succession at the pistol-wielding arm. Please, let her hit the nerve-centre.

The man yelped, dropped the pistol and clutched his arm. Jack jumped on to his back, embracing him in an unrelenting hug.

'Get the gun, Frances.'

She scrambled on her knees over to him. The pistol lay cold and heavy in her hands.

'Aim it at his stomach. It's a big enough target to hit.'

'What do we do now?' she asked. 'Take him to the police station?'

'The cavalry should be on its way,' he said. 'I met an urchin on my way and sent him to get Bluey.'

His captive struggled. Jack squeezed him tighter. The arm Frances had hit crunched. The man groaned. 'Can you hold up that gun another minute, kiddo? And where did you learn that sweet throw?'

'Uncle Sal. I hit him in the same spot once, and his arm went lame. I can also throw knives in case you're wondering.'

Jack smiled. 'I knew that you were good to have around.' He craned his neck. 'There are our reinforcements. Bluey!'

'Are you all right, Mr Jack? I'll take the gun, Miss Frances.'

She felt herself lifted to her feet. 'And Danny, too,' she said.

Danny's teeth gleamed. 'Your policeman mate will soon be here, Miss. Do you want to hang around or shall I bundle you home?'

'None of this,' Jack said. 'Take Miss Frances to the Chinese doctor in North Terrace to have a look at her ankle, and after that bring her to my apartment to clean up. Tell Ginny to fit her out with clean clothes.' His gaze met hers. 'You look like you've been dragged through the bush, kiddo, and we don't want your mother to get the fright of her life.'

'Wait,' she said. 'What's going to happen now?'

He arched his eyebrow. 'Good question.' He cupped her elbow and led her a few steps away, out of earshot.

'I can't let you stay, or your name will turn up in Phil's report, kiddo.'

'I know, but what about the other man?' She willed her voice to be firm.

'Phil should know what he's doing.'

'But what if he doesn't, and the boss goes free?'

'There's always that risk,' Jack said, holding her gaze. 'Do you have any idea?'

'Bluey and Croaky are about the same size, right? In the pictures, they'd swap coats.'

'And we'd turn up at Lake Torrens, with Bluey masquerading as Croaky, holding me at gun-point. I like that. But you have to go now, Frances.'

'Yes.'

'You'll be careful, won't you?'

'Always.' Jack said. 'Sweet dreams. I'll see you tomorrow.'

CHAPTER TWENTY-FIVE

*F*rances smiled all the way home. Dr Lum Yow had bandaged her ankle and provided her with a bottle of his famous 'Cure-All' tonic, Ginny had brushed out her clothes and produced a pair of real silk stockings from Dolores' stock, and, best of all, she and Jack were safe.

She sank deep into the plush upholstery of the car. She caught Danny's gaze in the front mirror. He winked at her.

She was too tired to do more than knock on her mum's bedroom door to let her know she was back, and have a quick wash. Her bed had never felt more tempting. She snuggled deep under the eiderdown and drifted off as soon as her head hit the pillow.

With Frances gone, Jack waited for the police. His prisoner struggled to get free, but the rough side of Bluey's fist shut him up until the police arrived.

'Phil?' He pulled him aside as two officers bundled Croaky into a van.

'You better come with me to the station for your statement, Jack.'

'Sure, mate, but later. I've got a plan you might like.'

Phil hesitated. Jack put an arm around his shoulder and whispered the details into Phil's ear.

'What if anything goes wrong?' Phil stroked his moustache.

'You want the boss-cocky?'

Phil nodded.

They drove down to the lake. Bluey squeezed into Croaky's coat and marched a resisting Jack step by reluctant step towards the water. He dug the gun into Jack's back.

Jack prayed that their target already waited for them in the shadows, and that the moon would stay behind clouds. Right now, the darkness was their best ally.

A whistle pierced the silence.

Jack and Bluey stopped.

'Closer,' a man's voice said.

Bluey pushed Jack forwards, until only six steps separated Jack and the shadowy figure.

'Time for a swim, Mr Sullivan. Your turn, Muggins.'

Bluey grunted and waved the gun.

'No gun. Slip him a knife if you don't have your cosh. It's quieter.'

Bluey put the gun away and fumbled in his pocket. Jack

lunged himself at the man, landed an upper-cut on his chin and pinned him to the ground.

The man spat in his face.

'Boss?' Bluey picked up the man and took him in a choke-hold until Phil appeared out of his hidey-hole and slapped handcuffs on him.

Maggie and Uncle Sal were all agog at breakfast. They didn't even notice that Frances dragged her left foot.

'Where's Phil?' she asked as Maggie put a piece of already buttered toast on to her plate.

'He had to leave at the crack of dawn.' Her mother's face shone with happiness. 'Would you believe it, our Phil snatched that horrid man who killed that poor Mr Petty. You can't imagine how much safer I feel.'

'That's wonderful.' She didn't know what else to say. Surely Phil had enough sense to keep her part out of it? Maggie would have a heart attack if she knew.

'Looks like you and Jack had a busy time yourself,' Uncle Sal said, lowering his right eyelid in a slow wink.

Frances busied herself with the jam.

'Mind you, Phil can't tell us much yet, because it's confidential and the investigation is ongoing, but the relief of it all.' Maggie sighed.

'I know how you feel,' Frances said. 'Now all he needs to do is catch the thief who took the funeral money from Mrs Jacobs', and all will be back to normal.' She heaved herself up.

'What's wrong with you?'

'It's a slight sprain,' Frances said. 'No need to worry, Mum. I've got Lum Yow's tonic, and my ankle should be right in a tick.' She blew Maggie and Uncle Sal a kiss, snatched her jacket and her cloche off their hook and limped into the crisp morning air to catch the tram, for once unworried about being spotted.

～

The telephone exchange had as busy a time as she could remember. The lines buzzed and hummed with the excitement as news leaked out that the police had made an arrest over the murder of Michael Petty. It felt as if a heavy blanket had been lifted from her beautiful city.

Jack knocked at the door one minute after her lunch hour began. She gave a start.

'It's all right, kiddo,' Jack said. 'I dropped in to say hello to Mr Gibbons and ask if I could be of any more help.'

Frances felt a smile spread over her face. 'You've done plenty already, haven't you?'

'I hope so,' Jack said. 'How's your ankle today?'

'Much better,' she said.

'Good. Now, where's your hat?' He opened the door for her.

'Where are we going? Balfours' again?'

'No. I'm taking you somewhere we can talk undisturbed, if that's all right with you.'

'Perfect.'

～

They sat under a white ash in Elder Park. 'Lakeside,' she said, looking at the softly rippling water.

Jack unpacked a picnic hamper bursting with grilled chicken, bread, tomatoes, cheese, fruit and pastries. 'Lakeside,' he said. 'Do you mind?'

'Why should I? It's lovely here, without cars and noise and unhappiness.'

He took out a bottle and popped it open, filling two glasses with a yellow liquid.

'That's not the champagne you were talking about, is it?' she asked.

'Smell it,' he said.

Frances sniffed. It was fruity and tangy, very much like ... 'Lemonade,' she said, surprised.

'I know I promised you champagne but that will have to wait until tonight.'

'Pity.' Frances sipped while trying to decide what to eat first. She took a chicken drumstick. 'What happened after I left?'

'A lot, thanks to you. Your plan worked like a charm. Bluey posed as Croaky, and Walker brother number two fell for it. Phil led us all the way to the police headquarters off Kilgore. Mug Muggins, or Croaky if you prefer, languished in a cell, and when we marched boss-cocky along, we flanked him and turned his head so it looked like we were deep in a friendly conversation.'

He chuckled. 'Mug couldn't wait to spit out the whole story in the hope of turning King's evidence.'

Frances stared at him, drumstick forgotten in her hand. 'Sweet!'

'I'll tell you the details tonight, over that champagne.'

'What about Ella-Mae? Was she in on it?' Embarrassing, how keen she was to hear the worst about the widow, but she didn't like her, or the way she'd ogled Jack.

'No. Her ex-boyfriend was, though, knocking on Ella-Mae's door a couple of times in broad daylight, so neighbours would remember for sure.'

'But why?'

'Because that way it would look as if she'd had something to do with the switched jewels. Randolph Walker worked for his older brother, who'd entered a partnership with Michael Petty, enabling him to get his hands on the choicest gems, replacing them.'

'But how did he get access to the safe in Petty's house?'

'If you know where to go, you can hire all kind of talent. My best bet is, he smuggled someone into the house while Ella-Mae was out and Petty was at work. The switch would have been undiscovered for a while, because Petty had no reason to open the safe or to examine every single item in the shop.'

'Why kill him, then?' She struggled to fit all the facts together.

'Because his mystery clients wanted to see his most precious jewels. Petty was good, seriously knowledgeable. He'd have been hard to fob off with a fake snake bangle once he had a close look.'

Frances put the chicken bone into a box and picked a mince pie. 'So,' she mused between bites, 'why on earth was Ella-Mae wound tighter than a spring?'

'Because of her chequered past,' Jack replied with more sympathy than she thought necessary. 'Just because she didn't mind a good time doesn't mean she wanted to go back to her old friends. Can you imagine her, when her new girl-friend, who incidentally is an item with our Randolph, deliberately bought cocaine in front of Len, boasting they had something to celebrate.'

'She wanted Len to hear.'

'She banked on him remembering the incident should the police have decided to investigate Ella-Mae.' He shook his head. 'You know, she might even have been fond of her husband. He gave her more than luxury, he gave her respectability, which isn't that easy to come by when you've grown up on the wrong side of the tracks.'

She finished off her meal with a melt-in-the-mouth lamington, grateful she couldn't be expected to answer with her mouth full. She rubbed her ankle.

'I'll clear away our picnic,' Jack said, 'and then I'll come and help you to the car.' He stacked and packed with brisk movements that spoke of experience. The rolled-up picnic rug fit into a strap at the side of the hamper, and another strap secured the silver-plated champagne bucket.

He led her to a wooden bench. His hand brushed her cheek. 'I'll be back in a coo-ee as my uncle in New Zealand would say.'

She stretched out her foot. She rolled down the woollen sock she wore to hide the bandage and slid her fingers down the ankle. The swelling was nearly gone. Maybe she'd made a wrong move for a jolt of pain to occur.

'Do you mind if I sit down, miss?' A lanky young man stood in front of her, trying very obviously not to look at her bared leg.

'Not at all, you're welcome,' she said.

'Thank you.' He gave her a smile that lit up his whole face. 'I'm new to Adelaide, and I've been hiking for hours getting a feel for the place.'

'Do you like it so far?'

'I love it,' he said. 'But then I'm from a place the size of a stamp, and any town would seem grand. But this ...' he opened his arms as if to embrace the city, nearly hitting Frances in the process, 'this is special for sure. And I've got a job as a junior clerk and a room in a boarding-house with only two other men to share.' His brown eyes sparkled. 'No offence, Miss, but you've been kind enough to offer me a sit and yack on, so I wondered, if maybe you'd join me for a cup of tea?'

Before she could decide on an answer, the young man was interrupted.

'This is becoming to be a habit, having to chase away other men as soon as my back is turned,' Jack said, sitting down next to her and pulling her tight. 'Sorry, my boy, but this lady's definitely with me.'

The End

CPSIA information can be obtained
at www.ICGtesting.com
Printed in the USA
BVHW070407160222
629080BV00004B/856